Love
Disguised

Love
Disguised

LISA KLEIN

BLOOMSBURY
NEW YORK   LONDON   NEW DELHI   SYDNEY

First published in the United States of America in July 2013
by Bloomsbury Children's Books
www.bloomsbury.com

For information about permission to reproduce selections from this book, write to
Permissions, Bloomsbury Children's Books, 1385 Broadway, New York, New York 10018
Bloomsbury books may be purchased for business or promotional use. For information on
bulk purchases please contact Macmillan Corporate and Premium Sales Department at
specialmarkets@macmillan.com

Library of Congress Cataloging-in-Publication Data
Klein, Lisa.
Love disguised / by Lisa Klein. — First U.S. edition.
pages   cm
Summary: After a mixed-up courtship with the Hathaway sisters ends badly,
eighteen-year-old Will Shakespeare jumps at the chance to go to London, where he
can pursue his dream of becoming an actor and where he is about to meet the girl
who will change his life forever. Includes bibliographical references.
ISBN 978-1-59990-968-4
1. Shakespeare, William, 1564–1616—Juvenile fiction. [1. Shakespeare, William,
1564–1616—Fiction. 2. Friendship—Fiction. 3. Disguise—Fiction. 4. Sex role—
Fiction. 5. Theater—Fiction. 6. London (England)—History—16th century—
Fiction. 7. Great Britain—History—Elizabeth, 1558–1603—Fiction.] I. Title.
PZ7.K678342Lo 2013   [Fic]—dc23   2012028912

Book design by Regina Flath
Typeset by Westchester Book Composition
Printed and bound in the U.S.A. by Thomson-Shore Inc., Dexter, Michigan
2   4   6   8   10   9   7   5   3   1

All papers used by Bloomsbury Publishing, Inc., are natural, recyclable products
made from wood grown in well-managed forests. The manufacturing processes
conform to the environmental regulations of the country of origin.

To R. R.
Thou, Love, art my Muse

Love Disguised

～⌐ Prologue ⌐～

London, October 15, 1582

Will Shakespeare dashed into the Boar's Head Inn, breathless and disheveled. This was the best day of his life and the worst.

"Meg, I have news. Dreadful news!" he called.

He made straight for the table in the public room where he did his best writing and dug papers and a pen from inside his jerkin. Time was not to be wasted.

"Meg? Come anon."

There was no reply. Long Meg was neither at the tap as usual nor serving customers.

A fat man looked up from his cup and said, "Long Meg? She's not here. And it's her I came to see."

"Then begone," said Will. "She's been known to thrash a man for gaping at her."

Chewing the end of his pen, he searched his brain for the right words. Writing a court brief was nothing like writing a play, and the law handbook he had stolen was of little help. Will was no more cut out for the role of a lawyer than he was for that of a glovemaker, the trade he had left behind in Stratford along with the bewitching Hathaway sisters. But in escaping to London, he now saw, he had sailed from one sea of troubles into an even stormier one.

"Will, why do you look so desperate?" It was the serving wench Violetta, small and with a dark cap of hair like an acorn. She placed a cup of ale before him.

"Because my friend Mack is in prison for assaulting and robbing the notorious villain Roger Ruffneck. He'll be hanged unless I can persuade the judge to free him."

Violetta gave a sharp cry and turned pale. She was a fountain of feeling, able to move the most stoic of playgoers to weep with her.

"Do you know Mack?" asked Will in surprise.

"He is . . . Meg's brother!"

"Yes. Therefore she must be told. Can you find her?"

The wench shook her head as if dazed.

"Well, look upstairs!" pleaded Will. "By tomorrow I must have another witness who can attest to his good character. Who knows him better than his own sister?"

Violetta nodded and scurried away.

It was fortunate that Will had stumbled upon Thomas Valentine as he was returning to the inn. The young doctor had agreed to testify against Roger Ruffneck, having seen him assault Will. London was a violent place. Why had he been so eager to come here? He was likely to be killed before he published a single play.

But the doctor alone could not prove Will's argument. He needed another witness. Why not the timid Jane Ruffneck, who was now hiding from her cruel husband at this very inn? *No*, Mack had insisted, wanting to protect her. Mack, hero to the downtrodden, now himself in dire need. Who would save him? It was up to Will.

He propped his forehead on his hands, not caring that the ink staining his fingers now marked his face as well. How unjust that Mack was in prison! Will longed to share Mack's suffering and thereby prove his true friendship. But having narrowly avoided that den of despair himself, he dreaded confinement. What did it lead to but starvation and death?—an early, tragic end to his fledgling dramatic career.

Not to mention his romantic hopes. The world of love was all before him. He thought of Anne Hathaway's soft lips, then of Long Meg, that strong and spirited maid with her nimbus of golden hair.

O brave Meg! What would she think of him scratching with his pen and fumbling in his handbook while Mack languished in jail? She would strap on a sword, a dagger, and a pistol and lay siege to the Tower itself, if her brother were held captive there. She dealt not in words but in deeds. In all of England there was no woman like her.

Will's thoughts were interrupted by the approach of a no longer timid Jane Ruffneck with Violetta trailing her.

"Let me help your friend," Jane said, her eyes blazing. "I will swear my husband deserved every blow Mack dealt him. I know that monster all too well!"

"I shall be there also to weep for Mack; that must move the entire court to pity him," said Violetta, wringing her hands.

Will groaned. It was reason, not passion, that must persuade the judge.

"I am gratified by your concern," he said. "But leave me alone to finish this writ. My friend's fate lies heavy upon me."

"And upon us as well," said Violetta.

"Why?" asked Will, puzzled, but Violetta and Jane were already hurrying away.

Alone again, Will bent over his page, which left him unable to see the black-clad figure, narrow as a shadow at sunset, creeping around the edge of the room toward his table.

A wrinkled hand reached out and touched his arm. Will jumped.

"Will Shakespeare?" said an old man's voice.

"And who are you?"

"One who makes his living by night," he said.

A thief! Will drew back. "Why have you come here?"

"She bade me, but I do it for the sake of my boy."

Was the old man a lunatic? Will didn't ask him to explain. He hoped he would vanish as suddenly as he appeared, like a ghost from the grave.

"I know something about your friend Mack," said the thief, his voice like the rustle of dry leaves.

Will's hopes revived. It seemed Providence had sent him a witness! He leaned closer.

The old thief spoke only briefly. He would not let Will question him. Nor would he be stayed. He finished his tale and slipped away. And when he had gone Will sat motionless, his brow furrowed and his jaw slack with amazement. The pen dropped from his fingers forgotten, and the handbook fell closed.

"By Jove, he speaks the truth," Will murmured. "I was a fool not to see it before!"

~◯ Chapter 1 ◯~

London 1579

Before she became the celebrated Long Meg and the muse of Will Shakespeare, little Meg Macdougall lived in a narrow house on Addle Street between Aldersgate and Cripplegate in London. Her mother, Jane, was a long, thin broomstick of a woman with strong, ropy arms. Meg's father, Jack, was a giant of a man who could lay a thousand or more bricks a day and drink a kilderkin of ale by night. Meg hardly seemed to belong to them. Her arms were puny, her knees knobby, her legs wayward as a baby fawn's. At mealtime her parents ate great quantities of meat as if filling the hollowness within their long bodies, while Meg was content to nibble a leg of a peahen or a crust of bread. But though she looked too frail to thrive, her eyes shone brightly in her thin face surrounded by hair the color of spun gold.

It was a happy household except when it was not. Jack Macdougall drank too much and Jane begrudged the waste of their meager resources. Their boisterous quarrels sent Meg scurrying to avoid the hurled brick or hot iron. Plaster crumbled from the walls and the very beams creaked and shifted.

All that kept the house from collapsing were the houses abutting it on either side, whose occupants shouted for quiet, only adding to the uproar. One night the constable came, and he would have arrested Meg's parents were it not for her earnest promise: "I will put them into their bed anon." When they had fallen asleep Meg poured out the rest of her father's ale and hid her mother's iron.

But Meg could no more cure her parents' failings than she could prevent the sun from shining or misfortune from striking. One night Jack was staggering home from an alehouse when he fell asleep in the street, and the next morning a cart rolled over his legs. Cruelly, the cart was filled with bricks. Lame and unable to work, he became a beggar, hobbling away every morning on crutches and returning with a few pennies, barely enough for bread. Jane worked day and night, bending over a boiling vat. All Meg saw of her was a cloud of frizzled hair and a pair of dye-stained arms. She ceased her labors only when the priest from St. Alphage came to bring a few coins of charity and teach her the scriptures. In his black robe, with his sharp, tiny eyes, he reminded Meg of a rat. She was glad her mother sent her away on those days with a bundle of wet laundry. In the fields outside the city gates, she would spread the clothes out to dry and play leapfrog with the other children or chase stray dogs. When the sun had bleached the linen to a blinding whiteness, she folded it and brought it home again.

On one such day it began to rain, and Meg gathered up the linens and ran home early. On the way she met her father leaning heavily on his crutches, a bloody bruise on his head. His cloak and every coin in his pocket had been stolen.

They turned onto Addle Street and Meg followed him into the house, clutching the mud-spattered linens, afraid of her mother's scolding. It was her father, roaring with rage, who thrust her out of doors again, but not before she caught a glimpse of the priest's hairy buttocks and her mother's surprised face.

"Harlot!" shouted Jack.

The priest scurried past Meg, clutching his black robe to hide his nakedness. A Bible flew out after him and struck his head.

"What was I to do?" Meg heard her mother cry. "He would not give me a penny of charity otherwise. O Jack, forgive me!"

Meg did not know what her mother had done, only that it was something wicked that shamed her father too. He left the house and did not return that night. Meg lay awake hoping he would forgive her mother, for surely whatever had happened was the priest's fault, not hers. But her father did not return the next day, and on the third day they learned he was in the Wood Street jail. He had been arrested for vagrancy because he could not produce a begging license.

Meg's mother stood outside the church and shouted at the priest, "You whited sepulchre! I'll never take your charity again!" The parishioners stared at her in alarm while Meg pleaded with her to return home.

"What is a sepulchre?" Meg asked her mother that night.

"A sheet that wraps a dead man," Jane replied dully. She heated up her iron and pounded the wrinkles out of a piece of linen until it became scorched. "A pox upon my boozing beggar of a husband and that skanderbag priest!"

Meg feared her mother was preparing a whited sepulchre

and that the priest was as good as dead. But he did not come to Addle Street again, and Meg and her mother no longer attended services at St. Alphage.

As Jane would not relent toward Jack, it was Meg who took her father scraps of food in prison. Because she lacked the penny to bribe the jailer, she could only thrust the food through the iron grate at street level and try in vain to touch her father's hand. She could dimly see how gaunt and begrimed he was. He shivered, for someone had taken his only blanket. But he was ever hopeful that his release would come soon.

A week later, on a morning after a night when the ditches and puddles turned to ice, Meg arrived at the prison with a cake, a blanket, and a penny for the jailer, only to learn that her father was dead.

When she told her mother, something in Jane broke. She became like an unlatched door swinging in the wind. She beat her forehead with her fists, crying, "I am the vilest of evildoers!" Such words alarmed Meg. She wondered if grief had addled her mother's mind.

Her own grief was of the silent sort. She dreamed of her father as a hearty bricklayer lifting her into his arms. When she awoke she hoped it was true and waited for him to come home. When he did not, tears slipped from her eyes. How could he leave her forever?

It was her mother's fault, Meg decided. "If you had gone to the jail and made them release Father, he would still be alive," she said, though she had no idea what the laws were and how justice was dealt.

Jane threw herself on her bed and drew her feet beneath

her. "See, the flood waters rise around me!" The unlatched door of her mind now hung by a single hinge.

The next morning Meg awoke to find herself alone in the house. Rain dribbled through the thatched roof and formed puddles on the floor. A feeling of dread enveloped her like a fog. Dressing quickly she left the house, hastened along Addle Street and down Wood Street, crossed Cheapside, and followed Bow Lane to Garlick Hill. The gutters in the middle of the street overflowed with garbage rushing downhill toward the river. Meg slipped in the mire but got up again. She searched along Thames Street, where warehouses opened onto the wharves and cranes stood like scaffolds for hanging criminals. At the end of a lane where steps led down to the water, Meg saw a pair of shoes. Her mother's shoes, neatly placed side by side as if she had just stepped out of them to bathe her feet.

"Mother!" shouted Meg. She gazed downriver to where the water surged beneath the arches of the great bridge. She called to the laborers operating a crane. "Did you see a woman go into the river?"

They shrugged and shook their heads.

Meg waited at the steps for her mother to return. The dread within her deepened into something with no name. Hours later, wet and bone-cold, Meg returned home to the house that sagged like a sorrowful face and leaked water like tears. She climbed into her parents' flea-infested bed. All night her eyes stayed open to aid her ears in listening for her mother's steps.

When she heard excited voices in the street she thought, *There is news of my mother.* She jumped out of bed and went outside but could not bring herself to question anyone and put her terrible fears into words.

At the grocer's stall in Wood Street she paid a farthing for some apples, hoping the grocer would tell her the news, but he turned away to help another customer.

The barber's son, a little magpie with bare feet and ragged feathers, ran up to her.

"Did you hear what happened last night? It makes me shudder to think of it!"

Meg hugged the apples close in her apron and dumbly shook her head.

"You don't know?" he said. "For an apple, I'll tell you."

Meg's hand shook as she gave him the fruit. "Did they pull someone from the river?"

The boy bit into the apple. He was going to make Meg wait.

"Tell me, was she dead or alive?"

"Dead," he said. "Murdered in his bed last night!"

His bed? "Who was murdered?" she asked.

"The priest at St. Alphage. His head was beaten in. I saw him wrapped in a sheet."

Meg stood, stunned. *A whited sepulchre.* She thought of her mother bearing down upon the linen sheet with her hot iron. Throwing the iron against the wall in anger.

"How did it happen?" she whispered.

"It was a strong arm that did it and a heavy weapon the murderer took away with him."

"Did anyone see . . . the killer?"

"Nay, he escaped before anyone saw him," the boy said, disappointed.

Meg's heart was beating wildly. She ran back home on

legs barely able to hold her up. Apples dropped from her skirt and rolled away. Once inside the house, she glanced toward the hook by the hearth where her mother kept the iron. It was gone.

"My mother—a murderess?" The horrible word slipped from her lips. She saw her mother rising at night and carrying the iron through the dark streets. But she could not imagine her beating the priest with it. Even in her bitterest fury, Jane had never struck Meg's father with the iron. But then she had never been so maddened and desperate as in the weeks since his death.

Now Meg understood that her mother had walked into the river with the iron, letting the bloody weapon drag her underwater. Grief and guilt over her deed drove her to kill herself. Her mother was a murderess twice over! Her father, a beggar who died in prison. How had it come to pass that she, Meg, was the daughter of shame and sinful sorrow and now alone in the world?

"I am no longer myself," she said, not knowing quite what she meant. She went to bed and slept for a long, long time, because there was no one to wake her up.

No one from the parish came to take Meg to the hospital where orphans were cared for. To keep from starving, she nipped food from the market vendors and ran away so fast, no one could catch her. The Fleet River provided fish; orchards yielded fruit into her hands. Meg began to thrive like a flower sprung from winter's withered stalks. Her hair became tangled and she cut it off. Her bodice was tight, so she filched some clothes she found drying on a bush. They turned out to be a boy's shirt and trousers. They proved comfortable and easier to run in than a skirt; thus she took to wearing them all the time.

Meg spent her aimless days in Moorfield, London's playground, watching the boys compete at stoolball and wrestling until they let her join their games. She gave her name as Mack. Soon she could strike the ball and fight as well as any of them. Davy Dapper and Peter Flick were the leaders, strong and unruly boys a few years older than Meg who seemed, like her, to have no parents. They never guessed she was a girl, not even when she emerged from a wrestling match with tears on her cheeks. She was not injured, but her chest ached with the longing to be embraced, however roughly. She threw herself into the next match and the one after that.

One day the landlord forced his way into the house to demand payment of the overdue rent. Finding the penniless orphan only stirred up his rage. He thrust his whelk-studded nose in Meg's face and shouted, "Give me three crowns, you puny maltworm, or I'll have you thrown in the clink!"

"I'll give you a crown—of bruises!" Meg grabbed a broken table leg and struck the landlord above his ear. "Now get out of here, you reeking pig's kidney!" She was learning new insults daily from her friends Davy and Peter.

"Surly boy, you deserve to die in prison like your father!" shouted the landlord, holding his head in his hands as he staggered away.

Meg sank to the floor and began to cry, at first without a sound and then with loud sobs. There was not a person in the world to comfort her, so it was some time before she was able to stop. She stared at her hands still clutching the table leg. It had felt so good to strike the landlord. Her own strength surprised her. Now she *could* imagine her mother beating the priest. Had she meant to kill him? Had Meg meant to kill the landlord?

She threw the table leg aside as if it were on fire.

Soon the landlord would return and fulfill his threats. Meg knew she had to leave at once. Her heart thudding, she packed a bundle of clothes and trifles to remind her of her parents: a button from her father's jerkin, a coif her mother wore to bed. On the stoop she hesitated, then threw the bundle aside. Empty-handed, she left the crooked, sorry house on Addle Street for good.

Or rather, for ill.

~⊙ Chapter 2 ⊙~

Stratford 1580

Will Shakespeare was a serious-looking boy with a wide, high forehead and wavy dark hair, the eldest son of a glover, former mayor, and chief alderman of Stratford-upon-Avon. That is, his one father, John Shakespeare, was all of these. The family's house sprawled over several lots on Henley Street and was a palace compared to Meg's half-ruined house on Addle Street. Will's mother, Mary Arden, came from a proud family who had once owned the entire forest northwest of Stratford. But her wealth had passed to her husband at their marriage and then through his fingers like sand. When Will was a little boy she would kiss him and say, "You are all my riches now." She taught him to read using a hornbook, and Will soaked up words as a field soaks up water.

While not an overly pious family, the Shakespeares sometimes graced the front pew of Holy Trinity Church. The priest there, unlike his counterpart at London's St. Alphage, did not meddle in the lives of his parishioners. But private misdeeds became public matters nonetheless. One of Will's first memories was of a woman shrouded in white and forced to stand while the preacher denounced her sin. Thus it was in church that Will first heard the words "harlot" and "lechery." He thought the faceless, white-clad girl with her head bowed was a ghost from beyond the grave, bound to return there after the service.

Will's family was a boisterous one, down through his brother Gilbert, sister Joan, and three younger siblings. The shouts of children playing and the clatter from the work-shop filled the sturdy timber house, along with the smells of his mother's cooking and the less savory odor of animal hides soaking in urine. Every night Will knelt to receive his father's blessing and heard him say, "Remember always your duty of obedience. Revere God in heaven and your father on earth."

A good son, young Will worshipped his father. He retained another early memory of standing on a bench watching a troupe of richly costumed actors perform in the guildhall. He danced with excitement to see them, while his father's arms about his knees kept him from falling.

"I want to be a player," Will said in great earnest. "Every-one will look at me and clap their hands." His father only laughed.

When he was about thirteen, Will realized that some mis-fortune had befallen his father. He stopped attending coun-cil meetings and no longer wore his black furred gown and alderman's thumb ring. He was sometimes drunk and his nightly blessing gave way to threats. Sometimes he beat Will or Gilbert, saying, "Remember, I am your father!" as if he himself had forgotten.

School offered Will an escape, and he gladly rose before

dawn to lose himself in studying history, ciphering, and Latin. His favorite work was Ovid's *Metamorphoses* with its tales of gods changing form and meddling with mankind. He was not often truant, save when a company of players came to nearby Warwick or Coventry. The master would duly whip him for missing his lessons, but his heart was not in it, for Will was his best student. Will himself hardly minded the punishment because the plays gave him such pleasure. He marveled how ordinary men, like Ovid's gods, could transform themselves and persuade him their feigning was truth.

As Will progressed through Stratford grammar school, the fortunes of John Shakespeare worsened. He sold some properties and mortgaged others. Creditors came to the house demanding payment, but Mary bargained with them until they went away. The bailiff delivered a summons to court, but John ignored it. He seldom left the house, and when he did Will was afraid he would be arrested. Fortunately the magistrate was an old friend of his father's and hesitated to enforce the warrants against him.

As his father declined, Will grew strong like a new shoot from a weak branch. His shoulders strained against his jerkin and his chin sprouted a few soft hairs he coaxed into the shape of a beard. He began to notice the female sex, their round and pleasing bodies. He would often recall the opening lines of Ovid's poem:

> *Of shapes transformed to bodies strange, I*
> *purpose to treat;*
> *Ye gods vouchsafe (for you are they that*
> *wrought this wondrous feat)*
> *To further this my enterprise.*

Restlessly he longed for change of any kind; sleeping and waking he dreamed of every sort of greatness and many a shapely girl.

But dreaming could not dispel his family's troubles. Often he heard his parents quarreling behind the closed door of the shop and leaned closer to listen.

"You have also profited from my wool trading," his father was saying.

"But I did not condone it. The first time you were fined I warned you to stop. If only you had heeded me!" His mother sounded tearful.

Will had often accompanied his father to the sheep fair. He helped with the shearing and filled the bags with fleece, enjoying the greasy softness under his fingers. There were now thirty or more bags—each weighing a tod, or twenty-eight pounds—in their barn. Will knew how profitable wool trading could be. More profitable than making gloves.

"You ask who betrayed you? Why, most likely some merchant whose honest trade you have usurped," his mother said.

"God rot him, whoever he is! I have traded wool for fifteen years without a license. Why should the Privy Council now enforce a long-breached law? I'll raise my rents to pay the fine."

"You have already done so. Your tenant over on Mill Lane, William Burbage, calls you a robber."

Will slipped away, keeping to himself the knowledge of his father's lawbreaking. One moment he felt contempt for him, the next moment pity. He wanted his father to be an honest glover and respected citizen again.

What did Will want for himself? Not to become his father,

for one thing. He thought of Ovid's Proteus, *changing aye his figure and his hue, From shape to shape a thousand times.* Will wondered what shape he would finally take. He might become an actor who, with a change of costume and a new manner of speaking, could be either a beggar or a king. He watched his own mind shift as wind stirs a field of wheat, until he found that his thoughts had ripened and were ready to harvest.

He went to his father. "I want to leave school." The sound of his own deep voice surprised him. "I have enough learning."

John Shakespeare laid down his needle and leaned his elbows on his work bench. "You do not want to become an Oxford philosopher? A lawyer at the Inns of Court?" He waved a hand at these airy fancies they could no longer afford.

Will eyed his father directly. "It is time for me to earn an *honest* living. To relieve our family's troubles."

John Shakespeare frowned.

Will realized it would not do to anger him. "Whatever I earn I will send home," he said with more humility.

"Don't beat about the bush. What labor do you intend to do?"

"I want to become a player." The words rushed from Will's mouth. "I'll join Lord Warwick's company if he will have me. I will gain such renown the queen herself will ask me to perform for her."

Again John Shakespeare laughed at his son's ambitions. "An *honest* living? A player is no better than a vagabond. Would you shame me thus?"

Will's retort came quickly. "You have already shamed this family by breaking the law with your wool trading." He could feel his neck and face growing hot. "And by selling Wilmcote, the last of Mother's estates, which was to be my inheritance."

John Shakespeare stood up and thrust aside his worktable, spilling its contents to the floor. He seized a strip of hide. It whistled through the air, snapped against Will's skin, and wrapped around his arm like a whip.

"Remember I am your father! You dare not speak to me so."

Will pulled his arm free and clenched his fists to keep from striking back.

"You *will* leave school," said John Shakespeare. "But it will be to learn *my* trade and none other."

You're a tyrant! Will wanted to shout. *But I am a rebel and will not submit!*

"But Father, I am not meant to be a glovemaker," Will protested.

His man's voice betrayed him, changing back into a boyish squeak.

⌒℘ *Chapter 3* ℘⌒

London 1580

When Meg left the house on Addle Street for the last time she could think of nowhere to go but Moorfields, where she told Peter Flick and Davy Dapper that her house had burned down, killing her parents.

"Did ye set the fire?" asked Davy. He seemed disappointed when she said no. He told her he had been apprenticed to a carpenter but ran away because the work was too hard. When he smiled Meg saw his teeth were starting to rot.

"I'm an orphan too," said Peter. "You're better off with no father than with one that beats you." He showed Meg his broken nose. It made a clicking sound when he moved it from side to side.

When dusk fell she simply followed Davy and Peter through the city, across the great bridge to Southwark, and down Crooked Lane to the sign of the cock, a ruined shop they called their den. There she slept on what remained of the second floor, a narrow loft reached by a ladder. The boys' den was crammed with broken bits of furniture, empty sacks, and moldering cloth. The single window was always shuttered, making it dark within, though here and there could be seen an unexpected gleam from a piece of gold braid, a ring, or an embroidered purse. Meg wondered but dared not ask how Davy and Peter had come to own such rich trifles. She was simply grateful for a place to sleep and companions against her loneliness.

Meg continued to pretend she was a boy. She had seen girls her age strolling along the wharves who were already bawds. She understood what had happened between her mother and the priest. She did not tell Peter or Davy that her mother was a murderess, though she suspected this would raise her in their esteem. Her companions talked much about crime. Davy had even been arrested. Through him Meg learned that the magistrate's mercy had a price. If her mother could have paid it, her father would still be alive. The sight of beggars saddened her, and when they were kicked and spat upon it roused her to anger.

Davy and Peter often resorted to St. Paul's Church. Meg accompanied them and was filled with amazement. No one prayed but rather strolled in a great crowd up and down the nave as casually as if it were a street. Peter thrust a purse into her hand and whispered, "Run!" She obeyed, fleeing so fast that her heels kicked her rump. When the boys caught up with her they were gleeful.

"How were we to know he was a fleet-foot?" Peter said as they congratulated each other. "He'll be an asset to our trade."

Meg asked what that was, for she had never seen them labor or trade in anything.

"Our business is to unburden persons of that which they take no proper care of," Davy explained, showing his black grin.

"Why, you are thieves!" said Meg.

"So are you," said Peter, scowling. "You'd be dead as a doornail if you hadn't been stealing food all this while."

Meg fell silent at the truth of his words.

"Come, you minnow!" said Davy, prodding her. "What wrong is there in relieving the rich of their excess? We will show you how it's done."

Meg, who was tired of being poor through no fault of her own, consented. It became her job to spy out a careless or aimless person and signal to Peter where the gull wore his purse. While Davy engaged him in conversation, Peter, with a flick of a knife against a horn-covered thumb, cut his purse strings. He passed the purse to Meg, who stuffed it down the front of her trousers, where its weight caused her no small discomfort. Her mind was also uneasy, but she put aside her misgivings rather than offend her only friends.

With Meg's small share of the purse she bought herself a simple doublet and hose and a velvet cap. She was keeping a close eye on her slim body lest it grow round and betray her. The way Davy and Peter talked about women caused her to blush, even made her a little fearful. She dropped the remaining coins through the grate of the Wood Street jail so the prisoners could purchase bread or a blanket from their jailers.

Davy and Peter spent their larger share on the fashionable clothing gallants wore and lost the rest gaming.

Not every day was given to cutting purses. Some days they enjoyed innocent pranks. Meg's favorite was to climb the bell-tower in the yard of St. Paul's. There they scraped off the pigeon dung with a knife and dropped it on the heads of passersby, whose outrage left the trio weak with laughter. But when a rival band of roisterers moved into the churchyard, Davy and Peter decided to seek out a new haunt across the city. What drew them to the Boar's Head Inn were the people crowding into the front gate. Whether the entertainment was a cockfight or a troupe of jugglers, a crowd meant an opportunity for thieves to ply their trade.

They paid a penny each to enter the innyard. The benches and galleries overlooking the wooden stage were nearly filled.

"I expect to be many times repaid," murmured Davy, rubbing his hands together.

"To it, Mack. Spy out a gull," said Peter.

Meg nodded toward an old man with his purse dangling in full view.

"I'll greet him now," said Davy. "Follow me, Peter; stay close, Mack."

But Meg's eye was caught by the movement on the stage. Two soldiers charged each other, their swords clashing. One groaned and blood seemed to spurt from him as he fell down dead. The very timbers of the stage shook.

"No, let's watch this action," said Meg. "I've never seen a play."

The victor began to deliver a lofty speech, whereupon the dead soldier sat up and thrust his sword into him. Meg gasped and stood on her toes, trying to see the wound.

"Come, Mack!" Peter's horn-thumb tapped the underside of his palm.

"Go snare him yourselves," she said in vexation.

Onstage the players ranted, fought, embraced their queens, fought again, and died a second time. Meg clapped until her palms hurt. She forgot about Davy and Peter, her petty crimes, her lost parents, everything but the present moment. The hostess of the inn passed before her carrying a pitcher of ale in each hand, her teeth as big as a horse's as she laughed at the stableboy trying to juggle oranges. One bright, round fruit fell to the ground. A woman seated beside Meg grabbed it and tossed the boy a penny. The players uttered words such as Meg had never heard before, words that fell on her ears like the measured beat of a drum. The woman with the fragrant orange leaned against Meg, called her "sweet boy," and offered her a slice of the fruit. Here was a new world of comfort and good cheer, and Meg's heart stirred with longing to be in it.

"Heigh-ho! Seize those scoundrels!"

Meg looked aside to see Peter and Davy pushing their way through the crowd. They leaped onto the stage and off again, pulling down the curtain on the startled actors. Two men pursued them across the stage. The audience roared with laughter, thinking this was a part of the play, until the actors began to curse.

My friends are in trouble, thought Meg, jumping to her feet and running after them.

"There goes a third one!" Meg heard the man's voice behind her and felt someone grab her cloak.

"I'll make you pay, thief!" The man's stinking breath assaulted Meg. He twisted the fabric at her neck, choking her.

She screamed. "Peter! Davy! Help me!"

They glanced over their shoulders at her but did not stop or even slow down.

Meg struggled against her captor. She managed to untie

the cloak, leaving it in the man's hand as she fled. She ran until the cries and footsteps behind her faded into silence. Peter and Davy were nowhere to be seen. She turned right and left, calling their names in a low voice. She was in a maze of narrow lanes, where she wandered until she emerged on the riverbank. Before her the swift-moving water glimmered in the twilight; the bridge was only a short distance away.

As long as she could see the river, Meg was not lost.

On her right hand loomed the Tower, a fortress where the worst criminals in all of England were kept. Meg imagined their moans and the clanking of chains. How close she had come to being caught! She knew that Peter and Davy would not rescue her. No, they had betrayed her. She never wanted to see them again.

Misery enveloped Meg like black water, and with a stab of sorrow she thought of her drowned mother. She turned her back on the river and huddled in the lee of an old stable, wrapped in growing darkness and knowing there was not a soul alive who cared for her, not even the woman at the Boar's Head Inn who had called her a sweet boy. She longed for another bite of that orange. But she was penniless again and lacked even the warmth of her cloak.

Perhaps Meg slept. When she stirred again it was long past curfew. The houses were all dark and the only light came from the pale moon. She sensed someone approaching and all her muscles braced for flight. The figure clung to the shadows, but Meg slowly made out the thin man carrying a long hook and creeping from house to house, looking up at the windows.

At once Meg knew how to save herself. She would have to commit another crime, but she promised herself it would be her last one. As stealing food had been necessary to keep from starving, so was this new misdeed necessary if she wanted to live an honest life.

Chapter 4

The man with the hook, a curber by profession, did not see Meg. She had the advantage of surprise. With a pounding heart she waited until he was upon her, then she leaped up and threw an arm around his neck, cutting off his breath. This was a move she learned while wrestling with Davy and Peter.

"Unhand me!" he cried, choking and dropping his hook as he tried to pull Meg's arm away.

"Do as I say," said Meg in a low-pitched voice, "or I'll raise the hue and cry and your profitable night strolling will end."

The curber tried to nod. Meg released him, satisfied to see that he trembled. "What's your name?" she demanded.

"Nick Grabwill," he said, rubbing his neck with a wrinkled hand. With a start, Meg realized she had assaulted an old man.

"Pick up your hook, Nick, and filch me a bodice and skirt," she said in a courteous tone. "Nothing cheap."

Grabwill sighed but proceeded through the silent streets, shadowed by Meg. He lifted a pillow from one open window, a man's shirt from another. The hook disappeared a third time, whereupon Meg heard sharp, high-pitched crying.

"Go to! Have you snatched a babe from its cradle?" she whispered.

Grabwill hurriedly withdrew his hook and they ducked into an alley. The babe's cries ceased. Meg's throat was dry.

"Give me the hook," she said. At the next open window, she guided the hook to where she imagined a bedpost with clothing hanging from it might be. Something—a lantern or metal cup—clattered to the floor inside.

"Who goes there!" came a man's voice at the window.

Meg ran, dragging the curber behind her. On a street by the wharf they paused before a three-storied house with its upper windows flung open to the fishy air.

Grabwill smiled. "Here's many a skirt to be picked up with ease. Let's try our fortunes within."

"What do you mean?" said Meg.

"Why, here is the best bawdy house this side of the Thames," he said, reaching for the knocker.

Meg struck his hand away. "I am not given to such lewdness!"

"What sort of boy are you?" said Grabwill, peering at her more closely than she liked.

"One who does not answer questions. Try your luck with the hook. Now!" She pointed to the windows but the curber stood still. He was losing his fear of her, so Meg reached out and cuffed his ear. She hated to hurt him but she had to have the clothing.

Angrily Grabwill fished in the window, his hook loudly

striking the window jamb as it emerged at last with the necessary garments.

Meg heard cursing. A half-naked woman leaned from the window.

"Is that you, villain Nick? A pox on you, hedgehog." She threw a bucket of night soil after them. Meg darted away in time but Grabwill was not so fortunate.

"Now my clothes are fouled and you owe me for the pains I've taken," he said once they had left the brothel behind. He was surly and Meg was eager to be quit of him.

"Take off your clothes," she said, seizing the hook from him.

Seeing his tool brandished against him Grabwill undressed, tripping as he removed his pants. With the hook Meg deposited his clothes in an open window. While he stood there helpless, Meg took off her jerkin and slipped on the bodice over the man's shirt she wore. She did this in haste, trusting Grabwill not to look at her closely. She put on the skirt, removed her hose underneath, and tossed the jerkin and hose to the curber.

"These are worth more than the rags you wore, and thus you are paid for your pains." In a softer tone she added, "I thank you, for now I am a reformed thief."

"The hat too," Grabwill demanded, pointing to her velvet cap.

Meg pulled off the cap and handed it to him. Even in the dark she could see his astonishment as her gold curls tumbled about her ears. He clapped Meg's discarded clothes to the front of his body.

"What are you, a doxy from yonder brothel or a devil from hell?"

Meg could not help smiling. "I am as honest a man as you are," she said. And then to spare him further shame she turned and ran away.

After an hour of searching Meg found her way back to the Boar's Head. The gate to the innyard was locked and quiet reigned. She curled up against the smaller postern door and thought of sweet oranges and laughter and strutting players. But when she fell asleep her dreams were not so pleasant. A vengeful Nick Grabwill pursued her with his hook, but she couldn't run because her feet were weighted with iron. Peter and Davy laughed soundlessly at her plight, the latter's maw full of black teeth.

When the door creaked open, Meg tumbled into the yard and awoke to see a woman with a broom looming over her. It was the hostess, her mouth a wide O of surprise.

"What sort of creature have we here?"

Meg got stiffly to her feet. By the morning light she saw that her bodice was of red taffeta and gaped in the front. Her skirt of yellow sarcenet ended a long way from the ground, showing her man's shoes and stockings. Even to herself she looked ridiculous. At least she no longer resembled Peter and Davy's companion from the night before.

"A poor but honest maid in need of shelter," Meg said humbly.

The hostess cocked her head. "How old are you, child?"

"I was twelve at my last birthday but I might be thirteen now."

"Where are your mother and father?"

Meg did not know where her father's body was buried or where her mother's drowned body had come to rest. "Dead," she said simply.

The hostess uttered a mew of pity. "How came you here?"

"By these two feet of mine." Meg looked at her shoes. "I ran from some wicked men."

The hostess stepped into the street with her broom raised and looked both ways. "You haven't led them here? I'll have naught to do with any villains. Did they harm you?"

"No, mistress." There was nothing more to say without unfolding her entire doubtful history.

The woman had her own suspicions. "Are you a strumpet? Your clothes look like they were taken from a bawdy house."

Meg gulped. How quickly the woman had hit on the truth— at least part of it.

"By this hand I am an honest girl," she protested. Tears sprang to her eyes. So much depended on this woman's mercy.

At that moment her stomach rumbled loudly.

"Bless me, you're starving!" the hostess exclaimed, dropping her broom. "Come with me anon."

Meg was glad to obey and followed her into the kitchen. She stared amazed at the hearth, which was wide enough to lie down in. It was fitted with pot hooks on swivels, spits for roasting meat, kettles, and stirring spoons. The hostess filled a trencher with porridge, bacon, and milk, which Meg devoured.

"Have you any kin?" the woman asked, regarding Meg with warm brown eyes.

Meg, her mouth full, shook her head.

"In all the world there is no one to care for you?" Her voice rose as if she might cry. She heaped more porridge onto Meg's plate and dribbled honey over it.

"No one," Meg echoed. The porridge tasted heavenly. She wanted so badly to stay.

"You have not run away from the Christ's Hospital?" The hostess stood with her hands on her wide hips. She was as round as a kettle.

"No, I lived alone until our house burned down." One lie could hardly hurt.

The hostess shook her head sadly. "What brought you to me?" she said more to herself than to Meg.

Meg chewed her food to avoid having to reply. She could hardly confess that she had first come to the Boar's Head with the intention of stealing from the patrons.

"Don't answer, for I already know." The hostess looked upward. "Providence brought you here, child, for just yesterday I said to Master Overby, 'I must hire a servant.' If you will work for your bed and board, then you may stay."

Meg leaped to her feet, threw her arms around the wide hostess, and—to her own very great surprise—lifted her right off the floor.

The woman's little feet scrabbled in midair. She let out a cry of protest, but when Meg set her down again she looked almost pleased. Her large teeth showed in a grin.

"You may call me Mistress Gwin or Mistress Overby, I care not which," she said, red-faced. "But I won't have you pick me up again unless I have fallen down."

"Yes, mistress!"

"What name did your parents, God rest their souls, give you?"

"Mack—*Meg*." She quickly corrected herself but Gwin seemed not to notice the slip. Then she hesitated. Her surname, Macdougall, was a reminder of her parents' shame and failure, which she preferred to forget. And yet her father had been a good man, not a thief like herself.

"I am Meg de Galle," she said at last. For this was to be a fresh start in her life and she needed a new, unsullied name.

~⌬ Chapter 5 ⌬~

Stratford 1582

The smell of the urine tubs stung Will's nose and made him gag. In the two years of his forced apprenticeship he had learned how to prepare the hides of deer, sheep, horses, and even goats. After scraping the skins and softening them with salt and alum, he soaked them in the urine tubs, then laid them out to dry. It always surprised Will that the resulting leather was smooth and soft, with no trace of foulness. But he would never get used to the awful smell. It stood for everything he hated about his father's trade.

After the first year it became Gilbert's job to tend the smelly tubs, and Will progressed to cutting the leather using special knives, patterns, and a glover's compass. He liked the precision of this work and laid out the patterns so as to waste none of the leather. But he hated stitching the pieces into belts, purses, saddles, and gloves. The needles pricked his clumsy fingers, the seams were always uneven, and his father berated his every effort.

Will's sister Joan worked the finer pieces such as women's gloves. Sometimes she lined them with velvet or flannel. The best ones were finished with gold braid, embroidery, and lace. John Shakespeare paid two sisters from Shottery, Anne and Catherine Hathaway, a penny for each glove they trimmed. Ever since spring, when he had held her nimble fingers in his and danced around the Maypole until he was breathless, Will had been in love with Catherine.

Will had known the sisters all his life. His father had purchased sheepskins and wool from their father, Richard Hathaway, who owned Hewlands Farm in nearby Shottery. But Hathaway had died, leaving his second wife to care for their five children. Anne and Catherine were her stepdaughters, but she treated them like servants. Everyone in the village pitied them for it.

Anne was twenty-six, eight years older than Will, with a mane of thick brown hair and freckles across her nose that gave her a look of sunny, robust health. When Will felt the first stirrings of manhood, he stole glances at Anne's round and shapely body just to feel his blood grow warm. But he could not forget how she used to carry him on her hip when he was a little boy and play with him like a puppy. Around her he always felt like a little boy tongue-tied with admiration.

Then he began to notice Catherine. What ho, Ovid! Almost overnight she had changed, and she now resembled Anne in height and shape so closely, they might have been twins. Will compared what he could see of their bosoms and found himself not more pleased with one set than the other. Even Catherine's hair was the same color as her sister's though sleeker, like the fur of a wet otter. She had green eyes and skin like fresh cream. She was shy, favoring Will with smiles but few words. And she was exactly his age.

On a sunny morning in mid-May Will followed the path from Stratford toward Shottery, crossing the brook and the meadows full of cowslips and honey-stalks without even seeing them. He cut across the hayfield belonging to Fulke Sandells, trampling the new wheat. Catherine's pale beauty was the only thought in his mind. And when he knocked at the door of Hewlands Cottage with its frame of hedge roses, it was his good fortune that she was the one to open it.

"Will!" His name was a breath issuing from her lips. A pink flush rose to her cheeks. She glanced over her shoulder and said in reply to a sharp voice that Will guessed was her stepmother's, " 'Tis only John Shakespeare's boy."

She turned back to Will and giggled. Her movements stirred up the scent of roses. He forgot what he had intended to say, content merely to look upon her.

The sharp voice sounded again. "Catherine, you lazy wench, you left the lid off the churn and there are flies in the butter!"

Catherine sighed. "I will think on you while I work," she said and withdrew into the house.

Will closed his eyes. The idea of Catherine with the churn held between her knees made him dizzy with desire.

A female voice said, " 'Only the Shakespeare boy.' I am glad it is not Fulke Sandells."

Will opened his eyes, surprised to see Anne where her sister had stood moments before. She smiled at him, her head tilted to the side, and waited for him to speak.

All Will could think of to say was, "Does your neighbor dislike my walking through his field?"

"Sandells's dislikes are no matter of mine," she said with a wave of her hand. "Why did you come here? I told your father I would deliver the finished gloves tomorrow."

Anne was never afraid to speak her mind. Perhaps that was why she was still unmarried. There had been gossip involving a betrothal and some misfortune, but Will had paid no attention to it. Now he wondered what the truth was.

" 'Tis a fair day for a ramble through the fields," he replied, satisfied that the answer made him seem aimless and free.

"Are you inviting me thither?"

"You and . . . and your fair sister," stammered Will.

"Catherine is not done with her chores," Anne said, stepping over the threshold and taking Will's arm. He had no choice but to walk with her. At the gate she plucked a sprig of lilac and tucked it behind her ear. The fragrance drew Will toward her. She reached up and touched his chin, saying she liked his new beard. Will was proud of this change in his features. He blushed and wondered if she was serious.

Laughing, Anne led him along a path toward the woods Will's ancestors had once owned. Before they reached its shaded precincts, a cloudburst drove them back to the cottage, where they took shelter under the eaves.

"So Nature keeps us from our pleasant purposes," said Will, leaning against the cottage wall and thinking of Catherine.

"I think I know *your* purpose, Will Shakespeare. Was it only the piecework you came for or something more?"

Her teasing tone confused him. Did she suspect he loved her sister? Without thinking, he said, "You are the piece of work I sought, Nature's own best creation."

It was the very phrase he had been saving for Catherine. But Anne was before him, buxom and redolent of lilac, her hair in damp tendrils around her face.

"Though it is a lesser work—the gloves—I must be content with," he added.

"You are a witty one," said Anne, slapping his arm lightly. "I'll fetch them for you."

Will hoped Catherine would come out so he could see her again, but Anne returned quickly, handing him the bundle of gloves. With no further reason to dally and nothing else witty to say, Will tucked the gloves inside his jerkin and said good-bye. At the end of the lane he glanced back and thought he saw Catherine's pale face at the window, watching him through the curtain of rain.

However Will contrived to speak to Catherine, it was always Anne who came to Henley Street on business or met Will in the marketplace and bade him walk her back to Shottery. He complied, for he always hoped to see her sister. When Anne took his arm, Will was afraid anyone who saw them would think he was courting her. At the same time he wondered what her body looked like without clothes. He wished that she were younger or he older. He felt guilty for dreaming about Anne when it was her sister he loved. But Catherine remained out of reach, a bud deep within a thorny rosebush.

Therefore Will conceived a plan to kiss Catherine during the Pentecost festival in June, when three days of games, dances, and mumming culminated in the crowning of the Summer King and Queen. But he required the aid of the pageant's organizer, David Jones, who happened to be one of his father's loyal customers.

When Jones came by the shop Will saw his chance.

"For you, Davy, this belt is only five shillings, not eight," he said, then skillfully brought the conversation around to the festival.

Jones admitted the pageant had become a burden to organize, with merchants, craftsmen, and aldermen all vying to create the best wagons and obtain places of honor in the procession.

Will hummed in sympathy. "I was thinking more of the play itself," he said. "Those ancient rhymes so twist the tongue and strain the sense that the audience groans to hear them. 'Tis no fault of yours," he added hastily.

Jones looked troubled. "If the play displeases the people of Stratford, I will suffer in their esteem."

"I have some skill with verses," said Will. "With your leave I will make the old pageant new, and you shall be praised for it."

Jones hesitated. He was paid a good wage for his yearly efforts and was unwilling to share it, Will knew.

"I want no payment. Only permit me to play the first shepherd," he said. Thus reassured, Jones gave his ready consent.

Will knew the old pageant by heart. He began revising it in his head as he worked. At first the words trickled through his brain like water in a dry brook. Why, it was easier to translate Latin sentences! But when he thought of Catherine the rhymes flowed freely. At night he scribbled down his new verses by the flame of a candle stub. A week later he visited David Jones with his finished pages.

Nodding as he read it Jones said, "I like it very well. The Summer Queen is hard of heart but women are ever so."

Affecting nonchalance Will said, "I care not who plays

the queen, but let the younger Hathaway sister be my shepherdess. She is nimble and can lead the others in the dance."

Will had carefully rewritten the lines he would say to his shepherdess to awaken thoughts of love.

> *Behold the queen, the mistress of disdain,*
> *Leading her king with a rose-red chain.*
> *When his lips are ready for their pay*
> *She winks and turns her lips another way.*
> *Come now you shepherds, all ye red-lipped lasses,*
> *Praise the god of love, ere summer passes.*

Jones punched Will's arm. "I see your plot!" he said. "I'll gladly smooth the path of love for you. She shall be in your arms by nightfall."

On the day of the pageant, the mayor's son and an alderman's daughter were transformed with flowers and green worsted capes into the king and queen, harbingers of summer. Will, wearing a sheepskin belted at the waist, spoke his lines to Catherine while straining to see through her gauze tunic. She pursed her lips until, cued by his verses, she smiled at him. But she would not kiss him as the other lasses did their shepherds.

"Please," he said. "It is written thus." But she only shook her head.

Though downcast by her refusal, Will grinned to hear the loud applause, which pleased him more than he had expected.

After the play, as everyone began to dance, Anne seized

Will as her partner and leaped lightly before him. "See, I can dance as prettily as my sister. But no one can rhyme like you, Will Shakespeare." And she kissed him on the cheek, leaving behind the scent of lilac. Will found himself blushing.

At least one citizen of Stratford was not pleased with the day's events. John Shakespeare, though he did not leave his house to see the pageant, heard about Will's role in it. That night Will felt his wrath.

"Did I not forbid you to be a player? Yet you deceive me and strut upon a stage before the whole town." Spittle gathered at the corners of his mouth. "I thought you had forgotten that disgraceful business. Writing verses! What profit is there in such vanity?"

"Thieving is more disgraceful than acting," Will shot back, "yet there is profit in it. Many a man, while seeming virtuous, milks the commonwealth for his good alone."

His father smoldered like a peat fire. "Hold your peace!" he demanded, reaching for his rod. "I abhor your disobedience!"

But Will could not be silent. "Next to a thief a player is honest; he takes nothing but the appearance of another and yields it again at the play's end." He watched the rod tremble in his father's hand but felt no fear.

"I will be a poor player and an honest poet before I will be a false glover."

Will's father turned and struck the table. With a loud crack, his rod broke and clattered to the floor in pieces.

~ Chapter 6 ~

Will had crossed an invisible bridge and was estranged from his father, though they dwelled in the same house. But in his mind Will was absent, always pondering how to leave Stratford. Should he ask the mayor for a letter of introduction to Lord Warwick, or should he hie to London and find employment there? One should not arrive in London penniless. Perhaps it would be wiser to work as a tutor for a year and save his wages. He considered his choices like a clerk comparing columns of figures. Should he leave in secret or tell his mother? And what about Catherine? There was the rub, the biggest hurdle of all. He wanted to marry her and take her with him, but he had yet to declare his love or even to kiss her.

On market days Will and his brother tended their father's stall at a prime spot, the stone cross where Henley Street, Bridge Street, and High Street converged. Often Catherine came to Stratford's market to sell the butter she and her sisters made. Will clipped and perfumed his beard and took to wearing a lace-trimmed shirt, hoping to look his best for her.

The effect was like spreading birdlime on a bush; a whole flock of fair admirers was snared. A few even bought gloves.

But Will's shy bird did not come flitting by until the last market day in August, when the fruits of the fields and gardens overfilled the many stalls.

Will was playing the role of a glover's apprentice to similar excess. "Such pretty fingers, goodwife!" he said, lifting a customer's forearm by her wrist. "Slip them inside this glove. A perfect fit! Last week Lady Warwick bought a pair just like these."

He and Gilbert watched the woman prance away, her newly gloved hands raised for everyone to notice.

"Confound me if I know how you persuaded a poor laundress she cannot live without a pair of embroidered kid gloves," Gilbert said.

Will did not reply. He had glimpsed a familiar brown-haired woman carrying a basket. One of the Hathaway sisters, for certain. As she drew near, his heart leaped. It was Catherine! She smiled shyly and held her basket in front of her. When she drew in her elbows her breasts swelled behind her bodice. *Breasts like golden apples*, Will thought, faint with desire.

"Lean closer, mistress, that I might see what's in your basket." It was Gilbert who had the boldness to speak.

Will cuffed him on the ear, knocking off his cap. With an oath Gilbert bent to retrieve it.

" 'Tis only butter," Catherine said to Will. "Would you like a taste?"

She stuck her forefinger in the soft butter and held it aloft. Unable to believe his good fortune, Will took her hand and slowly brought it to his mouth. Should he lick her finger or put it in his mouth? He did both, lingering until she pulled her finger away. Will's heart was beating. This was better than a kiss.

"When can we meet? I must be alone with you," he said in a low, urgent voice.

"Anne watches me like a hawk."

"Hoodwink her. Slip away while she sleeps."

Catherine raised her eyebrows. "You don't know my sister."

Will groaned. "Pray give me another bite, butterfinger."

"Close your eyes."

Will obeyed and opened his mouth in anticipation. He felt Catherine's breath in his ear.

"Meet me in the Forest of Arden, where the old oak lies across the stream and the rocks with the fairy rings jut from the ground. Tomorrow when the moon is at its height."

Will felt a tap on his nose and opened his eyes. Catherine had gone, leaving a dab of melting butter on the end of his nose. With dreamlike slowness he wiped it off. Then he realized the meaning of her invitation. She wanted him as much as he wanted her!

"Heigh-ho!" he cried, throwing his arms around Gilbert, who was waiting on the alderman's daughter, and knocking him to the ground. They struck a post, causing the tent to lean and toppling bridles and belts. While Will pummeled his brother with glee, the alderman's daughter glanced around in a furtive manner, picked up a kidskin purse trimmed in gold braid, and put it in her sleeve. Humming to herself, she walked away.

Will did not sleep a wink that night, nor could he keep his mind on his work the next day. His thoughts raced like deer before the hounds. Yet the hours and minutes of the clock crept like snails. He worried that he would become tongue-tied when he tried to speak his love, so he composed his thoughts into verses and memorized them. *Shall I compare you to a summer day?* Summer was almost past. *You are more lovely than the buds of May.*

By nighttime Will was so weary he was afraid to lie down, lest he fall asleep and miss his meeting with Catherine. He leaned on the windowsill, listening to the creaks and sighs of the house as his family slumbered. He watched the shadows shift along Henley Street until he judged it was time to go. Through the silent town and westward toward Shottery he hurried, his path bordered by nodding gillyflowers and daisies. A grove of alder and birch marked the entrance to the forest. Beyond, thick-trunked oaks all but blocked the moonlight overhead, casting long columns of darkness on the ground. It was the last of August, the night was cool, and his feet were damp with dew from the bracken. He heard the brook singing while the rest of nature slept. Across its banks lay a fallen oak tree and nearby loomed a large rock. This was the spot Catherine had described—but it was deserted.

Will made his way over the rocks and sat on the trunk of the oak tree, his back resting against a branch. The moon began its descent, darkening the glade. An hour or more passed. Doubt stirred in Will. Had she come first and left because he was not there? Or had she never intended to come? Was he being played for a fool? He called her name but the woods returned no reply.

Just as Will was beginning to despair, he heard a rustling and saw a figure wrapped in a hooded cloak. *Catherine!*

"I thought you would never come," he said, taking her hand as she climbed over the fallen tree.

She lowered her head, her brown hair spilling forward. "I was half afraid," she murmured.

The darkness made him bold, able to speak without stammering. "Let me see you," he said and reached out to remove her hood.

She intercepted his hands and held them. Ever the shy one, she turned her head to the side. So with his lips he ventured beneath her hood and found her forehead. Her hands released his and touched his face instead. A bolt of lightning traveled to the pit of his stomach. He drew in his breath.

"I have got my wish and you, your Will. So let us kiss and love each other still."

At once her mouth covered his, soft and wet. He closed his eyes and opened his lips and with his tongue touched her ivory teeth. Like an explorer he ventured into the cavern of her ruby mouth. He felt at once weak and mighty. And stunned to find her as eager as he was to travel farther.

"Now let us all the rites of love fulfill."

The words were like the sighing of the wind through the trees. Will opened his eyes, but the moon had vanished and he could not see her face. Could this be his shy Catherine? The darkness had emboldened her. She shrugged off her cloak and was looking down to untie her bodice. Her swift, decisive movements reminded Will briefly of Anne. He reached out and pulled her bodice open. She tugged at his shirt and the points of his trousers. This was no dream, he knew as he lowered her to the ground and felt her warm and willing limbs yield to him.

Afterward she said, her low voice mingling with the gurgle of the brook, "If we follow this deed with vows, then we are wedded one to another."

Will was weary with joy. His eyes were closed, the better to feast his other senses upon her. He lowered his head into the slight bowl of her belly. "I promise to be true to you, my Catherine," he said and fell asleep.

Daylight shone through Will's eyelids, forcing him awake. He was curled up on his side, shirtless. He sat up with a groan, wondering why he was in the forest. He remembered Catherine. She was gone. He scratched his head. Had he dreamed the night's events? He put on his shirt and drew a long, brown hair from the sleeve. No. Catherine must have returned home to avoid rousing suspicion. He smiled to think how easy his task had proven after all. Throughout the summer he had fretted and delayed. Now in a single night he had wooed and won his love.

Will's forehead itched from lying on the bracken. He raised his hand to rub it and noticed that the ring he usually wore on his little finger was missing. He did not remember taking it off. Had he given it to Catherine? Had they vowed their love? In the bright light of day, Will was not sure he wanted to be married yet. But he thought of Catherine's body and the pleasures it afforded him, and his doubts faded.

Beside him the brook babbled away, telling the secrets of all the lovers who had ever lain on its banks. Will stretched out in a patch of sunlight, letting it dry his dew-damp clothes. He knew he should be at work but cared not a whit for anyone's disapproval but Catherine's.

The day was far gone when Will finally returned to Henley Street. He knew the moment he entered the house that his father's toubles had flared again, this time into a bonfire.

John Shakespeare was shouting at his wife. "If I answer this summons, they will throw me into some hellhole of a London prison. Do you want that?"

"You might as well be in prison! You never leave the house." Seeing Will, she ran to him. "Alack and well-a-day, my son! We are ruined for certain."

"What is the cause, Mother?" he asked, alarmed.

Will's father answered, "Burbage has moved to London and is suing me for ten pounds, the amount of loans plus interest." He leaned on his desk and stared at an open ledger. "You must help me, Will," he said without looking at him.

Honeyed thoughts of love melted from Will's mind. Would his father be forced to sell his business and the house on Henley Street? Where would they all live? His own ambitions seemed frivolous. How could he go away and leave his family in such straits?

"What can I do more? I am already doing an honest man's work," Will said. If his father even hinted at something illegal, Will was prepared to defy him.

John Shakespeare took out a key and unlocked a heavy oak cabinet behind him. He removed a small casket, unlocked it, and spilled the coins onto his desk.

"Here are twenty-five crowns I was saving to pay the herald for a coat of arms. But I no longer have cause to be titled a gentleman." He sounded bitter and defeated.

Will had never seen so much money. Twenty-five crowns was equal to six pounds, the amount a craftsman might earn in a year. But it was only a portion of what his father owed.

"Take it, Will. Use a pound to hire a lawyer. Thomas Greene of Middle Temple knows me. Make him persuade Burbage to settle for half the debt." He searched the summons. "Or the case will be heard at the Queen's Bench in Westminster on the fifteenth day of October and a penalty determined."

Will blinked in amazement. It was not the lawsuit or the sum he disbelieved, but that two extraordinary wishes could be fulfilled in a single day. He struggled to speak.

"You permit me . . . to go? Nay, you *send* me . . . to London?"

The look Will's father gave him said what his words could never say: that he trusted Will to perform this business, knowing he could not make him return to Stratford. He was saving face, granting Will freedom without diminishing his own authority.

Gratitude and long-buried affection stirred in Will. He knelt to his father as he used to when receiving his nightly blessing and said, "I will find Burbage and persuade him to drop his suit. I will be diligent in all things, Father, and one day you will be proud of me."

Will saw the path of his life stretching before him, straight as an arrow's course. To London, by way of Shottery.

Will pounded on the door of the Hathaway cottage, calling for Catherine. He shook the latch, leaned his ear against the door, and strained to hear within.

"I'm here, Will."

He whirled around to face a surprised Catherine. Seizing

her hand, he drew her into an arbor where roses twined and bloomed and told her what his father had asked him to do, concluding, "Come away with me, Catherine, whom I have missed since last night, as Adam missed the rib taken from his side—"

"Nay, I missed *you*, Will."

"Then we have lacked one another, but no longer." He reached for her other hand. "Why did you leave the forest without waking me?"

She pulled her hands away and brought them to her bosom. "You are mistaken; I never went to the forest." Her look was troubled.

"Then was it a dream? No, these hands and lips swear they touched you."

Catherine shook her head violently. "Last night I was locked in my room. Anne was my jailer. And after I confided in her! She said she would not let me risk my virtue."

Will ran his hands through his hair. His thoughts were in a muddle. Why would Catherine lie to him? Did she regret her hasty vow? He looked into her eyes and saw a fury he did not understand.

Catherine stamped her foot. "O vile sister! Where are you hiding?"

Will drew back as from a tigress.

Anne emerged from the barn with a jug of fresh milk. Her cheeks were flushed and her eyes dark-rimmed as if she had not slept. She passed by Will and Catherine, her gaze fixed on the kitchen door.

"Stop, Anne, and hear me." Catherine's voice was hard.

Anne set her jug on the doorsill and stood erect.

"Will Shakespeare claims he made love to me last night," said Catherine, her voice trembling. "I say it was not me but an impostor. Some witch, surely. What say you?"

Anne said nothing. She swept her forefinger along her neck, pulling a narrow ribbon from within her bodice. Will recognized the ring dangling there and the truth hit him like a rock.

"It was you?" he asked unnecessarily. For even without touching her now, he knew that it was Anne he had kissed, Anne whose body he had embraced, Anne who drew from him, on the brink of sleep, the vow that was as binding as marriage.

How could he have mistaken one sister for the other? He looked at Anne, her hair brown like Catherine's, her height the same, her face only a little more lined. Catherine had the flighty manner of a girl, but Anne had the firm confidence of a woman. And, it would seem, a woman's cunning.

"You deceived me, Anne," he said.

"You were willing to be deceived, I think. And I never claimed to be my sister." She spoke softly.

"Why did you do it?" Will said, even as a voice inside him whispered that his own passion had done it, had blinded him.

"Because *I* am a fitting match for you, Will Shakespeare." Now Anne sounded defiant. "Not my sister. She is a child who does not know her own mind."

"I know you are a jealous harpy!" cried Catherine. She shook her balled fists inches from Anne's face. "You can't get a young lover without tricking your way into his bed!"

"O I am bewitched and bewildered!" lamented Will. He

had relished every moment he spent with Anne, believing she was Catherine. Did that mean it was Anne he loved, not Catherine? Now Anne, bold and sensual, was appealing to him. And her sister, whom he thought he loved, was behaving like a shrew.

Anne didn't reply to her sister, only slipped Will's ring on her finger and removed it, tucking the ribbon into her bodice again.

Catherine stiffened as she understood the significance of the ring. "No! You marry old Fulke Sandells. Let *me* have Will Shakespeare!" She was sobbing now.

Anne did not flinch but bore the assault as if she deserved it. Will saw the tears in her eyes. He knew he should be angry with her, but those tears stirred him while Catherine's frightened him. Gog's wounds, he was confused!

"I hate you, sister," Catherine said. "And you, too, Will Shakespeare, now and for all time." She stalked away, plucking up flowers and flinging them to the ground.

Will turned. Anne was touching his arm. Her cheeks were wet but she made no effort to wipe them. With her other hand she fingered the ring. She gazed on him with eyes full of sorrow and strange affection. She opened her mouth to speak but Will did not stay to listen. He turned and fled down the garden path, certain of only one thing: the desire to put Shottery and the Hathaway sisters far behind him.

~⌒ Chapter 7 ⌒~

London 1582

The pale morning sun crept over the innyard, making the cobbles shine with dew, and climbed the walls of timber and wattle to the sign of the Boar's Head, where it glinted on the beast's newly painted gold tusks. A thrush nesting atop the sign hopped to the ledge of a nearby window and began to sing. Below, a cloaked figure scurried through the patch of sunlight and disappeared around the corner of the inn.

Light streamed into a gabled room on the third story where Meg de Galle lay flat on her bed, the crown of her head pressed against the wall. Her gold curls tumbled around her face like the bloom of a flower. Her arms were bent and her hands, two folded leaves, rested on her stomach. Her body under her shift was slim and straight as a stem. Two graceful, long-toed feet rested flat against a heavy chest at the end of her bed.

Meg awoke to the song of the thrush but lay abed with her eyes closed, wishing for a few more moments of sleep. She heard heavy footsteps, the scrape of her door, and the voice of her mistress.

"How can you sleep like that? You look like the duchess on her tomb," said Gwin Overby, coming into her chamber.

Meg knew what Gwin meant, having seen tombs with stone effigies lining the nave of St. Paul's when she helped Davy and Peter filch purses there. Now her daily companion was a honest alewife, and true to her word, she had stolen not so much as a farthing since hooking the clothes from the bawdy house two years earlier.

"I'm not asleep," said Meg.

"How can a body rest in peace on a stone slab with people going by at all hours?" Gwin's words whistled through the gaps in her front teeth, which jutted forward as if they wanted to escape from her mouth. Some customers mockingly called her Mistress *Over-byte.*

"I believe the duchess rests quite well, being dead," said Meg. She sat up and rubbed the top of her head, which was sore from being pressed against the wall. "Will you measure me today?" She handed Gwin a piece of chalk and stood with her back to the door.

Gwin bunched up her skirt and with Meg's help climbed onto a stool.

"Don't slouch, bean blossom," she said, reaching over Meg's head. The chalk scraped on the wood.

Meg turned around and saw the new mark on the door—a finger's width above last month's. "It's not working," she said, glaring at the chest at the foot of the bed.

"You're fifteen and almost done growing," said Gwin hopefully.

Meg sat down on the bed and regarded her long legs with their sharp knees and long, narrow feet. They looked like her father's legs. Her long, sinewy arms were the same as her mother's. They had bequeathed her not a penny, but all their height and strength combined.

"It's bad enough being called Long Meg," she said. "But must they stare at me with mouths agape and slap their heads?"

"Don't mind them," said Gwin. "Somewhere is a good man who likes a woman who can reach the top shelf on her own."

"But would he would marry a girl whose lips are so high above his?" said Meg mournfully.

"There are worse fates than not being married," said Gwin.

Meg thought of her parents. It was not marriage itself but misfortune that had made them miserable. She did not tell Gwin that her father had died in prison and her mother had killed a priest and drowned herself. These were secrets she meant never to reveal. Nor would she ever speak of Davy and Peter, though some days she missed her old companions, missed the freedom of being Mack. Secure as she was under Gwin's wing, she longed for the excitement—yes, even the danger—of her old life.

"Get dressed and break your fast," Gwin said, passing through the doorway sideways because of her wide hips. She fed herself as generously as she did Meg, having a special fondness for butter and cakes.

Meg sat on her bed brooding. She had wanted to become a new person when she came to the Boar's Head, but her body had its own ideas of what that meant. Her limbs were long, her breasts like flatcakes, her hips narrow as a lath. She reached down to draw on her shoes—an old pair of the master's that had been chewed by Bandog, the mastiff—and noticed there were hairs growing on her big toes. *Was I meant to be a man? Did Nature err in making me?*

A new idea occurred to her. Taking an old piece of linen and a needle and thread, she sewed along the inner seam of her shift, making two large pockets.

In the kitchen below pots clanged, Master Overby shouted, and Piebald the cat yowled as if he were being skinned alive. Gwin called, "Be quick, Meg!"

"I come anon!" Meg laced up her bodice and stepped into her skirt. She took the stones she used to warm her bed, each one the size of her fist, and put them in her pockets, noting with satisfaction how they weighed her down.

"This *must* keep me from getting any taller," she murmured. She picked up the chamber pot and descended the stairs with care, pushed open the back door, and tossed the slops into the ditch between the inn and the mews.

"Watch it, Long Meg!" shouted the chamberlain, jumping to avoid the yellow liquid and dropping a pair of boots into the mire. "Beshrew you, wench!"

He was a surly fellow, Meg thought. "Fie upon you too, Job Nockney!"

Neither of them saw the cloaked figure in the shadows where the ivy grew upon the walls.

A growling Job Nockney picked up the boots and crossed the courtyard with his curious flat-footed gait. He looked up at the sign and frowned at the white smears on the boar's visage. "Dab, come hither!"

Job's son emerged from the stable scratching his flea bites. His hair, mixed with straw, stood on end.

Job thrust his finger upward. "I just painted that sign," he said.

Dab picked up a small stone, fitted it into his slingshot, and let it fly. The nest fell to the ground.

"You're a wicked boy, Dab!" Meg cried, running over to pick up the nest. She carried it inside and left in on the hearth, meaning to place it safely under the eaves after she finished her work. The thrush sang on, unaware that her home was lost.

Unseen, the cloaked figure had inserted a foot in the back door before it closed.

The inn had few guests besides the gentleman waiting for Job to clean his boots. Come September it would be teeming with travelers arriving for the annual Southwark Fair. They would sleep two or three to a bed and crowd into the public rooms to play at dice, drink, sing rowdy songs, and tease Meg, saying "How far up do those legs go?"

Master Overby and Gwin sat at a table in the public room, chewing cold venison and calculating their likely gains from the fair.

"We'll charge four pence for bed and board, two for a bed only—a fair price, considering the demand there will be for lodging," Master Overby said, jotting down numbers. "A penny to see the play and two for a seat in the gallery—"

"A shilling for a quart of canary wine; in drink will be our greatest profit," said Gwin.

"Two for a seat in the gallery!" Master Overby repeated, raising his voice. He did not like to be interrupted.

Meg shooed Piebald away with her broom. The cat jumped onto the table and meowed, nosing the greasy platter from which Gwin had eaten every bite.

"For entertainment I'll hire Sir Andrew d'Arke. That great swill-belly shakes the stage with his ranting, which pleases the—"

"And he is content to be paid with sack," said Gwin.

"Which pleases the audience!" shouted Master Overby.

Meg winced and looked away in time to see a figure cross the doorway.

"Are you looking for your boots, sir?" she asked, but got no reply.

Was the fellow deaf? Or was he a thief? Broom in hand she went after him. No one would sneak past her into the Boar's Head!

The sun had not yet lighted the dim hallway, but Meg could hear someone at the top of the stairs. She took the steps two at time and saw the hem of a cloak disappear into a far room.

"Who goes there?" she demanded, stepping into the room with her broom raised. No one was visible. The back of Meg's neck began to tingle. Gwin liked to tell of a merchant who had been murdered in his bed and whose ghost still haunted the inn. The door creaked on its hinges and fell shut behind her. She whirled around. Whoever had fled from her stood pressed against the wall. Meg stifled a scream as a pale hand emerged from the cloak and pushed back the hood. And she beheld not the transparent visage of a ghost, but the face of a living, breathing girl like herself.

Only much shorter.

Chapter 8

The breath rushed out of Meg and she dropped the broom. The girl barely came to her shoulder. She had dark, abundant hair, wide brown eyes, and a pink mouth shaped like Cupid's bow.

"Why are you skulking around here?" Excitement made Meg speak with the cant of the street she had learned from Davy and Peter. "Who is your marker? Speak, minion!"

"I do not understand you," said the girl, her eyes wide with terror.

"Your accomplice, thief. Where is he?"

"I am no thief! I am Lady Violetta Puttock. I saw you pick up that nest and thought you might help me too." She fell to her knees, threw her arms around Meg's legs, and uttered a cry of pain.

Meg winced. The girl had struck her head on the stones in her pocket. At every step they bumped against Meg's thighs. She could already feel the bruises.

"Be careful," said Meg. "I have very hard bones."

The girl sat back, rubbing her head. "Maybe it was a mistake to come here."

Meg considered her fresh, healthy features, her fine cloak

and blue damask gown, only a little muddied. This Violetta was well cared for.

"Then go back home to your family," she said roughly.

The thrush's plaintive song came to her ears. Had she discovered her nest was gone?

"I cannot. My father, Sir Percival Puttock, will force me to marry a man I hate!" Tears spilled from Violetta's eyes.

"There are worse fates than being married," said Meg, misquoting Gwin. "Why do you hate him? Is he old or ill-favored?"

"No. He is young and you might call him handsome. But he fawns upon me in a most offensive manner with flowers and love-tokens and flattery."

"How could you *not* love a handsome man who gives you gifts?" asked Meg.

"He always holds my hand to keep me near him," Violetta complained. "He studies me as if he were diagnosing a disease, for he is learning to be a doctor." She wrinkled up her nose. "He will spend every day letting blood, sniffing bottles of urine, and prescribing strange physick."

"Do you love someone else?" asked Meg. Violetta's distress was truly a mystery to her.

"I haven't had the chance! But I could. Indeed I *wish* to."

Even damp with tears, Violetta's face was still pretty. When Meg cried her face swelled and her eyes grew rheumy. Violetta had a rounded figure, narrow at the waist, and small, delicate hands. A green thorn of envy pricked Meg.

"What is the name of this offensive fellow?"

Violetta let out a deep sigh. "Thomas Valentine."

Thomas Valentine. The name was like music; it made Meg's lonely heart stir.

"If I were you, I would far rather be Mistress Violetta

Valentine," she said, drawing out the syllables, "than Lady Puttock. Even if your Thomas had a wen the size of a ducat on his forehead." The idea caused Meg to laugh merrily.

Violetta pouted. "I see you have never had the misfortune to be tormented by a lover."

"*I* see that *you* scarcely know what suffering means," Meg shot back.

"But I do! My father locked me in my room after I refused to marry Thomas. When my maid opened the door I escaped, stole some coins from him, and ran away." Her little chin was thrust out in defiance.

"Then keep running," said Meg. "If you stay here he might find you."

Violetta shook her head. "I have come all the way from Stoke Farthington and cannot go another mile." She considered the room with its neat bed, stool, washbasin, table, and chair. Narrow beams of light peeked through the shuttered window. "This place will suit me."

"It will cost you two shillings a night for supper, bed, and breakfast."

Violetta smiled. "Two shillings? That's not much, is it?" She opened a little velvet purse and tumbled the coins into Meg's hand.

"Is this all your money?" asked Meg. She counted five shillings, four groats, and three pennies.

"I had to pay the coachman two crowns."

"Two crowns? You were robbed!" Meg said, anger rising in her.

"I know nothing about money. I've never had to buy anything for myself." Violetta looked as if she would cry again. "I suppose I shall have to sleep on the church steps."

Meg sighed. She could hardly turn Violetta away. A kitten would have a better chance of surviving on its own.

"My mistress might hire you in the kitchen, for the fair begins soon and we will have many customers."

"Shall I learn to make pudding and pies, confections and conserves?"

"No, you'll learn to pluck poultry until you sneeze your head off and chop onions until your eyes are on fire," Meg said. "Do you have any possessions or were you cheated of those too?"

"I hid my bag beneath the trellis."

Meg thought for a moment and said, "Climb out this window. It faces the mews and no one will see you. Fetch your bag, go to the front gate, and ask for Mistress Overby. Tell her that her kindness is mythical. No, I mean *legendary*. Alack, just say you are my cousin."

Meg tied a sheet under the girl's arms and lowered her from the window. She weighed not much more than a sack of grain.

When Violetta was halfway down, Meg remembered something. "Psst! When you greet my mistress, do not stare at her teeth or note her girth."

Clutching the sheet with both hands, Violetta nodded.

When Gwin summoned her to meet her "cousin," Meg picked up Violetta and spun her around, feigning joy.

"By the veil of the Virgin, it's a miracle how you found each other!" said Gwin with a grin so wide it showed all her teeth and her gums as well.

Meg felt a twinge of guilt for deceiving her mistress but deemed it a small wrong because Gwin was so delighted.

Meg was showing Violetta the kitchen when Master Overby returned from an errand at the brewery. Gwin accosted him, still fluttering with excitement.

"Meg's cousin is here! All the way from Stoke Farthington the pretty maid came. She is called Violetta, after the flower. Where *is* Stoke Farthington?"

"I don't know. I've never been there," said Master Overby. "Didn't Meg tell us she had no living kin?"

"What does it matter!" said Gwin. "Let them be cousins if they will."

"I'll be keeping my eye on them both," said Master Overby. "This town is full of country-bred cheats who come here thinking to make an honest man their mark."

Meg glanced at Violetta and wondered if she was as innocent as she seemed.

"Pishery-pashery!" said Gwin. "There cannot be a wicked bone in her body if she is cousin to Meg. I'm already fond of her."

"You've always been soft," grumbled Overby.

"And you're hard as a stone," said Gwin with a low growl.

Meg heard the sounds of wet kissing. Blushing, she quickly steered Violetta outside.

"Speaking of stones," Violetta said, "why do you have them in your pocket?"

Meg was caught off guard. Had Violetta reached into her skirt while they were in the kitchen? Was she a thief after all?

"Don't ask questions and you won't be told lies," she said, glowering. It was the line she used on overly curious patrons of the Boar's Head. "Away with you."

Violetta looked stricken as she turned and ran inside.

The stones pulled Meg's shift tight over her shoulders, tugged at her waist, and weighed her down. Her legs ached with bruises. How foolish she was for thinking she could keep herself from growing taller! She wondered if her mother had put stones in her pocket before she disappeared into the Thames. Had she changed her mind at the last moment and struggled to be free of the muddy depths? Meg shuddered. She reached under her skirt, tore the pockets from her shift, and dropped the stones among the cobbles.

With a lightness in her step she went indoors, found the thrush's nest, and tucked it under the eaves outside her window, hoping the bird would return and lay her eggs there.

~⌒ Chapter 9 ⌒~

Violetta had to share Meg's room, for Master Overby would not spare a chamber for which he might earn two shillings a night. She was so small she took up very little space. Gwin sewed her a simple worsted dress and a coif to cover her hair.

"Neither my father nor Thomas would recognize me now," Violetta announced to Meg, pleased with her disguise. She made Meg promise to tell no one—not even Gwin—the real reason she was at the Boar's Head.

Violetta behaved less like a servant and more like a lady feigning humble circumstances. "What a variety of folk I shall meet living at an inn!" she exclaimed. "Scholars and pilgrims, simple men and great ones. Everyone comes to London, do they not? And they must sleep and eat somewhere."

Meg scoffed at her innocence. "You will see great men at the Boar's Head only when poor players pretend to be kings for our entertainment."

Violetta's eyes widened. "Father says players are wicked men. I fear to meet one."

"I think you would fear to meet a dragonfly," said Meg,

though she considered Violetta rather courageous to leave her father and come to London alone.

In practical matters Violetta was completely unskilled, having done no work more demanding than embroidery. The first time Meg told her to sweep the floor she said, "How shall I? For the chairs and tables are on it!"

"If you wish to discourage your suitor, let him see you trying to keep house," said Meg. "He would go choose a wife who knows how to use a broom."

She showed Violetta how to sweep around chairs and tables and gather the dirt into a pile. This took far longer than if Meg had done the work herself. Thoroughly vexed, she led Violetta to the innyard and gave her a bucket of water and a brush. She gestured to the expanse of dusty cobbles and said, "Tomorrow there is to be a play, so you must scour every stone."

Violetta knelt down, brush in hand. She was so meek, Meg felt a bit guilty. But she went back inside and from time to time peered out a window to note her progress. Violetta was slow at the task but diligent.

"God's pittikins, what are you doing?" The high-pitched voice belonged to Gwin. "Get up, you silly, simple girl. Meg, come anon!"

Meg had never seen her mistress so red-faced or felt the sting of her words.

"You ramping cat! A beastly thing it is to play tricks on my poor Violetta."

"I never thought she would do it," said Meg, pinching her lips to hide a smile. A small area of the dusty innyard gleamed. Violetta stood by, wet, begrimed, and expressionless.

Gwin snapped a wet cloth at Meg. "Begone, rumpscuttle," she said almost gently.

"Surely you knew it was a jest," Meg said as she passed Violetta. "Only a fool would try to scrub a yard full of stones. Why didn't you refuse?"

Violetta looked at her and said, "You may be strong and clever, but you do not know the art of making friends." She spoke calmly and with no rancor.

Abashed, Meg could only stammer. "I . . . I've never had a friend. One of my own sex, anyway." Peter and Davy hardly counted as friends.

"Now you do," said Violetta. She grasped Meg's hand.

Meg could not speak for fear she would cry.

Violetta nodded toward the circle of shining cobblestones. "If you had only helped me, we could have had the entire yard clean by nightfall."

Past the lump in Meg's throat, mirth tumbled out. She began to giggle and Violetta joined in with her own silvery laugh.

Although she was clumsy with a broom, Violetta had a knack for knowing victuals and drink. She could distinguish varieties of ale by their taste and knew malmsey from canary wine simply by the smell. She remembered what dish every guest had ordered. Moreover, she was small enough to slip between the crowded tables. Meg understood how Thomas Valentine had fallen in love with her. She smiled so agreeably that every man with eyes to see was smitten by her. But her judgment of wine was better than her judgment of men.

One day soon after Violetta's arrival, Meg found her in the lap of a frequent visitor to the Boar's Head, a lout wearing an oversized ruff around his neck. Meg marched up and leaned on his table with both hands.

"I don't like your familiar manner with my friend," she said.

"Go to, Long Meg! I favor this wench and she favors me." His wet mouth leered.

Meg's muscles tensed with the desire to strike him. "Unhand her, Roger, or I'll knock your soused head right off that dinnerplate you're wearing." She was referring to the large ruff around his neck.

In reply Roger squeezed Violetta's arm, making her cry.

Meg's hand shot out and grabbed his ruff. Her other hand seized his doublet, which startled him so that he released Violetta and let Meg pull him to his feet. His chair crashed to the floor.

"Don't tear my ruff," he pleaded. "It cost me six shillings."

Meg hauled him outside, dimly aware of the laughter and the wide-eyed stares that followed her. Roger's drunkenness was to her advantage. She easily tore the ruff from his neck and ground it underfoot. He drew his sword and she raised her long leg, strong as a stave, and kicked it from his hand, whereupon he stumbled away cursing.

When she returned carrying his sword, the patrons cheered and pounded the tables, crying, "There's a wench! You stowed him, Long Meg!"

Meg found Violetta sitting in their room with her arms wrapped around her knees.

"Why did you do that?" she said, frowning.

"To start a riot, of course," said Meg irritably.

"You embarrassed me."

"No, I saved you from shame." She set the sword upright in a corner. "And justly repaid a villain's rude mockery."

"*You* wronged *him*," insisted Violetta. "He only asked me to lean closer and speak directly in his ear. And by some mischance I fell into his lap. I was about to get up again."

Meg sighed. "Why is it that beauty and common sense seldom keep company in the same person?"

Violetta thrust out her chin. "I think you are jealous that the gentleman favored me."

Meg snorted. "Gentleman? If he is a gentleman I am Elizabeth, Queen of all England! No, that was Roger Ruffneck, a notorious villain. He has a wife and babe at home. And, 'tis reported, more than one bastard child." She was satisfied to see Violetta quake. "I advise you to be in less haste to find a husband."

Chastened, Violetta rubbed her arm where Roger Ruffneck's fingers had left a darkening bruise.

Violetta remained irrepressible, like grass that springs upright after being flattened by rain. Only days after Meg threw Roger Ruffneck from the Boar's Head, Violetta bounded up to her. "O Meg, yonder sits the fairest young man ever! He hails from the town of Straight Forward Uneven."

Meg topped off one pitcher of ale and started another. "He lies. I have never heard of such a place. Didn't I warn you, you'll find no fit husband here?"

"This one is not married, of that I am certain. I heard him swear to his companions, 'By my name, Will Shake-his-beard,

I love no woman.' I dislike that surname. But he does have a beard, though it is not long enough to shake even when he speaks." Violetta tugged Meg's hand. "Come and see. I'll be sworn he is not a rogue."

Meg looked askance at her. "Nay, he sounds more like a clown. Does he have a bauble topped by a bell that rings when he says something foolish?"

Not wanting her friend to fall into bad company again, Meg took a pitcher of ale and went to judge the newcomer for herself. She found a country-bred fellow holding forth, a goodly youth with wavy dark hair, a high forehead, and a trim beard. He was flanked by two companions, dandies bedecked with ruffs, rings, and feathers.

Meg felt her grip weaken and the pitcher start to slip.

One of the dandies had a crooked nose and his busy fingers tapped the table. The other held out his cup and smiled at her, showing a black cavity where his front teeth used to be.

Meg's pitcher crashed to the floor.

~∂ Chapter 10 ∂~

Will had hired a horse and left Stratford as fast as the spav-
ined creature permitted him. Twenty-five crowns were tucked
safely in his boot, and he carried the Burbage contracts, the
court summons, and three pairs of gloves to barter for favors.
The two-day journey took him eastward to Warwick then to
Daventry. In Towcester a pair of gloves bought him supper
amidst a lively company, a quantity of ale, and a bed that spun
beneath him all night. In the morning he had a pounding
head and a confused memory of having kissed more than
one wench. With so many pretty girls in England, it would
not be hard to forget the Hathaway sisters. He rode through
Brick Hill, Dunstable, and Barnet on a thoroughfare crowded
with horses, carts, and foot traffic bound for the city of his
dreams.

Will was feeling older than his eighteen years, a man of
the world, until he climbed the last hill before London and
saw the city for the first time. A veritable forest of close-set
rooftops, pierced at intervals by church towers, stretched
from east to west for a considerable distance. A wall with
towers and crenelations bound the city on three sides, and

the watery Thames made a fourth boundary. Like a vine sending out shoots, the city unfurled beyond the walls and over the rolling land. Thoroughfares lined with buildings reached out from the city in all directions, and smaller roads crisscrossed one another and meandered over fields. How in a place so vast, Will wondered, would he ever find employment? Where would he begin to look for William Burbage and Thomas Greene, the lawyer?

These misgivings almost made him turn homeward until he considered the troubles he was fleeing. He left the old horse with a dealer and pocketed the few shillings that were returned to him. At the statue of a griffin he paid his toll and passed through Aldersgate. He was in London! At once he was jostled from all sides and was glad he had taken precautions against pickpockets. With no fear of being robbed, he let the crowd carry him along into the widest street he had ever seen. He asked what it was called and was told "Cheapside." Indeed it was a thoroughfare given over to the buying and selling of everything imaginable. As far as Will's eye could see were stalls and carts heaped with fragrant bread, onions, apples, butter and cheese, and caged chickens and piglets whose bleating and squawking mingled with the cries of "Roasted ribs!" "Buy my hot pies!" "Three for a penny!" His rumbling stomach urged him to buy a pie, which he washed down with a cup of Rhenish wine. He wandered by stalls stuffed with bolts of woolen cloth, turkey carpets, pewter, ironware, candles, and shoes enough for every pair of feet in Stratford. So many diverse folk he had not seen in all his life: not only common housewives, tradespeople, and tattered beggars, but also proud merchants, noblemen in silks and velvet, and foreigners in outlandish clothes. The buildings on either side of him rose three, four, even five stories. Not even the guildhall in Stratford was built so fine and tall. He had paused before the shop of a goldsmith and was gaping at the carved cherubs tinted with gold when he realized someone was addressing him.

"Good day, fellow traveler. Did we not dine together at the inn at Chipping Norton?" The speaker was a man dressed in a plain cloak with the dust of the road on his shoes.

"No, we have never met, sir," said Will.

"You were not too soused to remember me." The fellow sounded hurt but he smiled. "Tom Treadwell is my name; I have forgot yours."

Not wanting to seem unfriendly, Will gave the stranger his hand—but not his name. "I was nowhere near Chipping Norton." He had never heard of the place. "I came from Stratford-upon-Avon, by way of Towcester."

"Forgive my mistake," said Treadwell politely. "Perhaps I had drunk too much." He bowed to Will and continued on his way.

Dazzled by new sights, Will instantly forgot the fellow. He peered down the many streets that fed into Cheapside like tributaries into a great river: Wood Street, Milk Street, Candlewick Street, and Ironmonger Lane. Now he knew where to buy wood, milk, wicks, and a cooking pot if the need arose. He stepped aside to avoid a band of roaring boys swaggering and swearing oaths that he would have been flogged for uttering. At Cornhill he was watching a tumbler perform his stunts when he was accosted again.

"Hail and well met! Upon my life, I know you," said a

pleasant fellow about Will's age. He appeared to be a gentleman's son, for his doublet and boots were of satin and he wore a porringer topped with a plume.

Will shook his head. "I do not know you, sir."

"By this hand, I have seen you in Stratford. It was a market day and you were about your business."

Will was astonished. He had expected to be invisible in London, but here was a man who had seen him selling gloves in Stratford!

"What was your business there?" asked Will, trying to recall seeing the young man.

"My horse had a broken shoe and your father shod him." He tapped his forehead, thinking. "Your name is John, like his!"

Will laughed. "Nay, my name is Will. Indeed my father's name is John, but he is a glover by trade, not a blacksmith."

"Then come with me, Will Glover—"

"No, it's Shakespeare. My forebears were soldiers of the king."

"A proud calling! I'll buy you a pot of ale if you'll share with me tidings of my friend the blacksmith and the good folk of Stratford. Ah, many times I have supped at the White Swan there."

"You must mean the Black Swan," said Will. Embarrassed at correcting the good fellow's memory, he added, "I shall be glad to sup with you."

The young man introduced himself and smiled, showing a gap in his front teeth that somewhat marred his appearance. As Will fell into step with him, he noticed a stroller holding up a sign.

"Davy, show me the way to the Boar's Head and I will buy you all the sack you can drink," said Will on an impulse. He was afraid he sounded like an overeager bumpkin.

His new companion hesitated but obliged him. On the way they happened to meet an acquaintance of Davy's. In his silver-hued doublet, Peter Flick reminded Will of a colorful fish darting through the crowded streets.

"Peter's a trusty fellow. But his wit's not so sharp since a robber struck him in the head with a stave," said Davy. He glanced sideways at Will. "A man has to judge well whom he takes for a friend."

"Have no doubts about me. I intend no harm to any man," Will assured him.

Davy clapped Will's shoulder as they passed through Aldgate and into Whitechapel Lane. At once Will saw the sign of a boar's head. He was pleased with himself for finding two friends *and* a play on his first day in London. At the gate he paid two pennies for the privilege of viewing the play from a bench and received a token. In the yard a man and a boy hammered a stage together. As the performance would not begin for another hour, Will and his friends went inside for some victuals. Davy and Peter showed a keen interest in his well-being, pouring him such a quantity of sweet sack that he in turn poured out all his troubles, confessing he had come to the city to repay a debt and to escape "two vile vixens."

"As my name is Will Shakespeare, I love no woman!" he declared to them.

A few moments later Will heard a crash, smelled ale, and

realized that a serving wench had dashed her pitcher to the floor beside his table. Why would she do such a wasteful thing? He blinked up at her. He had never seen so tall a girl. Her body was as slender as a sapling. With her crown of gold hair and fierce aspect she resembled a god of thunder and lightning. The sight so startled Will that he choked, spewing ale from his nose. No wonder she looked so angry. He must have been swearing like a shipman or pounding on the table. It was the sack making him rowdy. But it tasted so sweet! He knew he must stop.

"O you mortal goddess, why look you so wrathful?" He heard the words tumble thickly from his mouth. He bestowed on the goddess a smile designed to free him from the hook of his own misdeeds. But she wasn't even looking at him. Another wench, however, the short one who had been waiting on them, tilted her head and smiled at him. Faith, she was a pretty one! And she fancied him already.

"You are not welcome here, Davy Dapper," the goddess was saying. "Nor you with your filching fingers, Peter Flick."

"'Sblood, she knows me," said Davy, preening like a peacock. "Do I know you, maypole?"

"You should, knave. I am Long Meg. And I know how you cursed cuffins plan to gull this innocent yokel."

Will tried to stand up and found it difficult. "I'm neither innocent nor local but a sinful man from Stratford," he protested.

"My quarrel is not with you, sirrah, but with these two milk-livered villains."

Davy and Peter exchanged looks. Peter stood up and put his arm around Will to keep him upright.

"You insult my new friends?" Will said. "You, a woman!"

"Do you have your purse about you?" the giantess asked him.

Will smiled. He made a great show of patting his sides. He shook out his arms, looking puzzled when nothing fell from his sleeves. He reached into his pockets and pulled them inside out. "Have I been robbed?" he said, looking about with feigned horror.

"You are right; he must be a performer of some kind," the little serving maid said to the one called Long Meg.

Will put his finger to his forehead. "Aha!" he said and reached into the front of his trousers. He pulled out a purse and shook it. Coins clinked inside.

"Behold, I am in possession of my wealth. These men are not robbersh." Will heard himself slurring his words. He leaned over and chucked the little maid on the chin. "Fill our cups that we may drink to friendship."

Peter said something to Long Meg and sneered at her.

"Maypole, we'll go about you in a circle and tie you up, beshrew me if I lie," said Davy, getting to his feet.

Will blinked rapidly. Were his new friends now threatening this Long Meg? She did not seem daunted by them.

"Hear me, sirrah," she said to Will. "If you count these churls your friends, though you have a full purse you are a poor man."

"This tall woman has a tall wit, does she not?" Will said. Peter and Davy only scowled.

"You still don't know me, do you?" Meg said to them. "Your memories are as short as your mettle, cowards. You can't run from me again."

Davy and Peter started to bolt. The little maid shoved the bench into the backs of their knees, throwing them off balance. Before Will could react, Long Meg had seized Davy by his hair and Peter by his collar and haled them through the public room. Will watched his new friends shout and flail their arms, crash into tables, and upset alepots and platters of food. Cheers rose up from the other guests, men and women alike. "Huzzah! Huzzah for Long Meg!" Fists pounded on tables and heels drummed on the floor. *What a jolly tumult!* thought Will. It was almost better than a play.

When Long Meg returned, Will saw that she was flushed and her sleeves were torn. The uproar continued. Someone began a tune that everyone took up like a hymn.

> *Here's to our hero, Long Meg.*
> *She of the mile-long leg.*
> *Sing high, sing low, heigh-ho!*
> *To the Boar's Head we go.*

"More ale!" they demanded. The little wench whirled from table to table like a hurricane. Cups, bottles, and tankards were lifted to Long Meg. The host and his wife looked pleased at the happy riot she had caused, while the celebrated maid went about her work as if nothing had happened.

What exactly *had* happened? A giantess had dropped her pitcher, called his companions cowards and cheats, and thrown them out with her bare hands. But why? Will wanted to go after Davy and Peter and question them, but he wanted even more to see the play. So he picked himself up, went into the yard, and found a seat at the end of a crowded bench.

Will knew the tale of Pyramus and Thisbe from his favorite Latin book, *Metamorphoses.* It was a lamentable tragedy, but this play was more like a comedy. The actor playing Thisbe lost his false hair and with it, all pretense of being a woman. Fat Pyramus, his face aflame with whelks, was more suited to be a devil than a lover. When he stabbed himself and died the audience only laughed. Will joined in the hooting and hissing. He had seen better plays in Stratford.

When the play was concluded, Will looked up to find Long Meg standing over him.

"You owe four shillings and two pence for all that you and those rogues ate and drank," she said.

Will counted out the coins. He was sober and quite vexed. "I protest being forced to pay their reckoning, when you caused the commotion for no reason but to sell more drink."

She looked offended. "Sirrah, those two coney-catchers would have had all your money ere long. Shall I tell you how you were snared?" Without waiting for a reply she sat down. "A stranger accosted you on the street and claimed to know you."

"Yes," admitted Will, surprised. "But he went away again."

Long Meg nodded. "He is the barnacle, in thieves' cant. He relays the information he has gleaned to his confederates. A short time later the setter moves in. That was Davy Dapper. He compounds the barnacle's bit of knowledge with flattery and general truths, thereby drawing you into his acquaintance."

This was exactly what occurred, Will realized. First Treadwell, then Davy had by artful means persuaded him to disclose his town, his name, and his business. "What, are you a demigoddess, all-knowing?" Will said, suspicious. "Or are you in their fellowship?"

Long Meg's wide blue eyes narrowed into a frown. "You flatter me and then you insult me. Rather, you should thank me."

Will knew he had been careless but was loath to credit Meg for rescuing him. "I thank myself that they could not trick me out of my money. I kept a few coins in my purse and hid my real wealth close about me—"

"Stop! If you reveal that, you are a greater fool than they took you for."

But Will's hand was already creeping down his leg to the top of his boot. He wanted to be sure. His fingers probed inside, touched his right ankle. The purse with the twenty-five crowns was not there! Because it was in the other boot. He thrust his hand down his left boot. Nothing. A wild pounding started behind his ribs, reached to his head, and made his hands shake. Peter and Davy had been sitting on either side of him on the bench. Their knees and feet had jostled his beneath the table. Peter had helped him stand . . .

Will tugged off his boots, held them upside down, shook them, and threw them aside. He pulled off his stockings and stared at his bare, pale feet.

"Oh, fie upon the devil and his fiddlesticks!" he cried. "I *have* been robbed!"

~⊙ Chapter 11 ⊙~

Meg was surprised that neither Peter nor Davy had recognized her. Then again, she was no longer disguised as a boy, and in the two years since she consorted with them she had grown almost twelve inches, judging by the chalk marks on her door. She watched Will Shake-his-beard as he watched the play. She wanted to tell him that she had also been innocent, desirous of companionship, and easily betrayed by those same false friends. This awareness of what they shared drew her to him. Moreover she sensed in him a generous spirit. In his amazement at the sight of her he had not, like most men, teased or mocked her. Instead he had called her a mortal goddess, which made her stand up straighter, proud of her height.

When Will discovered he had been robbed after all, Meg did not doubt that Davy and Peter were the culprits. And it was her fault they had escaped.

"I wish I'd shaken them down before driving them off," she lamented.

"Let's go after those devil's minions, Long Meg," Will said, pulling on his boots again. "We'll catch them and get my money back. Rather, my father's money. It was to settle a debt."

Meg could not believe her ears. Will was enlisting her aid as if her sex were no disadvantage at all.

"I would gladly bash their brainpans," she said. "But they are long gone."

He gave her a searching look. "Why are you so willing to avenge my loss?"

"It was you who asked for my help," she said. But she knew that a host could be held liable if his guests were robbed. Master Overby, being weak-limbed, had assigned to Meg the task of keeping riffraff away from the inn.

Will was scratching his head. "Why did they run from you? Should they know you?"

Meg was taken aback. "They are afraid of me because . . ." She tried to think quickly. "They once betrayed my twin brother, Mack, as they did you." *A brother? Where had this idea come from?*

"A twin! How propitious!" exclaimed Will. "He must be a god in strength as you are a goddess."

Again he called her a goddess. She couldn't help but blush. "Your praise is undeserved," she murmured. After all, she had let Davy and Peter escape with his money.

"I must meet your brother," Will was saying. "And the three of us will overcome those paltry villains!"

"It would be unseemly for me to accompany you, for I am not a man," said Meg, beginning to regret her hasty invention of a brother.

"And I am no man but a giant fool if I do nothing. I hereby

vow to retrieve my fortune and be avenged on those who stole it."

"I'll witness your vow and do what I can to aid you," said Meg, though she had no idea how to help Will.

News of Will's loss had reached Master Overby, who declared that he must stay at the inn at no charge. Meg knew her master was afraid Will would go away and declare to everyone he met how he had been robbed at the Boar's Head, which would give the inn a bad reputation.

Will replied to Overby's offer by producing a pair of gloves, which he offered in payment of the night's reckoning.

Meg saw the gloves were made from a pale, buttery leather ornamented with gold braid. She longed to touch them, though she could see they would never fit her own large hands.

"What use have I for such gloves?" said Master Overby.

"None, I hope. You may give them to your wife," answered Will.

"Gwin? Have you seen the size of her hand? I think not."

Hearing her name, Mistress Overby elbowed her husband aside and tried in vain to insert her round fingers into the delicate glove. "Are you a peddler of gloves, young man?" she asked.

Will seemed offended. His mouth formed a thin line. He looked around the nearly empty innyard. Job Nockney and his son were already taking down the stage. Meg followed Will's gaze, which came to rest on the fat, whelk-faced player who was splayed out on a bench and drinking from a large tankard.

"No, I am a player," Will said. "And I would make a far better Pyramus than that ape!"

Besides the dauntless Long Meg and the toothy Mistress Over-byte, the Boar's Head could now boast a young trage-dian: Will Shake-his-beard, from Straight Forward Uneven, in Workshire. Will delighted in Violetta's mispronunciation of "Stratford-upon-Avon" and "Warwickshire," though Meg informed him that he did have a peculiar manner of speak-ing. He added false hair to his own beard so that it shook when he was in the throes of his stage passion.

The young tragedian promised to deliver a play that would please one whom he called his "great master, the poet Ovid." He needed three players: Thisbe, the beloved of Pyra-mus; a lion to threaten her; and a father to oppose her love for Pyramus. Overby agreed to play the father if the character was made a king, and Will persuaded Job Nockney to play the lion.

"But *I* want to play the lion," said Dab.

"You are too small and cannot roar loud enough to frighten the ladies," said Will. "You shall play the very famous Thisbe!"

"I must play the *girl?*" Dab's voice rose in protest.

"Yes, for you have the perfect voice for the lovelorn Thisbe."

Because she was tall and strong, Meg was the wall that separated Pyramus and Thisbe. She stood inside a painted prop and held it upright. It proved more difficult than she imagined to keep the wall still.

It soon became apparent that Dab was a poor Thisbe. He spoke every line with resentment and looked so sour when Pyramus tried to kiss him through the wall that even Meg laughed. The wall shook. Will was furious.

"Meg, there is no earthquake when Pyramus and Thisbe

meet. I would there were. Dab, you must pretend to love me—to love *Pyramus*. His breath smells like roses to you, not dead rats. Job, wear gloves to keep the splinters out of your paws, for you must roar only upon cue. And try to *lurk* more; you should be a cat, not a dog."

Through the gaps in the wall Meg watched the play, immersed in its every action and word. Soon she knew every line of the play by heart. She marveled at how Will held the stage like a captain commanding a ship. His voice set the very planks of the stage throbbing. His expression was so true, Meg blushed when she saw him pretending to kiss Thisbe and almost cried when he cradled her lifeless body. She was thankful to be hidden within the wall.

Through the wall Meg could also see Violetta serving the playgoers. Whenever Pyramus declared his love for Thisbe, she paused and stared at the stage with her lips parted. Her yearning for Will Shakespeare was as evident as the sun at midday.

The play opened the same day as the Southwark Fair. Travelers filled the Boar's Head. Master Overby was happy; he didn't care that none of the actors but Will had any skill. Will on the other hand was in great earnest, demanding so much of his players that Dab sat down in the middle of a performance with his arms crossed over his chest and refused to utter another word. His father leaped across the stage and threatened to tear him limb from limb, but the boy paid no heed. Will was forced to extemporize, lamenting that Thisbe had been struck dumb with fear. The play ended without the lovers' deaths, which blunted the force of the tragedy.

When the confused playgoers had left, Will exploded. "I'll

not stand onstage again until I have a Thisbe who can speak of love without mocking Pyramus."

Overby faced Will. "As the king, I decree we *will* have this play for the purpose of luring the fairgoers hither." Since taking on his new role, he spoke in a more elevated manner than usual.

"Then, O King, *mighty* King, bring me someone who can play Thisbe," said Will mockingly. "O Wall, upstanding Wall, know you of a proper Thisbe?"

Meg, who was not at the moment inside the wall, could not suppress her laughter.

"Here she is. Here am I. Let me be Thisbe." It was Violetta, wiping her hands on her apron. Her wide brown eyes glistened. "I can love Pyramus well."

"I cannot allow that!" spluttered Overby. "For a woman to appear on a stage is an offense against the law and Nature herself."

"But Meg is on the stage," Violetta protested. "Is she not a woman?"

"That is not the same," said Master Overby. "Within the wall she is invisible. She might as well be a man."

"I might as well be a *wall*," said Meg, her hands on her hips, "the way you talk about me."

"Why force Dab to play Thisbe?" Violetta went on. "Not knowing a woman's heart, how can he even feign to be in love?" Her voice faltered at the end.

Will stroked his beard and considered Violetta. "Can you feign being a boy pretending to be a woman?"

Violetta frowned as if she were doing a difficult sum in her head. "I can," she said. "Give me scissors and a comb."

Stunned, Meg watched as Violetta held her abundant dark

hair away from her head and proceeded to cut it off. What remained fell raggedly to her chin. She was still so pretty she would never be mistaken for a boy.

"Why have you done this?" said Meg.

As soon as she saw the look of delight Will bestowed on Violetta, she knew why.

The desire for profit persuaded Overby to allow Violetta on the stage. Finally Pyramus had a fitting Thisbe, and if the audience suspected that the curvy player was not a boy, that only seemed to increase their enjoyment. Pyramus courted his new Thisbe with renewed ardor. He railed against the wall for standing between him and his love. Meg felt it as a personal rebuke.

> Cruel wall, think you to keep us parted?
> I, Pyramus, and my love, true-hearted
> Thisbe?

Violetta thrust her hand through a chink in the wall and Will kissed it with a smack loud enough for the audience to hear. Violetta's eyes rolled upward and she panted her words.

> O Pyramus, I would thee wed
> And take unto my maiden bed;
> But cruel fathers oppose our love—

Violetta fell silent. She often forgot her lines. Pyramus waited.

"Though 'tis blessed by gods above," Meg whispered from within the wall.

Violetta repeated the line and no one was the wiser. She

feigned tears and the audience gasped when Thisbe discovered the dead Pyramus.

> *Asleep, my love?*
> *What . . . dead, my dove?*
> *O Pyramus, arise,*
> *Ope' once . . . thy lovely eyes.*

Again Meg whispered the words Violetta could not remember, and Thisbe's hesitation seemed the natural expression of grief. No one could see Meg's tears and for this she was glad.

When Pyramus did not awaken, Thisbe pretended to stab herself. She fell upon him and lay there until the applause roused them to take their bow. Meg knew she should be scandalized. Instead she envied Violetta and Will. How did they wring such emotion from an audience? Meg often murmured whole scenes to herself, enamored both of the words and of the mind that produced them—Will's mind.

At night in the room they shared, Violetta prattled of Will until Meg wanted to scream.

"O Meg, when I ran away from father and Thomas Valentine, I wanted to be in love and now I am! Don't you think Will handsome? When I am so near to him and his eyes are on me, I can't remember Thisbe's lines." Violetta sighed like a bellows, fanning the flame of her own love. "Truly I cannot say if he is handsomer than Thomas—nor can you, alas, not knowing Thomas—for I have heard love is blind and cannot see to judge itself. Therefore *you* must assure me. Is this not love?"

"How should I know what love is?" said Meg irritably.

Heedless, Violetta chattered on. "I dare believe Will regards me as I do him. I *feel* it. Do you see love in his eyes when he is Pyramus and I am Thisbe?"

Meg lay on her bed as unmoving as the wall that Pyramus cursed, as unloved, and as tall to boot. But filled with the kind of nameless longing a wall could never feel.

"Indeed," said Meg, sighing. "Pyramus loves his Thisbe eternally."

Chapter 12

Will's play drew so many spectators to the Boar's Head that Master Overby agreed to pay him a few shillings out of the profits from each performance. The fairgoers were an obstreperous crowd, however, and with Meg on the stage there was no one to keep order among them. One night they began to throw bread crusts and bones on the stage to make the lion roar. When Job flung them back, the audience was provoked to throw more garbage. Someone even tossed Piebald; Meg heard the cat yowling and felt his body thump against her wall. When someone jumped on the stage and stole Overby's tin crown, the irate king cried, "I do not condone rebellion!" and declared all further performances of *Pyramus* cancelled.

Now Will sat disconsolate, pondering ideas for a new play. Scraps of paper were spread out on the table before him. He groaned to see Violetta approaching. She seemed to relish distracting him.

"Sad Thisbe greets proud Pyramus this moonlit morn," she said, planting herself at his elbow. "Are you writing another play? Shall I be in it?"

"Not if you insist upon being Thisbe still," said Will without looking up. Violetta's nearness confused him. There was an ardor to her touch that reminded him of Anne and a coyness that recalled Catherine. Had he not left Stratford to forget those sisters? He moved his elbow away from Violetta.

"Can I be a queen? Like Esther from the Bible?"

"And who shall play the traitor Haman and be hanged onstage?"

It was not a biblical drama Will had in mind, but something from ancient history—the ill-fated love of Mark Antony and Cleopatra. Violetta had dark hair and her face could be smudged with coal, but she was too short for a queen of Egypt.

"Can you wear chopines on your feet without falling from them?" he asked.

"I will walk on stilts to please my Pyramus," said Violetta.

"Stop calling me Pyramus!"

"You would not die for me?"

"Die for you, no. Die *on* you, maybe." The bawdy pun slipped from Will but Violetta seemed not to mark it. "Don't you have some pots or floors to scrub?"

With a sigh she took her vexing presence from him, whereupon Meg appeared. It was like a scene from a play, Will reflected.

"Demigoddess, bring me some ale!" he called, pleased at the sight of her. When she came back with the cup Will asked, "Would you hear my idea for a play?"

Long Meg tilted her head to the side. "Is it about a young man seeking to recover his father's stolen wealth?"

"No, it is about a Roman general in love with the queen of Egypt," Will said defensively.

"Who will play in it? You know Dab is unreliable and Job Nockney has sworn never to take the stage again. Violetta's memory is like a sieve, useless for carrying wit or water."

Will rubbed his head. "Violetta's lines will be few and short. I shall write a part for you if you like. And one for Mistress Gwin. And the costermonger's daughter. Confound the laws, I'll have a whole company of women players. What a spectacle that would prove! We'll travel to every shire in England and dare the magistrates to punish us. Do you long to stand in the the pillory?"

Will knew his ranting was beside the point. The few shillings he had saved from playing Pyramus amounted to less than a tenth of what Burbage was owed. The rest he had spent on ink, pen, and notebooks. The court date, October fifteenth, was not three weeks away.

"How will my standing in a pillory enact your revenge against those two thieves?" said Meg, standing with her arms akimbo.

Will groaned. "Your words sting my remembrance."

"I am sorry," she said, dropping her arms. "You made a vow that I witnessed. I am only trying to hold you to it."

Talk of vows made Will feel guilty. He did not want to think of the Hathaway sisters or his promise to his father.

"You tell me, Meg, how shall I find those two shifty rogues in all of London? Can't you help me? Have you not a single word of encouragement?"

"Yes. Leave!" The sinews in her arm grew taut as she pointed to the door.

Will was stunned. "Are you throwing me out? What have I done?"

"Nothing," she said, exasperated. "Therein lies the problem. Who ventures to London and is content to see no more of it than the four walls of an inn?"

Someone who wants to hide, thought Will. *Someone shirking his duty.*

"Go out and find something to write about. You might also find the rogues you seek."

"I would gladly explore the city to feed my fancy, but I lack a single friend to keep me from the pathways of peril." He picked up his pen again. "I must write that down."

The nib of his pen scratched over paper. He looked at what he had written, then blotted it. Drivel! Meg was right; he had nothing to write about.

After what seemed like a long silence Meg said, "You can trust my brother."

"Your twin! How could I have forgotten?" Will jumped up and gathered his papers together. "Where is he now?"

Meg hesitated. She seemed flustered, glancing overhead as if her brother might be concealed in the rafters. "On Tuesday he has some business at Leadenhall Market," she finally said. "He will meet you at noon near the well in the courtyard." She lowered her voice. "Keep this a secret, for no one knows I have a brother."

Will was puzzled, even suspicious. Why would she hide the fact that she had a brother? But he was afraid to ask, lest she take offense and withdraw her offer.

"How shall I recognize him?" He deemed it safe to ask this much.

Meg raised her eyebrows at him. "He is my twin. If you know me you will know him."

Chapter 13

Once she was out of Will's sight, Meg clasped her head with both hands. "What have I done?" she murmured. The words "you can trust my brother" had simply rolled from her lips and could not be called back. Had her inward mind decided to hatch some plot unknown to her outward senses? It did irk her to see Will dreaming his days away and writing about ancient history while all of London, a very present place, awaited his discovery. Even more, she was irked that Davy Dapper and Peter Flick were still on the loose.

Having made her promise, Meg was determined to fulfill it. At a shop in Finch Lane she bought a slightly worn suit of men's clothes, yesterday's fashion at a cheap price. She pondered an excuse to be away from the inn and decided to tell Gwin she was doing charitable work at a parish far enough away that Gwin would not be tempted to join her. Violetta she was not concerned about. The girl was so consumed with thoughts of Will she didn't notice anything Meg did.

Meg set in motion her engine of deceit. The wheels turned with surprising ease. Gwin gave her four shillings for the poor, which made Meg feel guilty. Working secretly in her room, listening all the while for footsteps, she padded the doublet to disguise her breasts and embellished it with braid. Despite her caution, light-footed Violetta burst in and Meg had only a moment to throw a sheet over her work.

"I am full of woe!" complained Violetta. "For hours on end Will's pen makes love to his paper. He has not favored me with a glance all day." She dropped to Meg's bed, sitting on the edge of the sheet. "How shall I live without his looks?"

"The same way you lived before you saw him. From day to day rising, eating, working, sleeping."

"But every hour of the day and night he is on my mind!" Violetta wailed. She balled the sheet in her fist. Meg froze as the sleeve of the doublet peeked out.

"I hear Gwin calling you," Meg said. "Go see what she needs."

"I was not meant to be a servant. Thomas Valentine would have given *me* servants." Violetta pouted. "Yet here I am waiting on love. On one who hardly deigns to speak to me!"

"I do not think men love women who hang upon them like chains," said Meg.

"What I need is a friend to woo him on my behalf." She glanced sideways at Meg.

"Don't look at me so," said Meg.

"Please! Will is not in love with you nor you with him, so there can be no misunderstanding!"

"That may be true," said Meg, wounded, "but I will not be your go-between. It is your father's office to oversee your courtship. Now go away, for I would sleep."

"I have no father anymore!" Violetta wailed, pulling the

entire sheet to her bosom. She gasped at the suit of clothes lying in full view on the bed.

"Meg! Really!" She glanced around the tiny room and peered under the bed. "Where is he? It's not . . . Will?" Her voice trembled.

"Of course not!" snapped Meg. She snatched up the doublet. "I'm doing some mending."

"Don't pretend you have become a seamstress. You would not be so red-faced unless you had a lover." Violetta's voice fell to a whisper. "You can tell me who he is."

Meg was not about to lie and say she had a lover. But how could she explain to Violetta that she planned to impersonate a man in order to assist Will? Meg hardly understood this decision herself. She decided on a half truth that would please Violetta—if she believed it.

"I wanted to surprise you," Meg said. "Knowing how much you love Will, I planned to disguise myself as your cousin— that is, my brother, whom I'll call Mack—and persuade him to woo you."

Violetta clapped her hands. "I didn't know you had a brother. Is he handsome?"

Meg sighed. "I don't. It's a *disguise*."

"Oh, I see the purpose of the clothing now! How foolish of me to guess that you had a lover!"

"And why shouldn't I?" Though how such a thing would happen if she were running around as a man, Meg didn't know.

"You should, and someday you will," Violetta said with a wave of her hand. "But for now I shall advise you what to say to Will."

Meg was not listening. She had no intention of asking Will to woo Violetta. Her business was not courtship and love but helping Will find Peter Flick and Davy Dapper. But she had not considered the many deceptions her disguise would entail. Will was no fool; what if he recognized her the first time he and Mack met? How long before Gwin and Overby became suspicious? And could Violetta, who was still chattering like a jackdaw, keep from revealing Meg's disguise? She must be scared into silence.

"Violetta!" she said, interrupting her. "If you count yourself my friend, you will tell no one of our plan nor reveal that I am Mack. If we are caught in this scheme, eternal shame and ridicule will be our reward."

"You would take such a great risk for me?" Violetta whispered, touching Meg's arm.

Meg looked away to avoid meeting her eyes. "It shall be my pleasure," she said. For she felt a growing excitement at the prospect of meeting Will Shakespeare at Leadenhall Market and roaming the streets with him, freed for a time from the burden of being Long Meg.

Chapter 14

Will was at Leadenhall Market well before the appointed hour. The place made him uneasy, for it was not far from where Davy Dapper had accosted him. He wished Mack would hurry. He wondered if Long Meg was setting him up to be gulled. But she was so plainspoken, so upright, he did not want to believe she would deceive him.

The market teemed with harvest bounty and buxom wenches who made him think of Anne Hathaway. Despite what she had done he could not banish her from his mind. She was even in his dreams. Or was it Catherine? Her sweet features came to mind, her buttery fingers touching his lips—and the sound of her raillery, her vows of eternal hatred. How had he ever gotten entangled in their witchcraft? Even now he was not free of it.

"I won't let a woman deceive me again! Or a man for that matter," he declared, squaring his shoulders and striding back and forth as if daring anyone to try and trick him.

He recognized Long Meg's twin at once. He was taller than anyone in sight. As he drew near, Will could see that he shared her slender build, her blue eyes, and her curly golden hair, which peeked out from beneath a feathered cap. Of course he was wider in the chest and shoulders, and though he did not have a beard, his upper lip was darkened with fuzz. When he spoke his voice was deeper than Long Meg's.

"I am Mack de Galle and you had better be Will Shake-beard or Short-beard or whatever you call yourself, for the last two fellows I greeted denied they were and one took offense, for he was a No-beard with not a whisker on his face," he said in a rush of words.

Will smiled. He liked the fellow's wit. "I call myself Will Shake-*speare*, though I have none to shake." He noticed Mack wore a sword, as did most of the gallants in the streets. Almost no one in Stratford went around so strongly armed.

"If you would be true to your name you must have a spear," said Mack. "For safety as well as for show." He unbuck-led his sword and secured it around Will's waist.

Will gulped. "I have no skill with weapons."

"Wear it. It will make you look dangerous." Mack lifted the lower edge of his doublet to reveal a sheathed dagger and a pistol tucked between the points of his hose. "Gifts from my sister. Lost or confiscated at the Boar's Head." He winked. "I prefer my weapon to be hidden."

Will chuckled at the bawdy joke but Mack did not smile. So Will converted his laugh to a cough and placed his hand on the sword hilt like a man accustomed to doing so.

"Let us go now to Southwark, for 'tis the last day of the fair," said Mack.

He led the way past Eastcheap, where the street narrowed and became New Fish Street. Will's sword bumped against his thigh with every step. He could feel the dampness in the breeze and smell the river at low tide: mud, fish, and offal. A roaring filled his ears, and just ahead he saw the great bridge and the river surging beneath it. As he and Mack crossed the crowded bridge, Will gazed in wonder at the fair shops and dwellings on both sides. At the middle point was an old drawbridge from which Mack pointed out the tower of St. Paul's Cathedral, the city's heart. On the river below, wherries, barges, and boats of all sizes crossed to and fro. In the distance they looked like waterbugs skittering over the surface. Near the bridge the river slowed, waiting to pass through the arches clogged with branches, debris, and dead animals. On the other side the water fell several feet, churning and rushing seaward with the ebbing tide. The sight made Will dizzy.

"I wonder how many debtors and other disconsolate souls have jumped to their deaths here," he mused.

Mack suddenly strode away and Will wondered how he had offended him. On the other side of the bridge, where the road became a wide thoroughfare, he found Mack waiting for him.

"I hear those cunning foxes are still up to their crimes," Mack said. "Let's trap them in their lair before taking our sport at the fair."

Will's heart sank. In truth, he never wanted to meet Peter Flick and Davy Dapper again. The first time he had lost only his money. This time there was bound to be a fight, and he might lose an arm or a leg or even his life. No, he wanted only to explore the city in the company of this knowing and friendly Mack.

"Show me the way; I am prepared for some stout action," said Will, not wanting to appear cowardly.

He followed Mack into Crooked Lane, which indeed had a crook in it, beyond which the lane ended in an alley barely wide enough for two to walk abreast. Together they crept down the dirt path flanked by ruined houses and a foul-smelling stable. No sunlight found its way there.

"Call me Will Shake-in-my-boots if you will, but I like not this place," said Will, striving to sound lighthearted.

"Fear not; we are well armed," said Mack. "I have it on good intelligence that our two thieves used to resort here."

Misgivings crowded Will's mind. Was he being led into a trap? But why would Mack have given him a weapon if he meant to harm him? He gripped the sword and was about to draw it but realized the alley was too narrow for a sword to be of any use. He was sure to lose any fight in this dark byway. His body might never be found. Would death make his father proud of him, or would he berate Will's cold corpse for losing the twenty-five crowns in the first place?

Mack paused before a weathered sign of a cock over a decrepit door. He put a finger to his lips and drew his pistol. Will's mouth was dry. He wished he had Mack's dagger instead of the unwieldy sword.

Mack lifted his knee nearly to his chin and struck the sole of his boot against the door with such force that the door splintered. He fell backward into Will and they both tumbled to the ground. A loud blast sounded and the sign over the door fell with a crash. An acrid smell reached Will's nose. Mack's pistol had fired! Will could only lie on the ground wondering if he was still alive.

"Gog's wounds!" cried Mack, jumping to his feet. "Open up, you base knaves, you creeping caterpillars!"

There was no reply. A furry creature scurried over Will's hand.

"There goes a rat! Was that you, Davy?" said Mack. "Peter Flick must be inside." He motioned for Will to rise. "Come, men. Charge the door of this vile den!"

A sudden vigor surged through Will and he leaped up. He would not disappoint Long Meg's brother. The splintered door hung on a single hinge but seemed to be bolted from within. He drew his sword and hacked at the door until it fell off. His arm was jolted and numb. He stumbled through the opening into a room cluttered with chunks of plaster, dusty planks, moldy clothing, and broken furniture. In the dimness Will could discern not a single thing of value—no hangings or furnishings, no chests that might hold a robber's booty. There was not so much as a chair to sit on, much less the persons of Davy and Peter.

"This does not look like a thieves' lair," said Will.

"Maybe they are hiding in the loft," whispered Mack.

Will looked up. The ceiling was missing, the rotting rafters visible. "What loft?" he said.

Mack made a surprised sound.

"Perhaps there is a cellar," Will said, looking at the broken boards under his feet.

Mack shook his head. "There is not."

"How do you know?" Will asked. "Have you been here before?"

"Yes, but I . . . was outnumbered, so I went away again."

"You should have fetched a constable. What use am I to

you? Or did you bring me here for some dire purpose contrived by you and Meg?" Will felt his blood rushing in his veins, suspicion making him alert.

Mack looked furious. "Do you doubt my sister, a true and honest woman? Her manner may be rough, but she harms no man unless he deserves it." He thrust his weapons into Will's free hand. "Here, take these if you do not trust me."

Will fumbled with the dagger and pistol. "You burden my two hands with three weapons, knowing I lack the skill to defend myself with any of them. Now will you set your confederates upon me and rob me a second time?"

Mack rolled his eyes. Will had seen Long Meg do the same thing.

"Why should I contrive to rob you, Will Shakespeare? I believe you have no money."

Will felt his face redden. "I *know* I have no money. Therein lies all my trouble. Alack, I am Fortune's victim!" He tossed the sword, the dagger, and the pistol to the floor. They landed with a great clatter, raising a cloud of dust.

In the silence that followed Will heard a tiny sound, something between a whimper and a feeble laugh. "Even the rats mock me!"

But Mack was instantly alert. "Come forth, cowardly varlet," he said, fumbling in the rubble for the dagger.

Will's eyes followed the sound to a corner where there seemed to be a pile of filthy cloth. Something stirred there. Was it a dog?

He heard Mack draw in his breath as a skeletal creature crawled out of the darkness and stood up. It was a child with large eyes and lank hair, wearing only a ragged shift.

To Will's surprise, Mack dropped to his knees and in a soft voice coaxed the child nearer. He murmured and the child nodded.

"She knows our culprits," said Mack. "They chased her away when she came begging for food." He swept the child up and strode out of the house, leaving Will to pick up all the weapons. He tucked the pistol and dagger in his belt, sheathed the sword, and clumsily ran after Mack.

"Where are you going?"

"To buy her a meal and take her to the orphan's hospital. Her plight is now our fault if we do nothing to help her."

Will observed with what compassion his new friend fed the child and carried her to the nearby hospital, giving the matron four shillings for her care.

"I regret that I ever thought you meant to harm me," said Will. "You are a better man than I am."

"We shall see whether that is true," was Mack's cryptic reply. He strode ahead, veering into every tavern and alehouse in Southwark. He stayed not to drink but only to search for Davy and Peter, growing grim with his lack of success.

But Will was in the mood for revelry. Pots of bubbling ale and roasted meat beckoned him. Street peddlers hawked trinkets, mountebanks their magic cures, and drabs their darker pleasures. Goodmen strolled arm in arm with their wives and dandies with their doxies. Jugglers, musicians, beggars, and cutpurses with shifty eyes wove through the crowds. But why should Will worry? He had a staunch weapon about him. He was at Southwark Fair, where everything was for sale and promised delights he could no longer resist.

"Pick out a pretty wench and let's have some ale," he suggested, hoping to turn Mack from his vain pursuit.

"Mercy, no!" said Mack. "I cannot revel while thieves ply their dishonest trade, Justice closes her eyes, and starving children sleep on rotten blankets."

"Let wicked souls be heavy with guilt; yours should be light and fly upward. You saved a child's life today!" said Will. He put his arm around Mack's shoulder. "Dear friend, we are alive and well. We will find those villains next time. Now let us enjoy the present and one another's company."

Mack turned to him and smiled, his sorrowful look fleeing. In that moment he resembled Long Meg so closely that Will was drawn to him like iron to a magnet.

～ Chapter 15 ～

From a second-story window overlooking the crook in Crooked Lane, Roger Ruffneck was keeping watch. He was a member of Davy and Peter's gang, which included the smooth-talking Tom Treadwell and a thirteen-year-old boy, son of the old curber Nick Grabwill. Roger noticed a tall young man and a shorter, bearded one pass by. Their furtive manner aroused his suspicion and he summoned Davy. While Davy watched them, Roger tied on his ruff lest the occasion call for him to go out.

"Foh!" exclaimed Davy. "They've got that ragged kinchin."

"I tried to catch it once but it was too quick," said Roger.

"If they were at the sign of the cock they must be looking for us," said Davy. He started. "Why, that looks like the cuffin we robbed at the Boar's Head!" There was something familiar about the taller man as well.

Roger peered at him and growled. "I'll be sworn he has my sword!" He thundered down the stairs with Davy at his heels and seized a heavy walking staff.

"Don't hurt me, Master Roger. I'll do whatever you say!" Grabwill Junior cowered with his hands over his ears.

"Hold, you oaf!" Davy blocked the door. "Take off that vile ruff; it betrays you. We need a third man. Hie, Peter! Come anon! We must not lose them."

Davy thrust a pistol into Grabwill Junior's hand. "Wait here, toadlet. If they return, hold them until we get back."

Young Grabwill's father had placed him with Davy as an apprentice, that he might learn all the criminal arts. But he lacked ruthlessness and Roger tried to beat it into him. He knew he mustn't anger his elders. So he took the pistol; it was so heavy he needed both hands to hold it.

Moments later the trio of hounds were tracking their prey through the crowds of fairgoers, to the hospital, and from tavern to tavern.

"They don't even suspect we are following them!" said Davy, grinning. "Pudding-for-brains!"

"What was he called, the one we robbed?" Peter flicked his thumb against his fingers, trying to shake the name from his feeble mind. "He kept his money in his boot."

"Along his shank. His name was Shanks-board!" said Davy. "Or was it Shake-spire?"

Roger scratched his head. "How did *he* come by my sword?"

"Let's take them now," said Peter. "We are three cuffins against two."

"Well counted, Flick! But we are only spying in order to see where they lead us," said Davy.

"You are! I aim to get my sword back if I have to kill him," said Roger.

"Look at them now, as merry as playfellows," said Davy. "What is their purpose?"

"They're parting ways," announced Peter.

Davy seized Roger's bare neck. "Go after Shanksboard if you will. But if you kill him I don't know you from Cain. You'll hang, and I'll confiscate all your goods and sell every one of your precious ruffs."

"Unhand me, huff-snuff!" Roger said, shaking off Davy.

By now Davy and Peter had to run to catch up with the tall companion, who was climbing into a wherry. They jumped into another boat to follow him.

"I swear I know that fellow," said Davy.

"I heard Shanksbird call him 'Farewell Mack,'" said Peter.

"Was there not a boy named Mack with us once? His parents died in a fire," said Davy. "He set up our marks. He could outrun us both."

Peter scratched the dent in his head. He could not remember how he came by it.

"This cuffin somewhat resembles that Mack," said Davy.

"Which Mack?" asked Peter.

"The boy we left behind in the innyard, you clotpoll!" He shook Peter, causing the wherry to rock from side to side.

The shaking improved Peter's memory. "He was caught that day. I hope they cut off his ear. Did you see if Farewell Mack had both ears?"

"What would that prove, dolt?"

The wherry in front of them had landed. Now theirs touched the wharf. They followed their mark up Tower Hill.

"I can still see the look on the pippin's face as he begged for help." Davy laughed. "As if we would risk being captured."

"Why do you speak of him now? That happened long ago," said Peter.

"Because I think he is the same Mack."

"As who?"

Davy hit Peter with the back of his hand. "Since your head was staved in, you have become unbearably irksome. Look, he's passing through Aldgate."

"Oh, *that* Mack. We went to an inn together," said Peter.

"He's gone into the Boar's Head," announced Davy. "What if this Mack *is* the same one we left here two years ago?"

Peter shook his head. "Can't be. He was a pippin and this one is a giant."

"And you, Peter, are an ass."

Davy and Peter returned to their lair. Roger Ruffneck was still out, so Davy related their discovery to Tom Treadwell, who agreed that the connection to the Boar's Head was more than a coincidence.

"I remember now. Shankspit took us there to see a play," Peter said. "I robbed his boot. And that maypole threw us out."

Davy frowned, deep in thought. Long Meg—like Mack—surpassed the height of ordinary men. And her strength was greater than a woman's. He snapped his fingers. "Zounds, I have it! Long Meg is none other than our old companion Mack grown up. Disguised as a woman he enforces the peace at the Boar's Head."

"But why would he pretend to be a woman?" asked Tom.

"Maybe Mack *is* a girl," ventured Grabwill Junior. "Once a fellow forced my father to steal women's clothes, and when he put them on my father saw he really was a girl. It addled his mind."

"Stow it, toadlet," said Tom. "We are thinking." He shook

his head. "It shows unmanly cowardice for Mack to hide in such a manner."

"Worse, 'tis an abomination for a man to go about dressed as a woman," said Davy, his mouth twisted in disgust.

"Where have you been to church?" asked Tom.

"At St. Paul's. With you!" said Davy. He was out of all patience. "Do you pay no heed to the preacher as you fleece his congregation?"

"Long Meg threw us out of the Boar's Head. Let's go back and roast her ribs," said Peter.

"*Him,* you lackbrain. We'll roast his ribs and gripe his guts. Punish his ungodly transgression," growled Davy. "Now where the devil is Ruffneck?"

⌐⌐ Chapter 16 ⌐⌐

Meg had to arrive at the Boar's Head before Will, who might become suspicious if he found her absent. So she took a shortcut, crossing the Thames in a wherry. Despite her sadness over the child, she felt her spirits lift. Before she and Will parted he had called her "dear friend" and promised, "We will find those villains next time." She could hardly wait for another opportunity to roam the streets as free in her movements as a man. How easily adventure came to her! Creeping into Crooked Lane she had felt quicksilver flowing in her veins. Talking to Will was like opening a tap and letting wine pour out. It took some effort to curb her tongue, especially once she agreed to share a bottle with him. When Will asked how Mack had been betrayed, she told him how Davy and Peter had been his companions in mischief until the day they chose to save their own skins. She remembered at the last moment to leave the Boar's Head out of her tale. To Will's question about Mack's family she only said, "Our parents are dead. I raised Meg and she raised me."

"And what is your occupation now that you go about the city furnished like an armory?" Will had asked.

"Like you I am seeking my fortune." She winked and would say no more.

The drink that eased Meg's worries made Will melancholy. "A misfortune it was to lose your parents, yet I envy you."

"Will, are you so stony-hearted that you wish your own parents dead?"

"I mean that you are free to fashion yourself while I, like a hawk tied by jesses, am bound by this debt to my father."

Meg thought of her parents for the first time not with sorrow, but with resignation. "One day Death will come and cancel all debts, letting the hawk fly free."

"Unless he has a wife. Nothing binds a man more tightly than marriage," said Will, refilling their cups.

"Clips his wings, forsooth," said Meg, striving for the same manly tone. Curious, she added, "Why are you against marriage?"

Will filled Meg's ears with a tale of the two Stratford sisters, the one he had courted who turned into a shrew, and the other who let him believe she was her sister.

"I love them and I hate them," he said.

Meg only nodded, wondering, *Do all men have such complicated loves?*

"The bit in the horse's mouth, the bridle of his ambitions, the end of his youth, is marriage to a woman!" Will continued. He patted his doublet and dug in his pockets. "Drat! I have no pen to write down my lament of the disappointed lover."

He had looked so comical, Meg smiled at the recollection.

Her wherry touched the shore. She disembarked and was soon back at the inn. Quickly she changed her clothes and was Long Meg again, filling pitchers of thick brown ale.

At once Violetta was at her side, eager for news. "Why do you look so pleased? What happened?"

"I did a virtuous deed today," said Meg, thinking of the child.

"But what did you say to Will?" Violetta demanded. "Did you tell him my father is rich?"

"Ill news for you. He is averse to marriage."

Violetta looked dismayed. "You must change his mind!"

"Go away," said Meg. "He will arrive at any minute and overhear us."

An hour later Will had not returned. Meg decided he was exploring the city on his own. Patrons demanding ale and victuals kept her too busy to worry. Another hour went by. What if Will was lost?

"I can wait no longer. What did he say about me?" Violetta demanded, holding Meg's sleeve.

In truth Will had said not a word about Violetta. But rather than lie to her, Meg handed her a pitcher. "Go wash this," she said and vanished into the pantry. Moments later she felt Violetta jump on her back and seize her by the hair.

"Tell me what was said between you. Will he woo me?"

"Zounds, never! He abhors shrews. Let go of my hair." Violetta complied but clung to Meg's neck. "I confess I found no opportunity to praise you."

Violetta kicked the back of Meg's legs. "But you were with him for hours!"

"Yes, in taverns and dark alleys. Places hardly suited for courtship. Aaagh! He has an affinity for bad company—" Meg was having trouble breathing.

"And all the while you not once spoke of me?"

"—Making him a doubtful companion for an honest woman," she continued.

Violetta slid off Meg's back. She looked so disheartened Meg felt sorry for her.

"Why not write a letter and I'll give it to him," she offered.

"No. Next time walk in the fields and weave a garland of flowers. That will dispose him to love. If you do not advance my suit, I will reveal 'cousin Mack' for who he is. *You* shall feel the shame." She pinched Meg's cheek.

"Ow! You have my word; I shall win him for you," said Meg, surprised by Violetta's wrath. Did all women turned into shrews when their path to love was blocked?

Violetta reached up to tuck her hair back under her coif and Meg poked her under the arm. "Thus I repay you, acorn," she said.

"Stop, Meg! This is not a game." Violetta was almost in tears. "Tell me, where is Will? When is he coming back?"

"God's truth, I know not!"

Violetta's face showed alarm.

Meg wondered, *Where, indeed, is Will Shakespeare?*

Chapter 17

Will was lying with his face in a puddle not far from where he and Meg had parted. Someone was shaking him. He heard himself groan and felt himself shiver with cold. He managed to open his eyes. Two dark figures hovered over him. Pain surged in his jaw and neck, and he remembered the blow that had knocked him down. How long had he lain there?

"Are you hurt, sirrah? Will you let me examine you?"

Now this is a new stratagem for a robber, Will thought dully. To feel for broken bones—and hidden purses.

"Go 'way. I've naught left to take," he muttered and tried to roll over. The foul water caused him to retch, which made his head and ribs ache.

A second voice said, "Thomas, let us be on our way. This vagabond is not worth our time."

"Thomas Treadwell? You sapsucker, leave me alone," Will said. He blinked, trying to focus.

"No, by my troth. I am Thomas Valentine, a student of physick, and this is Sir Percival Puttock." He pulled Will out of the mire and helped him to sit up. He had a box with large handles, Will noted, something a physician might indeed carry. "We are newly arrived in the city."

"Within the hour, I see, for had you been here longer you would already lack your cloaks, your purses, and everything in that kit." Valentine was taking out a jar of ointment and a bandage. "I speak from experience—as the victim, not the thief, for I am an honest man. My worst vice is that I am a liar. I write plays."

Sir Percival drew his cloak aside to reveal a pistol tucked into his waist. "I will not be deceived," he said stiffly.

"I do not lie now," said Will hastily. "Except in the street where you found me. Alack, my poor head! I think my wit is damaged."

"I saw you take that blow," said Valentine, peering into his eyes. "Can you remember your name?"

"Will Shakespeare, by this hand." He held it up and examined it himself. All five fingers were attached and straight. He could still write.

"And what befell you?"

"A most undeserved blow felled me! A knave dressed like a courtier, but with a bare neck where his crimpled ruff should be, demanded my sword, and said it belonged to him."

"That is the very fellow who ran by us," said Thomas Valentine. "Go on."

"I said to him, 'Prove it by telling me what is on the hilt.' Like a dog he growled at me. 'R! R!' Those were the very letters engraved on the sword."

"You *are* a base thief, then," said Sir Percival.

"That is what he said but with the addition of vile swearing, for he was not a kind gentleman like you."

Sir Percival reddened.

Will addressed himself to Thomas Valentine. "I came by that cursed sword innocently enough, but I would not die by it. I flung it aside, whereupon the madman began to beat me with his walking staff."

Valentine had finished examining Will's limbs and bandaging his head. "Can you stand?"

Grimacing, Will stood up. "If you came to London to fix the head of every unfortunate in the street, you shall work until doomsday and never be rich."

The doctor gazed past Will and sighed. "I came looking for my true love, the lady Olivia. She has run away and I like a hound must run after, for she holds the leash around my heart."

Seeing Valentine was quite serious, Will held in his laughter. The fellow was a doctor after all, not a poet.

"Once we find the ungrateful thing, she is yours to wive, Thomas, and I am well rid of her!" said Sir Percival, whom Will took to be Olivia's unhappy father.

"O speak not unkindly of my sweet mammet, my only plaything," said the doctor.

Will didn't know whether to pity Valentine or Lady Olivia the more. "I'll be on my way now," he said. "It is growing late."

"Let us walk with you as far as your lodging," said Valentine. "I want to be certain you are well."

Will assented, for he still felt dazed, and the threesome made their way across the bridge and through the thinning crowds. Will's limp slowed their steps. Sir Percival kept his hand upon his weapon, and Valentine talked unceasingly of his beloved's many virtues. By the time they arrived at the inn Will was convinced of the doctor's devotion, but he had no clearer image of Olivia than he did of the Queen of Sheba.

Finally Will interrupted him. "I am poor and cannot pay a doctor's fee, but I can offer you food and drink here where I am well known."

"I would be glad to eat and drink with you, Will Shakespeare," said Valentine.

"Stop! I know that stratagem." Sir Percival narrowed his eyes at Will. "Do you take me for a witless rustic?"

A desire for mischief tickled Will. "Your suspicions are quite valid, Sir Percival," he said. "This inn is the deepest den of iniquity in all London. The serving maids are wantons. Ha-ha! And I am a varlet, a most *crafty* varlet—a poet and a player. Therefore trust nothing that I say—" Will was laughing so hard his ribs and his head pounded with pain.

Sir Percival drew back in alarm. "Thomas, you should not have aided this madman. Come away now." He grabbed the doctor's cloak.

"God go with you, Valentine, my good fellow," said Will, holding up his hand. "Come back and see my play in a few weeks. I have such a fetching and womanish actor playing Cleopatra, I swear you will forget your love for the lady Olivia."

"Let me die first!" said Valentine. He turned to follow Sir Percival, who was fleeing as if a devil were chasing him.

~~⊙ *Chapter 18* ⊙~~

Meg hardly noticed the man who stumbled to a table in the corner and leaned on it. His head was bandaged, his clothes torn and dirty. Someone shoved a stool beneath him and he sat down heavily, his head in his hands.

She heard Violetta shriek. "O look at poor Will!"

Meg felt liquid all over her hand. The tap was overflowing. She turned it off and hurried over with a dripping cup of sack.

Violetta glared at her. "I suppose you will blame *Mack* for this?"

"My brother would not hurt Will," said Meg, giving Violetta a stern look of warning. "Will, tell me who did this and I'll thrash the guts out of him."

Violetta tried to wipe the dried blood and dirt from Will's face. He turned his head aside with a grimace and took the towel from her.

"I would feign a good tale but my wit took a battering. In truth, it was no honorable fight; I dealt not a single blow in exchange for my hurts." Will gulped down the sack. "I gave up the sword to one who proved his ownership, and he thanked me thus!" He touched his bandaged head.

Violetta whimpered.

"Who was my assailant, you ask? 'Aargh, Aargh!'" Will groaned.

Meg nodded. "Was he wearing a ruff?" she asked.

"His *hands* were rough but his neck was notable for the absence of one," said Will.

"Certainly he was that notorious pimp and brawler, Roger Ruffneck," said Meg. He must have been following them.

Violetta gasped. "He is the same one who pinched my arm!"

"You're lucky he did not kill you, Will. It is rumored that he has murdered more than one of his rivals," said Meg. "It was I who took that sword from him, and I shall do it again and skewer him through the—" Meg stopped, for she saw Will looking at her in alarm. "Where was my brother when Ruffneck attacked you?"

"We had just parted," said Will. "Blame him not. He was excellent good company and we are already fast friends."

"I love him myself," said Meg, smiling to hear Will speak warmly of Mack.

"It was a *false* friend who left you in danger," said Violetta, frowning at Meg. "*I* would not have done so." She turned her attention back to Will. "Who tended to your wounds?" Her eyes brimmed with tears of tender concern.

"It was a young doctor in the company of an old, bald coot who would have left me in the street. The doctor himself was a good fellow named Thomas Valentine."

Violetta cried out again, putting her hand to her throat.

She leaped up as if to run out the door, then turned and fell to her knees, grasping Will's fingers and watering them with her tears.

Will gave Meg a surprised look. "Am I really such a pitiable sight?"

"Indeed you are," she said. Of course she knew the real reason for Violetta's distress. Her father and her faithful lover were nearby looking for her.

"You are drawing unwanted attention," said Meg, not unkindly. "Go and wipe your eyes."

"What prodigious tears!" said Will as Violetta scurried away. "Think you Cleopatra cried so over the wounds of Mark Antony?"

Meg shook her head. "Hers were crocodile tears. Violetta weeps with unfeigned sadness at your plight."

"It would seem she loves me then," Will mused. He looked a little dismayed.

Now was Meg's chance to speak on her friend's behalf. "As hard as Roger smote you, love has smitten her. The difference is *your* wounds will heal."

"What about you, Meg?" Will's tone was plaintive but his eyes sparkled. "Do mortal goddesses never weep? Do they fall in love? In Ovid's poetry they do."

There he goes again, calling me a goddess! Meg felt confident, even bold. Perhaps Meg could banter with Will as Mack had done. She tipped her head to the side and winked. "I soak my pillow every night with tears of unrequited love for Will Shake-his-beard." A hot blush rose up her neck. She wondered if she was being too saucy.

"So she loves me!" Will threw his head back and laughed.

The sudden movement made him wince with pain. "What can I do about it?"

"Woo her," said Meg. "She will tire of you, fall out of love, and you will be free again."

"I woo the indomitable Meg?" asked Will. "How shall I undertake that Herculean task?"

Meg did not know what "indomitable" or "Herculean" meant, but she suspected Will was referring to her great size. Once again she was Long Meg, the object of men's taunts.

"You misunderstand me and mock me to boot. I'll pluck your shaking beard for that!" she said, her teasing mood giving way to vexation.

"Peace, you Amazon warrior!" said Will. "I am wooing as you suggested."

"Not *me*, fool! We were talking about Violetta. *She* is the one smitten by love. Woo *her*." Meg didn't really mean it. Why should she encourage Violetta's silliness?

"Then you do not love your poor, wounded Will?"

"I do not, for you irk me on purpose like every other jack," she said, but to her surprise she was not angry.

"I shall not rile you further, Long Meg, for if you throw me out of here how shall I court the fair Violetta?" he said, letting out his breath in a sigh.

Meg rolled her eyes. "How indeed? You may stay, for though I do not love you, I would not add to your injuries. Now good night."

Wearied yet strangely excited by this contest of wits, Meg went up to her room. There she found Violetta tossing uneasily on her pallet.

"Did anything else happen?" she asked, sitting up and lifting her red, swollen face to Meg.

Meg nodded. "Your tears served you well, for in their aftermath I persuaded Will of your love and encouraged him to woo you," she said, pulling off her clothes. "I know that was to be Mack's office, but it was Meg who found the opportunity." She flopped on her bed. "I kept my promise. You keep my secret."

Violetta's eyes filled again. "My father and Thomas—how close they came to finding me!"

"Your father sounds like a harsh man. I understand why you ran away from him." Meg meant to be sympathetic but Violetta sobbed even louder. "Now, now. Thomas Valentine is a man of virtue. But who loves what is virtuous?" she said, adopting a lighter tone. "We love sweets and rare fruits that make us ill. 'Love knows no reason,' Will says." She yawned and climbed under the coverlet. "Perhaps I shall meet this doctor and against all reason he will fall in love with me. I will marry him and you can marry Will." Meg hardly knew what she was saying, and as soon as these words left her mouth she fell asleep, while Violetta whimpered like a kitten.

Will's injuries were not serious enough to deter him from adventure. The next day he asked Meg to arrange for him to spend a whole day with Mack. "This time you must come along and be my defender," he urged.

"You may borrow a poniard and defend yourself. Or better yet, I have a pistol," she said, just to see his eyes grow round. *I had better watch my tongue,* she thought.

Before going to meet Will, Meg asked Violetta for help with her disguise.

"You are strangely fixated on this clothing," said Violetta, looking askance at her.

"I do this for your sake. If he looks too closely at Mack and recognizes me, the game will be up."

Violetta obliged, paying particular attention to the fit of Meg's doublet. "If anything betrays you it will be your bosom. You had better wrap this cloth around your chest first."

Meg took off the doublet and regarded her breasts. Sometime in the last year they had grown ripe and round, probably while she was sleeping. "I should be glad, but 'tis an inconvenience now," she murmured to herself.

When Meg was swaddled and dressed, Violetta tucked the last locks of her hair under her cap and helped her smudge her upper lip and chin with ashes.

"You look nothing like yourself, save your height and the color of your eyes," Violetta said approvingly. "I would not know you myself."

~⊃ Chapter 19 ⊂~

It was a golden October day when Meg and Will ambled the length and breadth of London from Aldgate in the east to Ludgate in the west, from Moorfields north of the city to the harbor at Queenhithe. Meg loved walking down the street in breeches and breaking into a run if she felt like it. She held her head high, thinking what an advantage it gave her, this ability to see above the crowds.

Will was eager to relate his encounter with Roger Ruff-neck. It was a different story than the one Meg heard him tell at the Boar's Head.

"Seeing he meant to fight me for the sword, I threw it aside," said Will. "He had no weapon and I meant to make it a fair fight. So with my fists I met him blow for blow, blackening his eye and raising knots on his head. He contrived to fall in the direction of the sword, picked it up, and ran away with it. What a dastard! A base coward!"

"Well done, Will," said Meg, suppressing a grin. "I would have fared no better. Did the villain hurt you?"

"Not much," he said with a shrug. He was wearing a cap

that hid the cut on his head and trying not to limp. Meg learned something new about men: they liked to embroider their deeds as some women did pillow cushions to make them seem magnificent.

"Let's go to St. Paul's, which you showed me from the bridge," Will suggested.

Meg had assumed that the purpose of their outing was to find Davy Dapper and Peter Flick, but Will seemed more interested in exploring the city. So she decided simply to enjoy his company. Paul's Walk she found unchanged. Every sort of business was being conducted as usual in the nave of the church, which was thronged with merchants, lawyers, pickpockets, pimps, and even animals. Meg and Will left in disgust when a pack mule voided its bowels in an aisle and no one seemed to care. In the churchyard a crier sang the latest ballad and a troupe of tumblers entertained a happy crowd.

"Look up; heed those boys in the belltower," warned Meg. Just as she and Davy and Peter used to do, they were pelting passersby with pigeon droppings and rotten fruit.

But it was up to Meg to be watchful. Will was ambling from one printer's shop to another, pausing at bookstalls to read the broadsides and examine the tiny octavos and large folios. "This churchyard is heaven," he sighed. "But though I am a poor man—nay, *because* I am poor—I may not enter."

"So you cannot buy a book, but you can get a free sermon," said Meg, indicating the stone cross where a blackrobed preacher stood. With his arms spread he resembled a giant crow. He had to shout in order to be heard.

"You may see them in taverns, theaters, and even in hallowed churches, these mankind witches!" His thick brows were like caterpillars crawling up his forehead as he spoke.

"For God saith in His testament that a man who wears a woman's apparel is accursed, and a woman who wears a man's apparel is accursed also; verily they are monsters abhorrent to the Lord."

Meg felt herself grow crimson with shame and fury.

"Are there such creatures in London?" said Will, amused. "I thought all monsters dwelled in far-off Asia and Africa."

"The preacher himself is the monster—a dragon spewing poison," said Meg. "Come away."

"No, this is as good as a play. Listen."

"They are not fit for His house, but for the alehouse and the playhouse, those resorts of the riotous. Beware the dens of deviltry, the sinks of sinfulness."

"Even better!" said Will. "His eloquence inspires me to visit those places that promise so many pleasures."

"Let's go now, for I am thirsty," said Meg, hoping Will did not really intend to visit a bawdy house.

"A moment yet. Is that the chamberlain from the inn?" said Will, pointing to a man who stood rapt before the preacher.

Meg looked. It was indeed Job Nockney. When had he become a Puritan? Meg almost spoke her thoughts but remembered in time that Mack was not supposed to know Job. Nor did she want to risk Job recognizing her. She turned and strolled quickly away.

"Hold! Wait." It was Will, running to catch up with her, a notebook in his hand. "Let me sit and write down some choice phrases."

They entered the nearest alehouse, and while Meg quenched her thirst Will jotted in his notebook.

"Is it true, as my sister claims, that you write plays in

order to repay your father's debt?" said Meg, seizing the chance to remind Will of his blunted purpose.

"I wish I could deny that heavy reckoning!" he said with sudden feeling. "I write but to please myself and forget my sorrows."

"Ah, the sorrows of love. It was vile of those sisters to trick you. Or do you mean the sorrow of your bankrupt family?"

Will shook his head. "I've forsworn the Hathaway wenches! Let me love instead an honest and true-hearted friend such as yourself."

Meg's heart skipped a beat. Then she remembered Will believed he was speaking to Mack. She felt a tug of brief regret.

"Where does that leave my poor cousin who loves you distractedly?" she said.

Will groaned. It was not a sound that spoke of love. Therefore to plead for Violetta would be harmless, Meg decided. But how to praise her as one man might to another? She chose her words with care.

"Consider that Violetta has a pleasant temper as well as a pretty face—except when she cries at length, and her features remain swollen for several hours after." She paused. "Her father is a wealthy man, and she has every hope of an inheritance when he dies, if they are reconciled and if he does not spend it by then."

"That is faint praise," said Will.

Meg clapped him on the shoulder. "Do not think because I praise her I am in love with her myself! I have seen her but once or twice. My sister will vouch for her virtue, though it was nearly vanquished by the same villain who smote you in the matter of his sword. My sister took it from him, you know. At the Boar's Head." She glanced at Will to see his reaction.

"'Struth, Long Meg is a brave wench. She fears no man. And she has the most agile tongue of any woman I know."

To Meg this sounded like a bawdy remark. "Do not speak of my sister in that manner," she warned.

"Be content, Mack. I refer not to kissing, for her lips are beyond a man's reach. I refer to her quick and nimble speech. She confesses her mind most freely and with words well chosen."

Meg could not hide her pleasure. "In truth I got all my brains from her. Our parents had none to spare."

"Say, Mack, why don't you come to the Boar's Head? We three could indulge in a great feast of wit between us."

"I may not. And you must never speak of me there," she said with great feeling. If Will talked of Meg's brother, that would give her away, for the Overbys knew she had no family besides her "cousin" Violetta.

"Why should I not claim you as my friend?" said Will.

Flustered, Meg struggled to think of a reason. Finally she said, "One night I became boisterous, calling the hostess 'mighty Mistress *Over-byte*' and praising her *toothsome* fare. I meant the tasty food." She winked. "But her husband took offense and had Meg throw me out, whereupon my sister bade me never return there, for she feared to lose her position."

Will nodded sympathetically. "Meg is vexed with me too. I love to jest with her, yet she often takes it amiss."

Meg faltered, then found her riposte. "Can you blame her? How would you like to be a curiosity of nature, say, a man of uncommonly small stature?"

"I am already a curiosity, for no one respects a poet or understands him." Will sighed. "But you do, I believe.

Therefore disguise youself and come. You can keep me company while I write."

Meg started. *Disguise myself?* She glanced at Will, whose open look revealed no suspicion.

"With you present," Will went on, "Violetta might refrain from disturbing me."

The idea of sitting next to Will while his mind invented new people and gave them words and deeds greatly appealed to her. She had to shake her head briskly to remind herself to behave as Mack.

"You are too cruel to my cousin!" said Meg, more heartily than she intended. She took a swallow of ale. "Why do people flee from love?" She was thinking not only of Will and the sisters from Stratford, but Violetta running away from Thomas Valentine. "They should be glad of it. Is not the state of being loved preferable to that of being indebted?"

Again Will would not be reminded of his business. "To be in love is to be a slave to flesh and fantasy. It is to be speared with self-doubt and stretched on a rack, to have one's mind possessed with thoughts that find no relief but in wretched poetry."

Meg, who had never experienced the pains of love, could not help but laugh at Will's outburst. But she did so in a manly way.

Will took no offense, only nodded to himself. "'Stretched' and 'wretched.' Not a bad rhyme, don't you agree?" He dipped his pen and wrote.

"Your rhyme is fair but your raillery *far-fetched*," said Meg. "Love cannot be so vile as you say."

Will glanced up at her with an expression that conveyed, if Meg was not mistaken, admiration.

"Indeed it is a noble thing to love a friend as oneself—one's *better* self," he said, and the warmth of his smile made Meg blush.

Upon returning to the inn, Meg was forced to endure another of Violetta's inquisitions. She wanted to know everything Will and Meg had spoken to each other.

"I can't recall every word but their gist was, he is not disposed to love. He says love is a kind of torture, he would not be a slave, and more in that vein." Meg shrugged. "I cannot change his mind."

Violetta's face crumpled. "A slave? *I* torture *him*? He wrongs love who says such things."

"O I am weary of discontented lovers," said Meg. "You bottle your misery and pour it like vinegar into your cuts, which makes them hurt all the more." She undressed and placed Mack's clothes beneath her mattress. Taking her night shift from the hook on back of the door, she noticed the ladder of chalk marks there. How many months had it been since Gwin measured her?

"Violetta!" she said, interruping her friend's silent weeping. "Return me a small favor for the vast trouble I undertake on your behalf. Take this chalk and mark my height."

Since giving up the vain efforts to slow her growth, Meg was afraid to see how much taller she had become. At least two fingers, she guessed. She did not want to know and yet she was compelled to find out.

A sniffling Violetta climbed on the stool and stood on her toes. Meg heard the scrape of the chalk and ducked aside.

"Where is the mark?" she asked.

Violetta pointed. "Right on top of this one."

"No, you are supposed to make a *new* mark to show how much I have grown," said Meg impatiently. "I'll have to fetch Gwin."

"I know what I am doing," said Violetta. "The new mark is even with the old one."

Meg stared at the door. She stared at Violetta. She put her hand to the top of her head.

Violetta laughed through her tears. "You simple goose!" she said. "You have stopped growing."

Chapter 20

An hour ago Will had written *Upon the rack of love I lie, stretched / 'Til my limbs break, my heart wretched—*

He stared at the verses until his eyes crossed. How could he use them in a play?

His eyes strayed to the summons on the table that reminded him of the duty he was neglecting. He wished someone would come by and tell him what to do about it. Mack would be just the friend to advise him.

Early in the morning the public room was usually quiet, but today was all commotion. Through the open window he could hear Job Nockney shouting at Dab.

"You're a wicked boy. That you are my son I have only your mother's word and she was wicked too."

Will pitied Dab. Why did Puritans like Job see only evil in the world?

Violetta's voice issued from the kitchen. "I am not your slave, Gwin Overby! I was not raised to be a base servant, to labor at a common *tavern*. You forget I am a lady!"

Then came Long Meg's pleading voice. "She doesn't mean it, mistress. Do not send her away."

Piebald jumped on Will's table and meowed loudly. He stroked the cat's fur. Mistress Overby tottered through the door with Meg following.

"O Meg, everything is topsy-turvy here! Violetta has turned rebel and cries if you look at her cross-eyed. My husband lords it over me like an Orient king. Ever since that Will fellow came and put everyone in his play! Look at him scribbling his next piece of mischief."

Will stared at the scrap of poetry. It rebuked him as a failure.

"Next all men will walk on their hands, heels upward, and forswear strong drink. We shall go out of business!"

"Peace, mistress," said Long Meg. "At least *I* am not changed, no, not by a hair's breadth."

Meg and the hostess burst into laughter. The reason for their sudden glee was a mystery to Will. He would never understand women.

Meg skipped over to his table, her golden hair flying, her expression joyful.

"Good morrow to you, Will Shake-his-beard," she said, sitting down across from him and planting her hands on the table. "Write this."

Taken aback by her boldness and high spirits, Will picked up his pen and waited.

"Long Meg I am content to be, as there will be no longer me."

"Is this a riddle?" he asked, frowning.

"Tut, where is your wit today? I, Long Meg, will be no *longer* than I am now. I have stopped growing!"

"Aye, that is good," said Will, smiling at last. "I mean the verse and your news."

"Both well-measured, you should say," Meg said with a wink.

"Your brother winks in just such a way," remarked Will.

"'Twas my affectation first, for I was born before him," said Meg without hesitating. "Why are you not writing?"

Will sighed and pushed the summons toward Meg. "This writ must be answered on October the fifteenth. I have nine days to find my father's lawyer."

"There is a lawsuit?" Meg's eyes widened. "This matter is more serious than you let on. You could be arrested and put in prison!" With her forearm she swept Piebald to the floor.

"I know. I should have been seeking my father's lawyer instead of those two slippery thieves."

"A lawyer is but another kind of thief," said Meg drily. "Who is this barnacle you seek?"

"Thomas Greene, of Middle Temple." Will laughed but it came out more like a bark. "What, are lawyers gods that live in temples? Where is this church of litigation?"

"I know not but surely Mack does. He will take you there tomorrow," Meg promised.

The next morning a grateful Will met Mack at the Ludgate, the city's westernmost gate. As they passed through it Will noticed a dark house pitched steeply over a foul-smelling ditch. Its closed shutters were barred with iron. It was Fleet Prison, Mack informed him. Will shuddered.

Where Fleet Street met Chancery Lane they came to a gatehouse leading to a fair and stately building. MIDDLE TEMPLE, the sign read. A stream of young men poured from the gate, all clad in black robes and hats shaped like small pies. Will regarded them with some envy. Had he not been forced to leave school to assist his father, he might have been among them, preparing for a profession that would make him rich and well-esteemed. In all the kingdom was there an actor or playwright who was regarded as anything more than a talented vagabond? What made Will think he would be an exception? He wondered if it was too late to change his life's plan and choose a more conventional path.

"Come, Will!" Mack's voice interrupted his thoughts. "The porter says Thomas Greene is within."

Passing through a foyer hung with banners and escutcheons, Mack and Will followed the sound of voices to a large common chamber. There an elderly man with a wisp of hair over his bald pate was lecturing to his fellows.

"Let us consider whether in a case of willful manslaughter it is more just and fitting to strike off the felon's hand at the place of his crime and then proceed to the place of his execution, or to punish and execute him in the same location, to wit, the site of the crime?"

"Shall it be always his right hand that is stricken off?" said a second lawyer. "What if he committed the crime with his left hand?"

"A murder of crows!" whispered Will, viewing the black-robed assembly.

"Pssst! Fetch me Thomas Greene," Mack whispered, nudging a clerk who picked at the threads of his gown.

Will wanted to hear what the lawyers decided about the felon's hands, but at that moment the threadbare clerk returned with one who confessed to being Thomas Greene.

His eyes were indeed green. He had red hair, a red face, and round, fat fingers. Will thought of a sausage about to burst from its casings.

"D'you know my father, John Shakespeare of Stratford? I am his eldest son, Will."

Thomas Greene made a move as if to disappear into the flock of lawyers, but Mack gripped his arm and said, "My friend has need of your services."

Thus compelled, Greene led them to a dingy chamber and sat down at a table littered with parchment, books, candle stubs, and bones from past meals. He shoved aside the mess and waved his hand, urging Will to hurry.

Will handed Greene the writ, the red wax seal dangling like a clot of blood. He watched the lawyer mash his lips together and twitch his nose as he read. Will realized he was nearsighted.

"'Tis too late to plead. The judge at assizes has found for the plaintiff." Greene shrugged. "It remains but for Westminster to punish the debtor."

"Punish him?" Will's voice rose. He cleared his throat. Would they cut off his hand? He hunched over and tucked his hands in his armpits for safekeeping.

"It is your father's debt, not yours. Why look you so worried?" said Greene.

Mack, standing behind Will, spoke up in his defense. "Because he is the one who must face the judge."

"Rather *you* must on my behalf," Will said to Greene. "Unless we can find Burbage and persuade him to a settlement. Do you perchance know him?"

Greene made a sudden farting sound with his mouth.

"Never even heard the name. And he would be either a fool or a saint to forgo a claim on ten pounds."

"Then draw up a writ to delay this action or appeal the judgment," Will pleaded.

"Lex dilationes abhorret," said Greene pompously. "The law abhors delays. Yet there might be extenuating circumstances or irregularities in the judgment." He picked up a small handbook and began to discourse of arcane subjects: courts of *nisi prius; postea*, the records of trial; the plea of *non est factum*, that the deed is not that of the defendant.

Thanks to his grammar school Latin, Will was able to follow Greene's ramblings. "These writs and subpoenas. How quickly can you prepare them? And what shall be the cost?"

Greene bent over a piece of paper, his nose inches from the desk. He made a list and announced, "Two pounds, ten shillings, and seven pence!"

"Merely to begin a suit with no certainty of success?" Will cried. "I don't have that much money."

Greene leaned back in his chair and exhaled like a giant bladder. "Then you waste my valuable time, Will Shakespeare."

Will slapped his hands on the summons and pocketed it along with the scrap of paper. He dug into his pocket and tossed two shillings on the desk. "Here is recompense for your precious advice, Master Greene."

"Are you crazy?" said Mack. "You owe him nothing!"

With surprisingly deft fingers Greene pocketed the coins.

Will grabbed Mack's arm. "Come, let's leave behind this temple of turpitude."

When they reached the street Will burst out laughing.

"How can you laugh?" said Mack. "That stuffed gut grows fat with his fees while honest folk starve."

"I laugh because I have got the best of him. Quick, before he realizes it."

When they were well mingled with the crowds on Fleet Street, Will drew a small book from his pocket and tapped its cover. *"The School for Lawyers,"* he read.

Mack's mouth fell open. "Did you nip that from Greene?"

"No. I purchased it with my two shillings."

"What! Who will be your lawyer now? Zounds, what if *he* sues you?"

"Peace, Mack. I don't need a lawyer." He held out the book. "Study this. With a little Latin and some logic *you* shall be my lawyer."

Mack stepped back, holding up his hands in refusal.

"Come, I shall countersue Burbage, outwit his lawyer, and share my gains with you," said Will. "Think of the sport to be had!"

"There is no sport in prison if you lose," said Mack. "I won't be a party to such folly."

Sudden worry gripped Will's guts. Mack was right. He was acting foolishly and without regard for the consequences. He was expecting too much of Mack.

"I am sorry I asked for your help," Will said, unable to hide his disappointment.

"No, Will, *I* am sorry." Mack sounded sad too. "I am ashamed."

"Why?" Will laughed bitterly. "You are not the hapless and penniless son of a man who shirks his debts."

"What I mean is that I regret I cannot help you, my friend," said Mack. He fiddled with the braid on his doublet and avoided looking at Will.

Will did not understand Mack's reluctance. He tried again, holding out the book and speaking with softer persuasion. "I ask only that you study a little with me and play the lawyer for one hour in court." He paused. "Pray tell me, how hard can that be?"

Mack stared at the book, then into Will's eyes. He let out all his breath at once.

"Damned hard, Will Shakespeare, for I cannot read!"

~∽ Chapter 21 ∾~

London

Meg wished a bear would come lumbering down the street and drag her away in its teeth. Or that the street would open up and swallow her. Anything to escape the disappointment that crossed Will's face.

"You cannot read!" repeated Will in perplexity.

It was hardly something to be ashamed of. Meg knew very few people besides Will who could read or write. "Am I no longer worthy of your companionship?" she asked, striving to keep her voice from trembling.

"Of course not. I mean—yes, you are. Fie upon my tongue." Will rubbed his mouth. "Not a word?"

Meg decided the best strategy was to be bold, not shamefaced. "I could no more read that lawyer's book than I could swim to France with my hands tied together."

"You could swim to France with those well-turned legs alone," said Will with an admiring glance below.

Meg felt herself blush. There was no way to hide the shape of her legs while wearing close-fitting hose. "Believe me, I would do it if it would help you in this case."

"Would you do something easier and less dangerous?"

"If it were in my power, yes," said Meg warily.

"Would you pretend to be someone you are not in order to help a friend in need?"

Meg's heart pounded against her ribs. Had Will uncovered her secret?

"Speak plainly," she demanded.

"If I read the lawyer's part to you, could you memorize it for the judge?"

Meg let out her breath slowly. *Of course I can*, she thought. She was already performing a role. Not once had she slipped and forgotten to speak and behave as Mack. But could she doubly disguise herself to play Mack and a lawyer at the same time? Meg scratched her head through her cap. *How shall I know my cue?* She opened her mouth to ask, then remembered Mack knew nothing about acting.

Instead she said, "What if the judge asks me a question I cannot answer? I shall be exposed as an imposter."

"All the world is a stage on which we wear costumes to flatter ourselves and deceive one another," said Will.

"Do you accuse me of false intentions?" asked Meg, feigning offense as Mack yet wondering if Will *had* discovered her to be Meg and was baiting her.

"What I meant was that no clothing could improve what Nature made perfect in you, dear friend."

"Are you suggesting I go about naked?" she said roughly, hoping her red face would be construed as irritation.

A laugh exploded from Will. "Wear whatever you will as long as you agree to learn the lawyer's part." He was on his knees now. "Dear friend, do it for my sake."

Will was in such earnest that inwardly Meg melted. She

had to remind herself that he was appealing to Mack. Yet how could she deny the pleasure it gave her to have a fair young man kneel before her? How could she refuse him? It might end their friendship and thus her adventures as Mack. And it would mean Will's defeat in court. If he were fined or imprisoned she could do nothing to help him.

"You look like a besotted lover. Get up before someone notices you," said Meg, pretending disgust. "I hardly know you, Will Shakespeare, and yet I trust you. We will meet again in two days." She turned to leave, then said over her shoulder, "Do not make the lawyer's part too difficult!"

As usual Meg returned to the Boar's Head by a different route and quickly became Long Meg again. When Will came in she asked, "Did you find the lawyer?" and pretended to be shocked when he showed her the book he had stolen. When Will said he had persuaded her brother to play the lawyer, Meg put on a doubtful look.

"He will need several days to study the role," she said. "His memory is not so quick as mine."

"First I must write it," said Will and commenced working as if a fire had been lit under him. He paged through the stolen handbook, jumped up from his table and gave a speech to the air, then fell to his stool and scratched furiously with his pen. Meg watched in amazed silence.

"My head aches, Long Meg. Fetch me some ale and listen to what I have written."

Meg brought him a cup and peered at the mysterious scribbles. How she wished she could read it for herself!

Will recited his new words for her. "Are these not fine

phrases? I have mingled the Latin with the English to sound more learned."

Meg tried to hide her panic. She was afraid to say anything.

"Why do you look so distressed?" asked Will. "Do you not like it?"

"Like it? I can make no sense of it! How shall my brother learn it? What if he makes a mistake before the judge?"

Will touched her hand to calm her. "I have confidence in him. He is as brave as you are and almost as witty."

Meg's hand tingled. She did not draw it away. "And what if he is arrested for impersonating a lawyer?"

Will waved his hand as if brushing away a fly. "Many an *ignoramus* passes as a lawyer because he can curse in Latin. Under my tutelage your brother will seem as wise and logical as Aristotle."

Already Will was using foreign words. Meg feared he might lose his purpose while studying this lawyer's book.

"Tell me, Will, can a painter work from a description in words or must he see the subject with his own eyes?"

"Is this a riddle?" he asked eagerly.

Meg plucked the book from Will's hand and placed it on the table. "Have you ever been to court or heard a lawyer speak to a judge?"

Will kept his gaze on the book. "I see your point," he said. "But I say a man may play a king without living in a castle. Surely he can play a lawyer without being in a courtroom."

Perhaps he was right. But Meg was afraid of the unknown realm of the judge. She had seen the outcome of their decisions: a man in the pillory bleeding from his ears, a prostitute in a white sheet standing before the church. Once she had witnessed a hanging on Tower Hill during which Peter had filched several purses from unwary bystanders. But foremost in her memory was the Wood Street jail, the dark, miserable hole where her father suffered without any cause and died without recourse to justice.

"A court of law is not a mere stage, Will Shakespeare," said Meg, striving to check her strong feelings. "Feign what you will but remember that a judge in fact sends men to prison. He takes away their freedom—and sometimes their lives."

She swept up the empty cups and turned away so Will would not see the tears in her eyes, threatening to fall.

~⟡ Chapter 22 ⟡~

Hewlands Farm, Shottery

At the dawn of an October day the village of Shottery presented a peaceful aspect. Crofters with their sickles and carts headed to the fields, wearing cloaks they would throw off when the sun had gained strength. Haycocks dusted with frost dotted the fields like pieces in a game of nine-men's morris. The sheep grazed in the still-green meadows, growing their winter pelts, while cows lowed in the lee of stone fences where falling leaves also gathered. Sleepy housewives swept the dirt from their doorsteps and gazed over their gardens going to seed.

Anne Hathaway was blind to the day's glory. With a yoke across her shoulders she picked her way carefully over the rutted ground. Leaves cascaded around her and fell into her milk buckets. The rising sun cast a long shadow behind her that shifted with her every step. At the kitchen door she eased the yoke from her shoulders and sat picking the red and gold leaves from the creamy surface. She was so tired lately. Her whole body ached. Especially her heart.

She heard Catherine giggling. The sound irritated her like

a burr trapped in her stocking. She tiptoed down the garden path and peered through a tangle of briars and wilted roses to see her sister head to head with a young man. So early in the morning! Anne worried about Catherine's virtue, but what could she say after spending the night with Will herself?

The fellow turned and Anne saw that it was Gilbert Shakespeare, who had been keeping company with Catherine since Will left for London. He possessed little wit and even less charm, in Anne's view. And Catherine? She was like a child who forgets a toy as soon as it is out of sight.

Anne knew why Catherine could so easily shift her affections from Will to his brother. She had not lain with Will. Had not heard him whisper, *Let us kiss, and love each other still.* These words Anne could not forget. She knew that it was *her* body Will had loved, *her* ears he had spoken into, *her* lips he had kissed. Not Catherine's.

She crept back to the kitchen door, leaned against it, and closed her eyes. She asked herself for the hundredth time, *Was Will deceived? Or did he recognize me and willingly lie with me?* It made a difference to her. It made all the difference in the world.

Once Anne had seen a biblical play in Coventry about two brothers, smooth-skinned Jacob and hairy Esau, and their father, Isaac, who was old and blind. Jacob covered his body in furs, pretending to be his brother Esau, and tricked their father into giving him the blessing that was due Esau. She thought about that play often and wondered if Isaac was truly deceived. Could he not tell his sons apart by touch or by their voices? Perhaps Isaac knew Jacob was the more deserving brother. As Anne was more deserving than Catherine, who, as her current behavior proved, never really loved Will.

Anne insisted to herself that she did not regret sleeping with Will. Did not regret the cloak that, like Jacob's furs, led Will to think she was Catherine. But she did rue the breach with her sister. Catherine had said hateful things to Anne, accused her of being jealous, deceitful, and a thief.

You do not deserve Will, was Anne's defense. *I know what love is, and you do not.*

Marry an old man instead. Someone your age. Catherine's contempt was like a dagger.

Alas, marriage to Will was now out of the question despite their vows, for he had fled to London and no one had heard of his whereabouts since.

A cat, her belly sagging with unborn kittens, rubbed against Anne's leg. She sat down and stroked it. "I am so unhappy. Nine people live under this roof. Father's wife treats me like a servant and expects me to take care of her children," she murmured to the cat. "I am twenty-six years old. I want my own household. And my own children."

Her life was not supposed to be this bleak. Six years ago she had fallen in love with the neighbor's son, David Burman, a frail fellow with gray-green eyes and brown hair. They first kissed in a meadow beside the River Avon and a year later plighted their troth before their fathers. Anne waited two years for David to save enough so they could be married and set up their own household. They never consummated their love, though David often begged her and she was sorely tempted. But she feared that once she lay with him he might leave her. By denying him she thought she could hold on to him.

David did leave her. He contracted a fever in the spring and within a week was dead.

Anne still remembered the sensation of grief. It sucked all life and light into its blackness, like a bog. She had stood on Clopton Bridge trying to summon the strength to jump into the swollen Avon flowing beneath her. If only she had lain with David! If only she had a babe with gray-green eyes to remember him by. If only.

And so five years of her life were lost, three to unsatisfied desire and two to grief. Then Fulke Sandells, her father's friend, asked her to marry him but she declined. He was forty, almost an old man. She did not want his or anyone's pity.

Then one day she noticed Will Shakespeare. She had known him from childhood. In the interval of her own love and loss he had changed from a schoolboy to a man. He had apparently never heard of her misfortune. In his presence a heavy weight lifted from her shoulders, leaving her heart lighter. She felt herself flourish again and become the young woman who had fallen in love with David Burman. She contrived opportunities to see Will and permitted hope and desire to burgeon within her.

Yes, she had stolen Will's love from her sister as Jacob stole Isaac's blessing from his brother. But she regretted neither the deceit nor the deed. The memory of delight was something she could hold fast to. That and the possibility that she did love Will even if he hated her.

On one point only was Anne tempted to regret. She hoped she was mistaken in her calculation. All of September and seven days of October had passed, yet she had not bled since August. With sad dismay she asked herself, *Have I gambled everything for love and lost again?*

She opened her eyes. She was still sitting by the kitchen door. The household now stirred with footsteps, childish voices, the clang of pots. Sunlight fell across her lap. The cat licked the milk-dipped leaves on the ground.

⌐⌐ Chapter 23 ⌐⌐

Will had apparently considered Meg's worries, for when he met with Mack again, he suggested they observe a session of court. "It was your sister's advice, which I am glad to heed because she is a very wise and comely wench."

"Did we not discuss the perils of flattery but two days ago?" Meg said. "I cannot be moved by praise of my sister."

"I speak the simple truth," said Will. "Now, which way to Westminster?" He was all business today.

"It is far and we will spend too much time getting there. The chapel in St. Paul's is closer. Offenders against common morality are tried there."

"The bawdy court!" said Will. "I have heard 'tis like a play, such lively scenes occur there. Let's go."

Dozens of idlers crowded the chapel, some munching on bread and cracking nuts. Meg and Will pushed their way onto a bench. A woman charged with slandering her neighbor was being sentenced to wear a bridle to curb her tongue.

"I knew a notorious scold in Stratford that would not submit but bit her bridle so hard she broke all her teeth. Thereafter no one could understand her ranting and railing."

Meg chuckled. "A wayward horse is wiser than she was."

Then came a tenant accused of lewdness toward his landlady; his lawyer argued that because his client was drunk, he was not aware of his acts and therefore not guilty.

"*Qui peccat ebrius, luat sobrius*," intoned the judge.

Will gave a rueful laugh. "That is true, without a doubt!"

"What did that gibberish mean?" Meg asked him.

"He who does wrong while drunk must be punished when sober."

"Were you drunk when your father's money was taken from you?"

"That is not the point in my case," said Will irritably.

"Well, if the judge tells me to 'quee peck it,' how should I reply?"

"Neither admit nor deny, but equivocate. Say, '*Quaeritur, prima facie*'—on the face of it, the question is raised."

Meg whispered the phrase, trying to commit it to memory. "Kway-it-tour preema fock-ee-ya." It sounded like a lewd insult.

The next defendant was a woman accused by her husband of adultery. She bore an expression of such abject misery that Meg's sympathy was stirred. With no lawyer to plead for her, she raised her hands to the judge and denied that she had ever been unfaithful to her husband. She was interrupted in midsentence.

"Your Honor, I have two witnesses who will swear that they beheld the defendant *in flagrante delicto*, in a close, lascivious, and unlawful embrace."

"That is the husband's attorney," said Will.

"Assuredly a rogue. Note his shifty eyes," said Meg.

"Produce the witnesses," ordered the judge while he stared at the woman with disdain.

Meg gasped. Standing before the judge and wearing gentlemen's finery that belied their baseness were Peter Flick and Davy Dapper.

Will glanced up from his book. His arm shot out to the side, striking Meg in the chest.

"Ow!" Meg's breasts hurt. She hoped Will did not see her cringe.

"It's them! What should we do?" he whispered.

Meg put her finger to her lips. "For now, listen."

Davy was calling the defendant a lascivious woman and stamping his satin-booted feet for emphasis. Peter clasped his filching fingers and swore that the plaintiff, Roger Ruffneck, was an upright and faithful man.

Meg started. She had seen the man in the gargantuan ruff. "All three villains are here in one place!" she said.

"They outnumber us, Mack." Will pulled his cap over his eyebrows.

"We'll waylay them outside," Meg whispered.

The judge was now speaking. "Jane Ruffneck, have you no one to vouch for your . . . *virtue?*" He hemmed as if the word was stuck in his throat. Meg heard scornful laughter from the observers.

Mistress Ruffneck stood without bending. Her self-pity had fled and her eyes flashed with anger. "Who is the man you accuse me with?" she demanded of her husband. "Where is he?" She glared at Peter and Davy.

Roger masked his villainy with a false face of innocence. Peter tapped his fingers against his leg and eyed the crowd for his next victims.

"These men all lie," said Jane to the judge. "But as God is my witness, I am a true wife. I am the one abused by my husband." She pulled up her sleeve. Dark bruises covered her arm.

Meg covered her mouth to keep from crying out. She recalled Roger pressing Violetta's arm hard while attempting to seduce her. She could not count the number of times he had come to the Boar's Head with lewd women. He, not Jane, was the one guilty of adultery. Meg swelled with fury.

"A man may rebuke his wife. Indeed it is his duty if she is wanton," said the judge loudly. "*Per curiam*, the defendant is guilty. I grant the plaintiff a divorce."

A hubbub ensued. Jane Ruffneck's voice rose over the commotion. "Your Honor, how shall I feed myself and my child?"

Meg felt herself jostled as the wardens forced the unruly observers from the chapel. "Where is Truth? Whither Justice? They have deserted these proceedings!" Meg heard herself shout.

Will grabbed her elbow. "Were this a morality play, Mack, lightning should strike all those devils!"

"It's *not* a play," said Meg, her voice low and steely. "Come with me, Will."

In the crowded churchyard Meg threw her gaze from right to left, but it was Will who spotted them.

"Over there in the cloisters!" he announced. "Ruffneck and his lawyer!"

Meg advanced toward Ruffneck while beckoning Will to follow. All her attention was on the villain framed by the arch of the cloisters with the monuments to the dead ranged behind him. He was giving his lawyer a purse, saying "I thank you, Weasle, and you also, Peter and Davy." The face of Death, painted on a stone wall, oversaw their transaction.

Like an avenging angel she drew her sword and said, "It's the devil himself dividing the spoils of the innocent among his foul minions."

Four sets of startled eyes looked up at her. Roger drew his sword. Weasle clutched the purse to his chest. Peter and Davy glanced at each other and ran.

Meg decided to let them go. "Give me that purse, Weasle. Give me all your money, your rings, and jewels. Make haste before Death claims you loathsome, lying dogs."

Roger made as if to strike her but Meg, quickened with fury, smote him with the flat side of her sword. He dropped his weapon and fell to his knees clutching his side. Meg sheathed her own sword and picked up Roger's.

"I took this off you once before, did I not?"

As soon as the words left her mouth, she realized with horror her mistake. It was Long Meg, not Mack, who had taken the sword the first time, at the Boar's Head. She hoped that neither Roger nor Will noticed the slip.

She turned to Weasle, who cringed. "Don't take my purse, sirrah. It's my fee. Let me keep my fee!"

"You put your money where your heart should be. Shall I cut it out of your chest?" How good it felt to let her words flow and shape themselves into fearsome threats!

Weasle dropped the purse and pulled off his rings as if they burned his fingers. Meg scooped them up, then motioned toward Roger. "Now strip him of his valuables."

Weasle stumbled to his knees and groped in his client's pockets, tugged at his fingers. Roger cursed and tried to shove him away, but Weasle managed to poke him in the eye.

"What ho! No fighting in the cathedral precincts!"

Meg turned to see a constable approaching.

"Arrest him! He broke my ribs," Roger cried, trying to point at Meg.

"Sirrah, 'tis only a scuffle among friendly rivals," Meg said with a laugh. She lifted Roger's sword. "While I hold this they cannot harm one another."

"Help, my eye is bleeding," moaned Roger.

The constable took another step toward Meg but she blocked his way.

"You might get hurt yourself," she said in a threatening tone. She pulled a gold coin from the purse. The constable hesitated for only a moment before taking it and turning on his heels.

A shaking Weasle got to his feet and handed over Roger's purse and jewels. There was a considerable sum inside, Meg thought with satisfaction as she hefted it. "This may help to right a few of your damnable wrongs, Roger Ruffneck."

"Now give me back my sword," said Roger. His ruff was in shreds.

"Do you want it through your leg or in your gut?"

Roger shrank into himself like a turtle.

"Now give me the rings you put in your own pockets, thief," said Meg to the lawyer.

Weasle produced two large gold rings set with precious stones. "By gog, I'll sue you."

"I'm not afraid of snakes, rats, or weasels," she said scornfully.

A grimacing Roger shook his fist at Meg. "I know who you are, Mack."

Meg felt courage seep from her sinews. What did Roger

know? How had he discovered Mack was not a man? She must not let him call her bluff.

"You know nothing. This game is not up yet." It took effort to keep her voice steady.

"And we know who Long Meg is," growled Roger. "You can't hide from us."

Meg's heart jumped but she was ready with a comeback.

"I know Long Meg well. She is more of a man than you'll ever be!" As she hoped, Roger looked both insulted and confused.

"Come, Will, let's go," she said, feeling triumphant. She turned but Will had disappeared.

Chapter 24

When Peter and Davy ran, Will ran after them. He did not stop to think. He knew only that he could not stand by like an idle lackey while Mack took on Roger Ruffneck. Without a sword he was swift and agile. He had Mack's pistol securely tucked inside his belt. The desire for revenge pulsed through his veins.

Will's mind was working as fast as his legs. What would he do if he caught Davy and Peter? The odds were against him in a fight. He would demand their purses, and if they had twenty-five crowns between them he would take the money and let them go. If they tried to overcome him he would fire the pistol. What if he happened to kill one of them? His dreams would die at the end of a hangman's rope. He decided he would only threaten to use the pistol.

Keeping Peter and Davy in his sight, Will dashed through the maze of streets, dodging chickens and small children. Slowly he gained ground. He was close enough to smell the cloying French perfume that trailed Davy like a cloud. He could see the dandy's boots coming apart, the heels flapping.

"Just take them off," Will heard Peter shout.

"Nay, these cost me ten shillings!" said Davy, mincing along on his toes.

Will saw the crash coming. But Davy was looking over his shoulder at Will while the handcart piled with straw and dung creaked its way toward him. By the time he turned around again, the cart was upon him and he ran headlong into it. The carter lost control and tipped his load and Davy into the street. With a loud crack the cart broke into pieces.

Will supposed it was a sort of thieves' honor that made Peter stop running when Davy fell. Or it was dumb surprise. Will soon caught up with them, halting just short of the malodorous mess.

Davy crawled out of the slime and shouted at the carter, "You rank and crusty dung dealer! I'll sue you for ruining my clothes."

"The devil take you! I'll sue *you* for breaking my cart." The enraged carter began to beat him with a shovel.

Peter pushed the carter, who growled and turned on him. Will heard the crack of a bone breaking. Peter howled and grabbed his twisted left arm with his right. The carter swung around again and hit Davy in the head. He was a powerful fellow with arms as big around as hams. Will knew he should act and stop the mayhem. He put his hand on the pistol.

The blast stunned even Will. The carter dropped his shovel and fell backward onto his buttocks.

"You killed him!" said Peter.

Will stared at his hand holding the smoking pistol. The carter didn't appear to be bleeding. About three feet away was a blackened, bowl-shaped hole in the street. Will's relief was immense but momentary. He was holding three miscreants at bay with an empty pistol.

"Hold, all of you. I'll shoot the next man who moves!" he said.

Fortunately his foes were in no state to run away. A whimpering Peter cradled his broken arm, and muck-covered Davy his sore head. Will hastily sprinkled fresh powder into the pistol.

"Who are you?" demanded the carter.

"I am a notorious bandit in these parts. These villains know me well," said Will. He carefully waved the pistol at Davy and Peter. "I trusted you and you shook me down. Now you will taste my vengeance."

"It was not me that robbed you," lied Peter. "See, my arm is broken."

"Stow it, Peter. Your brain is broken. And you, Will Shankspeer, are a white-livered bumpkin. Ha!"

Will thought he was behaving quite boldly and Davy's accusation made him furious. "You ingrate!" he said. "I saved you both from that dunghill madman. You owe your lives to me. For twenty-five crowns I'll spare you. Empty your pockets and your purses."

"You go first," murmured Davy.

Moving only his eyes, Peter glanced toward the black hole in the street. "No, you. He said he would shoot the first one of us who moves. I am afeard of pistols."

Neither of them stirred. Will knew that if a constable arrived he would be the one arrested, for he was brandishing the pistol. Davy smirked, for he knew it too. The carter was getting restless.

"Yield every penny to me. Now! Or you shall not live to regret it," said Will.

Uttering yelps of pain, Peter struggled with his good arm to reach his opposite pocket and managed to throw his purse at Will's feet. Davy dropped his in the mire.

Will picked them up, emptied them, and quickly tallied the coins. His heart sank. The total was less than five crowns. He pocketed the coins and threw down the empty purses. "You are still twenty crowns short."

Peter held his arm and looked at the ground. Davy shrugged.

At once Will knew where they kept their money.

"Take off your shoes and give them to me."

Peter removed his shoes and shoved them toward Will with his bare foot. Davy reluctantly stepped out of his boots. The satin was soiled, the heels hanging useless. Will shook the boots, peered inside, then tossed them away. He examined Peter's shoes, wrinkling his nose at their rancid odor.

Nothing.

He flung the shoes down in disgust. What a disappointing ending to the scene of his revenge!

"Can I have my boots back?" said Davy. "They cost me ten shillings."

Will picked up Davy's boots and Peter's shoes and tucked them under his arm. He would let the foul thieves walk home on bare feet.

"Aren't you going to shoot us now?" said Davy with a sneer.

Will considered his pistol. He did not trust the thing. He put in in his belt, making sure the barrel was pointed away from his body.

"I gladly would, but I purpose to get my twenty crowns from you yet," he said, turning to leave and finding his way blocked.

"My cart is broken." The carter had resumed his grip on the deadly shovel.

"'Tis not my fault, sirrah," said Will. "Let me pass."

The carter stood his ground like a brick wall. The sight of the money had made him bold.

"'Twas that knave's doing and he owes me." The carter nodded his head toward Davy without taking his eyes from Will. "But you took his money. So now *you* owe me."

Will could not argue with his logic. But he was not about to relinquish his hard-won five crowns. "Then sue me, varlet," he said, slipping to the side in order to escape.

The carter was quicker than Will expected. He grabbed Will by the jerkin and hoisted him off the ground. His hot breath, fouler than the stench of his dung, assaulted Will's nose. He imagined himself lying in the street with dogs gnawing his limbs. His fingers found the coins in his pocket and he dropped them to the ground. They fell into the powder-blackened hole.

The moment his feet touched the ground, Will ran. Penniless again, he clutched two shoes and a pair of boots with broken heels.

~⌒ Chapter 25 ⌒~

Meg's pockets were heavy with riches. But she was sore at Will, for he had not stayed to witness her triumph over Roger Ruffneck and his lawyer. She wanted to find him but her task here was not yet finished.

She left Roger and the lawyer berating each other in the cloisters and called, "Jane Ruffneck, where are you?" until she saw the short woman hurrying away. Meg quickly caught up with her.

"Don't be afraid of me," Meg said. "I am Mack de Galle and I want to help you."

She gave Meg a wary look. Her face was lined with suffering. "You are that fellow Roger hates. He calls you a monster and a womanish man." She tipped her head toward Meg. "What he calls me is much worse. I thank you for knocking him to the ground. The dirt is where he deserves to lie. Now, good day."

"Wait," said Meg. "Where will you go?"

"Why, to fetch my child and then to the poorhouse." She stepped around Meg.

"Why do you avoid me?"

"Because if my husband-no-more sees us talking, he will believe that I put you up to beating him, and I shall suffer further at his hand."

"Alack, do my good intentions already go awry?" said Meg. She showed Jane her bulging pockets. "I took from him the riches that are rightfully yours. But if I give them to you here, you will become a victim again, for this churchyard is thick with thieves."

"Why have you done this for me? This is not your quarrel," said Jane. She seemed moved.

Meg permitted no one to see the dark place within her where suffering dwelt and from which her hatred of injustice issued. "Trust me, it is," she said quietly.

"I shall trust you," said Jane, her eyes filling with tears. "For Roger's enemy must be my friend."

"For your safety, you and the child must come with me to the Boar's Head Inn."

Jane nodded and led Meg to her house, where they collected little Ned, who was about seven years old, and a bundle of their belongings, making haste to avoid Roger's return.

As they neared the Boar's Head Meg began to sweat. Her disguise was again the difficulty. She paused, took out Roger's purse, and handed it to Jane.

"Other business summons me now, Mistress Ruffneck, but you shall be welcomed at the inn by my sister, Long Meg." She lowered her voice and said in a serious tone, "Do not speak of me to the host or his wife or any of the guests, lest one of them betray me to your husband's minions."

"You would leave me already?" said Jane sadly.

"I shall be watching this place. You will be safe here," Meg assured her. "Now, farewell."

Meg retraced her steps and approached the inn via the alley. Gwin blocked the way, squabbling with a boy over the purchase of some eggs. So Meg ran toward a leaky and unused part of the stable where she had hidden spare clothing beneath the straw. She tore off Mack's clothes, jumped into her skirt, and fumbled with the laces on her bodice. With her sleeve and some spittle she wiped the sooty beard from her face and dashed toward the kitchen door, nearly colliding with Gwin in the entryway.

"Meg, where have you been all day?" She frowned and batted at Meg's skirt. "There's hay stuck to you."

"In the barn. I confess I was shirking but now I shall work doubly hard," she said, not waiting for further rebuke.

In the public room Violetta was serving Jane and the boy, whose face was buried in a bowl of milk. Meg entered carrying a broom and pretended not to notice them.

Jane jumped to her feet. "Are you Long Meg? You look remarkably like your brother!" Her eyebrows shot up and she clapped a hand over her mouth.

Behind Jane, Violetta was tapping her head with her fingertips like a ninny.

"Did he send you here for lodging?" Meg asked, shifting from Mack's manner to her own.

"Of course. You know that." Jane stared at Meg with a strange expression.

"Mother," said the milk-lipped Ned, "why is she wearing that hat?"

Meg drew in her breath. Her hands flew to her head. She

felt Mack's cap still fitted there, hiding her golden hair—and baring her careful disguise.

"Drat!" she said, tearing off the cap. Her hair tumbled about her shoulders. "Will's not here, is he?" she whispered.

Violetta shook her head.

"Why, you are not a man at all!" Jane said in wonder.

"That's true." Meg sighed. "I am sorry for deceiving you."

"Don't be sorry. By my troth, I am glad that it was a *woman* who vanquished my husband," said Jane. "If only I had your courage!" She seized Meg's hands. "Why, I was half in love with Mack for coming to my rescue. And now my admiration deepens, for my champion is one of my own sex!"

Pleased by the praise but afraid Will would walk in at any moment, Meg said, "Hush and keep my secret, please, for if it is known that I am Mack—" She broke off, no longer certain of the consequences. Instead of being appalled, Jane was delighted. How might Will react if he learned Mack's true identity?

"Then your deeds would be all the more celebrated," said Jane, finishing Meg's sentence.

"What deeds?" Violetta asked Meg.

"Never mind, Violetta. Take Mistress Ruffneck and her son to a room."

Violetta stamped her foot. "What did Mack do today? I think it was *not* wooing Will Shakespeare on my behalf."

"Peace, I pray you!" said Meg. She saw that Violetta was like a squib about to explode in a shower of sparks. Meg picked up the bundles herself and led Jane and her son upstairs.

Violetta's petulant voice followed her. "Does Will worship you like she does? Does he find Mack so remarkable?"

"Save me from ever having such jealous thoughts," Meg said under her breath.

When she went downstairs again, Will had returned and was regaling Overby, Violetta, and some customers with a riotous tale involving a brute with a shovel and his cartload of dung. On the table, instead of his usual notebook and papers, rested a pair of shoes and two ragged, broken-heeled boots. Davy Dapper's boots.

Meg drew closer to listen and deduced that Will had caught up with Davy and Peter but recovered none of his money. He was hiding his disappointment well.

"That's a merry tale, Will. Save it for a play," said Overby. He pretended good cheer but Meg could see he was vexed. "I must have another one soon or it *boots me not* to let you stay here longer." He picked up the dirty footwear and dropped it to the floor.

"A good pun, Overby. I shall make use of it in *Cleopatra*," said Will. "It is a heroical romance with scenes of battle to please the men and tragic lovers to make the women weep. I am almost finished with it."

"A comical tale will profit me more, for laughter disposes men to celebrate with drink."

"There shall be a clown in it," said Will, eager to please Overby. "I will have him chased by a crocodile."

"Do not forget that I must be the king again," said Overby.

"Certainly you shall play the noble Caesar and wear a gilded robe," said Will.

Thus satisfied, Overby returned to his tap, dispensing

brew with his chin in the air. Will's listeners drifted away and Meg sat down. She could see his merry mood had departed.

"What shall you do now?" she asked. She knew that he had put aside his new play in order to prepare for his day in court.

"To satisfy Overby I must have a rehearsal," said Will. "Come, Cleopatra, 'tis time to learn your part!"

Violetta clapped her hands. "Another play! A new audience every night."

"That's not what I meant," said Meg to Will. "The fifteenth is less than a week away."

Will ignored her. Apparently he did not want to be reminded of the doomsday.

"Violetta, you are stagestruck," he said. "I'll go and fetch your part."

"Rather I'd say you are Will-struck," said Meg when Will had gone. She was irritated with both of them. "Why do you want an audience to behold your display of love? What if Thomas Valentine happens to see you on the stage?"

"You think you know my heart?" said Violetta, sticking out her lower lip. "No one here knows me or what I wish for."

"I know you think that being a servant debases you, yet you are clamoring to be an actor, someone who is even more reviled."

Meg had provided just the spark to kindle Violetta's dry tinder.

"You call *me* debased and reviled? You mannish creature not content with being a woman!" She lunged toward Meg.

"Hold off, you mincing dwarf!" said Meg, taking Violetta's hands and forcing her to sit. "You know I disguise myself to help Will Shakespeare avenge those who robbed him."

"I thought it was to win his love for me!"

Meg was taken aback. "I *did* praise you to him. Now in spite of my efforts, you will caper about as Cleopatra and woo him yourself."

"Why, I think you are jealous," said Violetta with slow amazement. "You want to be seen on the stage and not be hidden in a wall. Or under a doublet! Are *you* in love with Will?"

"In love with Will?" Meg echoed. It was a question she could not answer. She knew that what she felt for Will Shakespeare hardly resembled Violetta's fiery passion. "Will and I are friends. That is, Will and *Mack* are friends. How should I know love anyway?" She tried to laugh but the sound came out as a croak. "Is madness the certain sign of it? Being hot then cold, hopeful then despairing?"

"Yes! For that is precisely what I feel," said Violetta.

"I think you love yourself more than you do Will," said Meg, exasperated. "In a few days' time he will face a judge over a debt he cannot pay. Help me turn his attention to that more serious matter."

Violetta drew back. "A man's money and his debts are no concern of mine. Will has asked me to be in his play. That is all of *my* business. And you are trying to keep me from it!"

Meg sighed. It was no use appealing to Violetta's nobler feelings. "I was trying to protect you. If you are recognized on the stage, you could be arrested and greatly shamed."

"*You* should worry about being arrested," retorted Violetta. "How many men have you attacked lately? What do you do when you go out as Mack? And what shall I do if a constable comes to arrest you?"

"Tell him Long Meg will bastinado his brains if he does not leave at once."

Violetta's eyes filled with tears. "That's no matter for mirth."

Oh no, thought Meg, *there she goes again, weeping like a fountain.* "Save it for the stage; Cleopatra sheds many tears before she dies. Now I am going to bed."

It had never occurred to Meg that Violetta was worried on her behalf as Meg was worried on Will's behalf. Was that concern the same as love? If so, how could Violetta claim to love Will and not care about the consequences should his performance in court prove a failure?

~⌐ Chapter 26 ⌐~

Will's head ached. His brain felt like a tennis ball bandied back and forth. Duty called him to finish the lawyer's part for Mack. Desire called him to finish his Cleopatra play. Mark Antony himself was never so divided. Now Overby was demanding a play and Will hoped a rehearsal would placate him. For if he were evicted from the Boar's Head, he would be a vagrant with no means of earning a living. Whereas if his Cleopatra play and the ones after it were successful, he could easily repay Burbage. But he was more likely to end up in the clink first, unless he finished those legal writs and Mack recited them ably before the judge.

The usual dreams that filled Will's sleep—of meeting a rich lord who would pay him to act and publish his plays— did not come that night. Instead he dreamed of want, pain, and penury, of his mother and sisters huddled in darkness like the little girl Mack had rescued. He awoke with the firm resolution of finishing the lawyer's part for Mack immediately after the rehearsal. While Overby summoned his employees, Will shoved aside the tables in the public room, ignoring

Mistress Overby's complaints that he was turning everything topsy-turvy again.

"Violetta, sit over there and study your lines," he said.

"Let us play one scene of excellent pretending and make it look like perfect art." She smiled. "I have got that line at last."

"Like perfect *honor*," said Will, correcting her. "But that is not the scene for today." He took the sheet from her and turned it over. "Here are your cues. Now to assign roles." He clapped his hands for attention. "Job, you shall be the crocodile."

"I'll not pretend to be any such devil," Job said, indignant.

"It requires no pretending," murmured Will. "Let me see you crawl and snap your jaws."

"I will be the crocodile!" said Dab eagerly. He cried out in pain as Job grabbed his ear and twisted it.

"No Dab, you must be Iras, the queen's attendant," said Will.

"Is that a girl? I will not wear a skirt and false hair again. If I can't be the crocodile I will be a soldier. See, I have hair on my lip already."

Will sighed. He needed Dab in his company. "What if I make Iras a young man and let him carry a sword?"

Dab clapped his hands in delight. "Then let Long Meg play the crocodile! She can frighten anyone. But I'll kill her with my sword."

"Hush, you bug. I'll squash you with my thumb," said Meg.

Will noticed she stood with her arms crossed over her chest. Why was she sulking? What distressed her? Perhaps she wanted a role too. But she was too tall even for the crocodile. The beast must not be longer than the hero.

"Meg, will you speak the prologue? It describes the argument of the play, in which the triumvir, Mark Antony, loses his share of the Roman Empire for love of the Egyptian queen."

"I'll do it. It befits me as the host," said Overby.

Will ignored him and watched Meg hopefully. "You may speak in your own voice. It will be no use to put you in a man's garb, for the audience will still know you."

Meg regarded him with an expression he could not fathom. She seemed to be hiding something from him. No, she looked apprehensive. Women were such mysterious creatures.

"You have a fine, strong voice," he said to encourage her and held out a page. "Will you also read the parts that have no players yet?"

Meg pressed her lips together. She looked almost angry. Was she unhappy that Violetta and not she was playing the queen? What had he done to offend her but ask her to read . . . ?

Will smacked his forehead. That was it! Like Mack, she had never learned to read. He turned away to spare them both further embarrassment and plunged into his hero's speech.

> *Duty, duty, drew me, Antony, to Rome,*
> *While love did call me to my other home,*
> *Egypt, whose queen I made my heart's*
> *sovereign.*

Will bit hard on the words "duty" and "Antony." He *was* Antony. His duty was to pay his father's debt. Stratford was his Rome and London his Egypt, where he would pursue his true love. A woman? No, a mistress who would not betray him: Poesy. To bring more feeling to his utterance, he thought of the Hathaway sisters and his own mistaken passion.

> *I made these wars for Cleopatra's sake,*
> *Whose heart I thought I had, for she had mine.*
> *But she false-play'd my glory, betrayed me*
> *Unto an enemy's triumph.*

Will motioned to Violetta and Overby and said in his own voice, "Now, Cleopatra, betray me. Turn to Caesar and exchange the document for the stone, which will be painted to signify a great jewel."

"Why is Caesar the enemy?" demanded Overby.

"He becomes Antony's enemy but triumphs over him in battle. Therefore be content until the end."

"What are my lines when I give her the jewel?"

"It is a dumb show. Therefore you do not speak, though you shall in another scene, I promise." Will tried to be patient, knowing the entire production depended on Overby's goodwill.

Now came the scene of Antony's death. "Meg, you must play Eros, Antony's friend. I beg you to slay me, for I have been shamed by my defeat and by Cleopatra's betrayal. But you are unable to kill Antony because of the love you bear him. You say, '*Turn then from me your noble countenance*' and when I do, you stab yourself instead. Thus."

Will demonstrated by falling to the floor and Meg did the same. Will turned toward her, knelt, and lifted her by the shoulders. To his surprise she was soft and yielded in his grasp. Her hair brushed his face. He had to remind himself that she was a soldier.

"Eros! You are nobler than myself, and with your sword teach me how to die." He was aware of Meg's startling blue eyes on him as he drew his sword. He fell on it and rolled to the side.

All the company gasped. Meg sat up and reached out a tentative hand.

"Lie down!" ordered Will. *"How not dead? I live? Guard, dispatch me!"* he shouted into the corner of the room.

"Enter now, Violetta. This line is your cue." Will fell back, supporting himself on his elbow. *"See me, I am dying, Egypt, dying. Give me some wine and let me speak."*

Violetta rushed to him with a high-pitched cry.

"Not so!" Will rebuked her. "Cleopatra enters in a stately manner and only her face betrays her pain."

Violetta twisted her features. She looked as if she were being tortured. Will sighed and bade her go on with her speech.

"Noblest of men, would you die?—"

Will interrupted her. "You are not asking me to die, you are begging me *not* to. Go on."

"Have you no care of me? Shall I . . ." She faltered.

"Abide in this dull world," Meg supplied, still lying down.

"I was getting there!" snapped Violetta.

Will groaned, then whispered, "The sound signifies that I, Antony, am now dead."

"Right," said Violetta and began to recite, *"O the crown of the earth does melt, and there is nothing left remarkable beneath the visiting moon."*

Will banged his head on the floor.

"What? Antony lives?" said Violetta.

"No, that was me, Will." He sat up. "Violetta, you are a queen who has just seen her lover die a noble death. You should be overcome with awe and grief."

"Does Caesar win the queen now that Antony is dead?" asked Overby.

Will ignored him and continued speaking to Violetta. "Remember with what passion Thisbe loved Pyramus? Cleopatra worships Antony a thousand times more."

Job, who had been observing from a distance, jumped to his feet. "Fie! Here is Satan's dissembling stage! Such lewdness will damn you all," he shouted. No one heeded him.

Violetta's mouth quivered. At last she was summoning the passion Will wanted to see.

"But I do not know if *I* do," she said. "Love Antony, that is."

Will felt like pulling his hair out. "That is not the point! You *feign* passion, as I do. We are players." What had gotten into Violetta? She had been such an eager Thisbe, Will had almost believed her love was real.

"She's no Cleopatra, I'll warrant," said Overby, shaking his head. "The audience will mock her and make me a laughingstock too. And then they'll go to Burbage's new playhouse instead."

Burbage's playhouse? Will pricked up his ears like a fox scenting an elusive prey. "Master Overby, did you say 'Burbage'?"

Overby scowled. "I did. James Burbage. I don't know the fellow, but he owns a public playhouse in Shoreditch."

His words were like twin lambs frolicking before that hungry, lucky fox.

"Burbage owns a playhouse?" Will repeated in amazement. Questions rushed into his mind: *What does it look like? Who are the players? Might James Burbage lead him to William Burbage?* If so, there was yet hope, for Will was confident he could persuade Burbage to settle his father's debt and avoid the judge's sentence.

"Then we shall go there anon and see how a play ought to be performed!" he said, silently thanking Fortune for unexpectedly uniting his duty and his desire.

Chapter 27

The name that so surprised Will also dispelled Meg's uncertain mood. She knew that Burbage was the one to whom the Shakespeares owed money. She welcomed the opportunity to visit the playhouse, for it was a diversion with larger purpose. She had not been so excited since she was a child and her parents took her to St. Bartholomew Fair to see the morris dancers with bells on their feet. She had never been to a proper play. Overby had explained that noblemen went to the queen's palace or Blackfriars, where the actors were boys and the Master of Revels decided what could be performed. But the idea of a playhouse that would admit anyone, rich or poor, was new. Two such places stood in Shoreditch, which was beyond the reach of the London authorities. Petty criminals abounded there and Meg felt it her duty to safeguard her companions, Overby, Violetta, and Will. Job would as soon go to hell as to a playhouse, and he made Dab stay at the inn with him.

Meg knew she would have to watch herself, measure her every movement. As Meg she hardly knew how to behave outside the walls of the Boar's Head. She must not slip into Mack's voice and manner and thereby betray herself to Will. During the rehearsal she had been certain he was playing cat-and-mouse with her. Saying it would be no use to put her in man's clothing because the audience would still recognize her. Giving her a page to read and pretending to be disconcerted that she could not do so. She must give him no cause for suspicion on this outing. She would watch Violetta to learn how a lady should conduct herself.

Meg peered in the glass as she tried to plait her hair and weave in a green ribbon. Her face was flushed with the effort.

"Why, you look uncommonly pretty, Meg," said Gwin. "If I didn't know better I'd swear you are sweet on that madman Shakespeare."

Meg rolled her eyes. "It is Violetta who loves Will," she said. "Therefore tease her."

But she had a doubt about the ribbon. Was it a good idea to encourage Will to look closely at her?

"I dare not, for she will start leaking tears like a cracked pot," murmured Gwin.

For the moment Violetta looked happy enough. She was wearing the blue damask skirt and the fine cloak, long since cleaned, in which she had arrived at the Boar's Head. She had gone nowhere since then for fear of being seen by her father or Thomas Valentine. Why was she now so eager to go to the playhouse? And why in their rehearsal had she spoken Cleopatra's lines like a wooden fencepost? Meg wondered how a man could tolerate any creature so inconstant and inscrutable as Violetta, however beautiful she was.

On the other hand everyone knew what to expect of her,

Long Meg. She was not changeable since she had stopped growing. But did she not spend some days masquerading as a man, changing her clothing and her manner and deceiving everyone about her? The more she persisted in her disguise, the more perilous it became and the more complicated was her life. How long could she keep it up?

And—she dared to ask herself—why must she?

But now was not the time for questions. She tossed a cloak borrowed from Gwin over her shoulders, fastened it with a brass brooch, and declared herself ready to go to the playhouse.

From Whitechapel the foursome passed by St. Botolph's outside Aldgate and the gun foundry. They followed the lane where a row of narrow houses faced the foul-smelling Houndsditch. Eager Will was in the lead; Meg and Violetta hurried after; and Overby lagged behind. Outside Bishopsgate they turned north toward Shoreditch. They passed Bethlehem Hospital, where the poor and those distracted from their wits lived. Houses grew more scattered, and between them Meg glimpsed fields crisscrossed by paths where walkers hastened, their heads bent against the wind.

Will paused to lift Violetta over a large puddle in the road. He took Meg's hand and she jumped across, feeling an energy from his grip the way lightning sometimes caused her skin to tingle. She thought he held her hand a moment longer than necessary.

"I wish your brother were along," said Will.

"Am I such unpleasant company?" Meg realized her reply sounded coy. She was never coy. It must be the hair ribbon and the brooch that made her feel so different.

"I only meant that if I should encounter William Burbage, I need my lawyer to help me deal with him."

"That may be unwise, if you mean 'deal with him' the way my brother dealt with Roger Ruffneck—" Meg caught herself, remembering that Will had not seen her get the best of Roger in the cloisters. She contrived a small lie. "Jane told me that Mack robbed her lying husband and his lawyer and gave her all their money and jewels."

"Zounds, what a hero your brother is! Did he spare me twenty-five crowns of it? That would solve all my troubles."

"For shame, Will Shakespeare," said Meg. "That was all Jane's fortune and none of your deserving." She added, for she wanted to tell of Mack's triumph to someone, "Ask my brother to tell you the story when you see him again."

"Aye, and in turn he shall hear how I almost shot a carter with that loose pistol he lent me! We were lucky to keep our souls in our bodies."

Meg sighed. "Promise me you won't assault Burbage until later, for I do not wish to be run out of the house at the point of a sword before I have even seen the play."

Will laughed. "I promise, dear Mistress Meg, for I long to see the play as much as you do." He took her hand again, though the puddle in the road was behind them.

Dear Mistress Meg? What words to savor! She let her hand rest in Will's. It would be rude to withdraw it. But if Violetta turned around and saw them she might fly into a jealous passion. Had Will purposely fallen behind and taken her hand? What nonsense her brain was capable of. And why must her face betray her by turning scarlet? She withdrew her hand.

"I hope the company is in need of another player," Will

was saying. "I shall be content to perform any part, be it the hero's or the clown's, so long as I am in a *real* company."

"Would you leave the Boar's Head?" Meg could not keep the disappointment from her voice. "And your play of Cleopatra undone?"

"No, I shall finish it and see it performed in a theater so full of people it will seem an entire world." Will spread out his arms as if trying to embrace something vast that only he could see.

Meg had not realized the greatness of Will's ambition. It seemed to expand, filling the openness and heating the air between them like a flame. Meg relished the warmth. She loved the way Will's words made her feel as she held them in her mind. She did not want him to leave the Boar's Head.

The playhouse was easy to find. A colorful flag fluttered from a staff atop the thatched roof. The three-story timbered building, not quite square but not quite round either, was situated where the road and the paths through the fields converged. A painted signboard proclaimed it to be simply THE THEATRE.

"Keep your purses close," warned Meg as she spotted a pickpocket. She intercepted his fleeting gaze, scowled, and squared her shoulders. He moved away. Meg reminded herself that she was not Mack, once a thief and lately Will's rowdy companion, nor was she Long Meg, keeper of order at the Boar's Head. She was just Meg going to a playhouse with her friends, and she must behave as such. She was not sure how to be simply herself.

With the others she paid her penny and entered the playhouse. The interior was a large yard strewn with sawdust and open to the sky. A thatched roof covered the galleries and the stage, which was built at the level of a man's chest, enclosed beneath, and curtained at the back. It was a far cry from the stage at the Boar's Head that had been put up and taken down so many times it wobbled dangerously. A trio of musicians played the pipe, tabor, and drum. The firstcomers had already taken their places before the stage, planting their elbows on it as a mark of possession and beating time to the music.

The playgoers were as diverse a collection of humanity as Meg had ever seen in one place, including St. Paul's. There were housewives and gentlemen, shopkeepers, servants, apprentices, schoolboys, trulls and thieves, sturdy yeomen, merchants and men of fashion, and nobles in velvet and fur who made their way through the baser sort to the galleries above.

"Look, Meg," said Will. "There is one of those foppish men I heard the preacher condemn. He called them 'more fit for the playhouse than God's house.' "

Meg followed his gaze to see a slender gallant with big-buckled boots. Lace cascaded from his doublet like a bush of full-blown roses, and a plume stirred in his cap like ripe grain in a field.

"He aims to outdo his mother, Dame Nature," Meg said with a wry laugh.

"He?" said Will. "I think this hybrid creature is a woman who wishes herself a man. Are the features not soft and the shoulders slim?"

Meg was alarmed. Had Will ever stared at Mack with such suspicions?

"Does the chest show signs of a woman's twin wonders?" Will continued. "Which we men long to have, and that is why we constantly stare at women's bosoms."

More amused than offended, Meg laughed. But she was eager to end this dangerous conversation. "It is certainly a young man, for the shadow over his lip is proof of a mustache," she said, though she knew a smudge of ash could produce the same effect. She also wondered if this person was a woman, why she would dress to *attract* notice.

"Whether a man or woman, it is as eager to see a play as we are," said Will. "Come, here is a good place to stand."

The house was now almost full. Hawkers pressed their way through the crowd selling roasted nuts, fruits, and pomanders. These fragrances mingled with the earthier smells of sweat, wool, and dung trailed in from the streets. Meg was grateful to be so tall, for she could see over the heads of the other playgoers. Tiny Violetta, however, was at a disadvantage.

"I can't see anyone!" she wailed. "Even standing on my toes." She seemed almost desperate. "Please, Master Overby, may we sit in the gallery?"

To Meg's surprise Overby dug in his purse again and paid a burly fellow for access to the gallery stairs. Moments later Meg found herself seated between Violetta and Will, overlooking the yard.

"I hope that was not Burbage," said Will. "He did not look forgiving."

Meg for her part was wondering about Violetta's strange behavior. She did not attempt to change seats with Meg so she could sit beside Will. And instead of being pleased with her clear view of the stage, she commenced leaning forward and backward, craning her neck to see into the opposite galleries, even bending over the railing to peer among the groundlings.

"Do you have a burr in your bodice?" whispered Meg. "Something surely is pricking you."

Violetta subsided onto the bench, but Meg could see her eyes still darting about as if she was looking for someone. Whom could she possibly know in all of London?

Will had bought an orange and as he peeled it, the scent reminded Meg of the night she had gone to the Boar's Head with Davy and Peter and a woman had offered her a bite of an orange. The same longing stirred in her again: the desire for a home, for sweetness on her tongue and laughter in her ears. She felt a nudge. Will held out a piece of the fruit. Meg could only stare at it and wonder how Will had known what she was dreaming of.

"Wake up. Take it," he said, lifting her hand from her lap and placing the pungent fruit on her palm.

She brought the orange to her lips and bit it. Nothing had ever tasted so good. She licked her fingers and murmured with pleasure.

A fanfare sounded. Sweetness *and* joyful noise! A man came onstage and shouted what Meg guessed was the prologue. The audience quieted and the play began. It was about a goodwife named Gammer Gurton who lost her one and only needle while mending a pair of breeches for her servant Hodge. She drew the entire village into the trouble of finding it, and such slapping, tumbling, and rudeness ensued that the audience hooted with laughter.

"I cannot hear. What did he say?" Meg whispered to Will.

Will waved his hand. "No matter. The words are slight. The actions are what gives delight. I will have clowns in all my plays."

But Meg could not laugh at the foolishness. It left her strangely saddened.

Will turned to her. "Don't you like Diccon the beggar?" he asked. "He is the cause of all the trouble, yet even he grins."

Meg stared at the ragged player. "My father became a beggar," she said softly. "And that was the beginning of all our troubles." The words came to her lips and she made no attempt to hold them back. She didn't care if Will heard them.

In the next scene a drunken parson was mistaken for a thief and beaten bloody with a stick. The audience roared its approval and Will whistled through his fingers. Meg could not even smile.

"Come now," Will said. "This is no tragedy."

"Oh, but it is!" said Meg, blinking back tears. "Such a priest abused my mother. He was killed, as he deserved to be." She could not admit that her mother was the killer. "And my father did not thrive by wickedness, like Diccon, but died despite his goodness."

She closed her eyes. Sounds came to her as if from a great distance: Gammer Gurton's high, false voice, the stamping of feet in the galleries, Violetta giggling beside her. What had caused her to reveal her secret sorrow now—in the middle of a play—to Will Shakespeare of all people? Next would she throw off every stitch of clothing and confess to Will that she was her brother, Mack?

No. She would pretend she had said nothing. She opened her eyes again. "I like your plays much better, Will."

He ignored the compliment. "Could you but laugh, would it heal the hurt?"

So he had heard every word! She felt herself redden, knowing his eyes were on her.

"I don't think so."

"I bid you try it," he said.

He looked so earnest and yet so lively, his face divided in halves, that Meg could not help smiling. It was not hard.

The servant was now running about the stage making farting sounds. Meg did not suppress a giggle.

"Eww!" said Violetta, grimacing.

"It's nothing but air!" Will said. "He has a bladder in his sleeve."

Finally the lost needle was found in the very breeches Gammer Gurton had been sewing. When the constable slapped Hodge on his rump, driving the needle into his buttocks, and Hodge shot upward, cursing inventively, Meg truly laughed. She drew in her breath and released it into the air, where it dispersed like her secret, a brief story no more terrible than Gammer Gurton's lost needle.

She felt herself glowing with inner warmth. This was happiness. To be free of sorrow and secrets. To sit in a theater beside her friend Will Shakespeare, laughing together.

Chapter 28

When the play ended Overby stood up and let out a loud, long fart. "Henceforth call me Hodge," he said. Laughing, Will stumbled down the gallery stairs.

Violetta was not so amused or appreciative. "How will this teach me to play Cleopatra? There were no lovers and no one died."

Will remembered the reason he had brought them and sighed. Indeed, what could such a light play, so lacking in poetry, teach them?

"It was almost a tragedy," said Meg. "For the silly needle occasioned as much woe as a lost kingdom."

"Almost a tragedy, yes," said Will, gratefully seizing on her words. "A comedy is a tragedy averted by unexpected good fortune. That is our lesson."

It was more complicated than that, Will knew. While watching Meg he had been surprised at how the simple matter of the play moved her. Was it possible that comedy as well as tragedy could touch the heart? That it could have a purpose beyond inducing laughter? Perhaps despite its exaggeration, a comic tale could hit the truth like a hammer on the head of a nail. For this slight comedy had uncovered a part of Meg's soul, the sight of which affected Will also. A tender feeling mingled with his merriment, confusing him.

Overby was poking Will in the chest. "You must put a mad beggar and a farting clown in your Cleopatra play. Too much dying makes me melancholy."

Will could barely hide his annoyance. "I will, and you shall play them both," he said, though he had no intention of adding such ridiculous characters to his play. If he were around to finish it.

Mirth departed and dread settled over him. "I have some business and will return to the inn anon," he said. "Come with me, Meg."

Meg stepped to his side and Will felt a surge of confidence. There was no one—not even Mack—he would rather have with him for this meeting. Was it because she really was striking to behold?

"Sirrah!" he called to the burly fellow heading toward the stage. "Will you take me to Mr. Burbage?"

He nodded and Will and Meg followed him through a small door behind the stage. There the players were putting costumes and props into trunks. The boy who played Gammer Gurton doffed a nethergarment stuffed with bombast that gave him a woman's shape. Will wanted to linger and talk to him. More than that, he wanted to pull aside the curtain and stand on the stage and imagine what it would be like to perform there.

"Do you have business with me?" The peremptory voice startled Will. A man with a graying beard stood with one foot on a bench, leaning on his knee. "I am James Burbage. I built this theater and manage this company."

How like a god he looks! Creator of his own world, thought Will.

"I commend the skill of your players and their pleasing performance," he said, aware of sounding like a flatterer. "I am William Shakespeare, formerly of Stratford, now staging my own plays at the Boar's Head Inn." This was an exaggeration, for Will knew that once he refused to put a madman and a clown in his new play he would be out of a job. "It is my ambition to be in a company such as yours."

"You are the third fellow this week to ask me for work. The first one is sweeping garbage from the galleries and the other two I sent away." Burbage brushed something from his knee.

"Tell him your true purpose before he is out of patience," Meg whispered.

Will said that he was looking for William Burbage. He fully expected to be directed elsewhere when James replied, "He is my brother and a shareholder in this enterprise. William!"

Will fought the urge to run. Meg's hand on his arm restrained him.

A bald-pated man reeking of wine sauntered into the room. Will saw with relief that he was an ordinary sot, not the bugbear he had feared. Now was the moment to reason with him, to appeal for mercy and thereby avoid the dreaded sentencing. And yet he was loath to discuss his father's debt before James Burbage, the one man in London he wished to impress.

As soon as Will identified himself, William Burbage began to abuse the name of Shakespeare, calling Will's father a crooked cheater and a villainous varlet.

Will grew hot. His neck and forehead throbbed.

"He is as dangerous as a rabid dog," Meg murmured, stiffening.

"Hold your peace, for this is not the Boar's Head," Will whispered back.

"My father, like all men, has his faults," said Will, striving to be conciliatory. He explained that his father had dispatched him with enough money to settle half the debt, but it had been stolen from him and he was unable to recover it. "Will you accept payment as I earn it?"

"I'll have the entire ten pounds now," William Burbage barked.

"I am all but penniless," Will said in a low voice.

"Then I'll see you at Westminster and to prison after."

Will summoned all his courage and said with a bravado he scarcely felt, "My lawyer has grounds on which to challenge the debt. He shall present a witness and ask the judge to void the prior judgment. You shall get nothing." Will was pleased with this hasty invention but it only enraged William Burbage.

"I'll smoke your skin, Will Shakespeare. Roast your ribs for every farthing your miserable father owes me," he said, advancing toward Will.

James Burbage stepped in front of his brother and said, "Go home; you're soused."

"Let's away, Mistress Meg," said Will. "All is lost. 'Tis time for me to fall on my sword like a good Roman."

"Wait! Will you savor humiliation or turn it to victory?" said Meg, seizing his sleeve. She turned to James Burbage and intoned, *"O the crown of the earth does melt, and there is nothing left remarkable beneath the visiting moon."*

Will stared at her in stark surprise. Meg drew a deep breath and went on.

> "Good sirs, take heart,
> We'll bury Antonio, and then what's brave,
>   what's noble,
> Let's do it after the high Roman fashion,
> And make death proud to take us. Come away,
> This case of his huge spirit now is cold."

One of the players began to applaud. Will swelled with pride.

"What is that speech?" said James Burbage, looking at Meg in amazement.

Meg nodded toward Will.

"Queen Cleopatra beholding the deceased Mark Antony," said Will. It was no surprise to him that Meg had committed Cleopatra's entire speech to memory. But what moved her to speak it now?

Meg nodded toward the player. "You should hear Will Shakespeare as the Roman general. His dying would move a stone to weep."

"Is that Kyd's work?" asked James Burbage. "The tragedian Thomas Kyd," he explained, seeing Will's blank expression.

Will drew himself up to his full height. "No, it is mine. You would honor me by attending its performance at the Boar's Head in Whitechapel."

"Now hear Cleopatra as Antony is borne away," said Meg, and her clear voice rang out again. *"Come, we have no friend but resolution and the briefest end."*

Meg beckoned to Will and with long strides swept across the backstage. She was a galleon sailing through the waves! Will bowed, exulting in Burbage's astonished expression. He turned to follow Meg, a proud Mark Antony trailing after his brave and beautiful queen of Egypt.

Chapter 29

Meg soaked up Will's praise like a flower garden soaks up rain.

"Oh, that was brave! Well spoken in the spirit of Cleopatra herself. What made you do it?"

They were walking back toward London, warmed by the bright October sun and a sense of triumph.

"When you spoke of dying on your sword, Cleopatra's speech naturally came to mind. I've heard Violetta practice it a hundred times." She rolled her eyes, because Violetta still did not have it memorized. "I thought if Burbage knew of your genius he might help in the matter of the debt."

But Will did not want to talk about the debt.

"He was impressed. He compared me to Thomas Kyd, who must be a great playwright."

"Do you think he will come to the Boar's Head?" asked Meg.

"We must be prepared for it. The performance must shine." Will paused and scratched his head. "What am I going to do about Violetta? She was a passionate Thisbe, but her fire is all turned to ice as Cleopatra."

Meg shrugged. "I think she is cold because you spurn all her advances. She believes you do not love her."

"She is right," Will said. "Though she is pretty, her wit is too slight for my liking."

"It is good news for me that there are men who prefer cleverness to beauty," Meg said lightly. She fingered the ribbon in her hair. It was making her downright flirtatious. She must be more serious. Will's situation was dire.

"Can you at least pretend to like her? Pick up the honeyed looks she sends you and return them." She was not in favor of more deceit, but she wanted Will's play to succeed.

Will marched his fingers up her arm and said playfully, "This fruit is nearer. I would rather pluck it."

His touch pleasantly tickled her. But she swiped his hand away. "Off, you bug. What do you mean, going after my fruit?"

Will put up his hands. "Don't be angry, sweet. I mean *you* must be my Cleopatra."

"Me?" Meg trilled. She was too stunned to say more. *He calls me sweet!*

"Did you see how moved James Burbage was by your speech?"

"I think he was merely astonished to see a woman declaiming in verse." Why not play Cleopatra? She knew all the lines. She loved the words. If Violetta could play Thisbe, why couldn't Meg play a queen?

"How can I feign love for Mark Antony?" she said, thinking aloud.

"I wish you did not need to feign it." Will sounded hurt.

Meg glanced at him. Was he serious? His eyes twinkled as he smiled. It was time to end this uncertain conversation.

"You're flattering yourself, which is only worse than flattering me," she said. "Now forget Cleopatra and James Burbage. It is William Burbage who must concern you. How many days until you meet him in court?" Meg knew the answer but she wanted Will to acknowledge how short the time was.

Will sighed and pressed his forehead. "Three days."

"Three days," Meg repeated. "If you are not worried, I'm sure my brother is. Does he know about this new witness? Have you prepared him, or must he extemporize before the judge like a player without any lines?"

"If his wits are as quick as yours, he will learn his part on the way to Westminster," said Will. His eyes widened. "Though perhaps *you* would be a better advocate."

"What judge would listen to a woman?" said Meg, striving to keep an even tone. "Nay, your best chance is to trust my brother."

"A woman cannot be a lawyer," agreed Will. "So disguise yourself as a man. You could easily do so!" He sounded gleeful.

Meg's head began to spin. Did Will already know about her disguise? She struggled to remain calm.

"I would not risk it for love or money," she said firmly. She pulled ahead of Will with a few long strides. Now he could not see her face and divine her worried thoughts. *If I can memorize Cleopatra's speech, surely I can learn a few Latin phrases. If I can move Burbage to amazement, why shouldn't I be able to move a judge to mercy?*

Meg arrived at the Boar's Head just steps ahead of Will to find a tempest breaking within.

"You went to that mad, wicked playhouse, leaving me undefended. When he came in Bandog crawled under the table and didn't even bark. I could have been killed!" Gwin's voice was tremulous, her mouth a wide *O* framing her teeth. Her hands tore at the edges of her apron.

"Your wits are all a-jangle, woman. I see nothing out of order here," Overby said.

"There he is, the cause of it all!" said Gwin, pointing to Will. She rushed over and gripped Meg's arms. "O Meg, I had such need of you! He was the most vile-looking fellow, with a broken face and a great pistol in his belt."

"Did he hurt you?" asked Meg. "I will find him and triple the injury."

"What did he want?" said Overby. "Did you know him?"

"No, I never saw him before. He said, 'Give up Mack that lives here.' I would have given him anyone he asked for, but I don't know any Mack." She trembled at the recollection. "I had to swear it by the body of my poor dead mother."

Cold fingers crept down Meg's back. Who was seeking Mack at the Boar's Head, unless they knew of her disguise? Meg remembered Roger Ruffneck's threat. *I know who you are, Mack. You can't hide from us.*

"He came to the wrong inn. He won't be back," said Overby, trying to sound tough.

Meg was not so sure. She asked Jane Ruffneck, who was helping Violetta serve customers, if she had seen the man. Jane nodded but said he was no one she recognized. So Gwin's unwelcome visitor was not Roger or Peter or Davy. Besides them, whom had Meg offended? Or rather, Mack? She could think of no one who could be so determined to find her. Yet, being prudent, she decided to take measures to protect herself.

"This has gone too far, Meg," said Violetta, watching Meg

strap a small dagger to her lower leg, where she could reach it at any time. They were preparing for bed. "What has Mack done that someone seeks to harm you? Does it have to do with Jane and her son being here?"

"I do not know," said Meg honestly. "And we need not worry. He is looking for a man, not for Long Meg."

"But that puts you in danger every time you go out as Mack!" Violetta was now truly distressed. "You must forgo wooing Will on my behalf. That foolish disguise has no effect anyway."

Meg winced, for Violetta had struck the nerve of her own doubts. What *was* the point of her disguise? As Mack she had done nothing to help Will catch Davy and Peter. As Meg, however, she had helped bring his verses to James Burbage's attention. Why persist in being Mack if she could aid and befriend Will as Meg? Did she dare admit that her disguise, which at first had granted her freedom, was now a burden? Yet to reveal her deceit would put Meg in the same company as the two sisters who had betrayed Will. To what a difficult pass had matters come when to be honest would destroy her friendship with Will! Rather, two friendships: Meg's and Mack's.

"Then woo Will Shakespeare yourself!" Meg snapped. "Forget what is proper for a lady and what is not."

With tear-filled eyes Violetta implored her. "Oh friend, dear Meg, could I but unfold the contents of my heart to you—"

"You do. I wish you would stop," said Meg.

But Violetta went on. "Can true feeling be rekindled in this undeserving servant? Can something lost be restored by wishing?"

"What do you mean?" A brief, sad thought of her mother passed through Meg's mind.

"I don't know." Violetta shook her head and the tears spilled over. "I'm asking you."

"Honestly, Violetta, how should Will or any man understand our sex? For I am a woman like you, yet you present an unfathomable mystery to me."

Through her sobs Violetta managed to say, "No, they understand us better than you think."

Chapter 30

In the churchyard of St. Botolph, one gravestone stood for the judge and another for the plaintiff as Will instructed Mack in the proceedings of a courtroom. All Will's knowledge was gleaned from the lawyer's manual he had taken from Thomas Greene.

"Look at the writs in your hand before you speak. Gesture thus as you deny the basis of the judgment," he advised.

Mack easily grasped the arguments Will had written, but he struggled when it came to learning the Latin phrases meant to buttress them.

Will repeated them again and again. "*Non est factum.* It is not his deed. *Debita sequuntur personam debitoria.* Debts follow the person of the debtor."

Mack threw up his hands. "Take your nonfacts, your debits and debitors, your sequent persons, and hang them all on Tower Hill!"

Will burst out laughing. "I must remember that line for a play. You shall join my players and perform it."

"You forget I am barred from the Boar's Head," said Mack.

"I can persuade Overby to overlook your old slight to his wife. He is ambitious to compete with the new playhouses. Say you will consider it."

Mack's reply came slowly. "Once the case is settled and everything else is sorted out, perhaps."

It was not a refusal. Encouraged, Will said, "You are even fair enough for the woman's part. Speak with a trill for me."

"No!" Mack smacked the writs against the stones. "I'll take my leave of you right now if you do not heed this grave matter."

"O excellent pun!" Will suppressed a laugh, for he was afraid of Mack's threat.

The fifteenth of October dawned with auspicious sunshine, but Will arose with a cloud of foreboding over his head. It followed him darkly as he dressed and ate a breakfast of cold mutton. He still had not found in the handbook any cause for a counterclaim. He must depend on the judge's mercy, which in turn depended upon Mack's powers of persuasion. Then again, he reflected, probably Burbage could afford to purchase whatever outcome he desired.

Will's dire meditations were interrupted by the sight of his friend waiting for him at the Cornhill, where they had first met only weeks before.

"Good day, Matthew Mandamus!" Will hailed Mack by the name they had agreed upon and gave him a black robe dearly purchased for the occasion.

"Don't lose this; it will make a handy costume someday. Your present cap will do. I have all the documents." Will patted his pocket for the dozenth time.

On Mack's advice they hired a wherry for quicker passage

to Westminster, which was a mile west of London. The thick-armed boatman rowed against the river's current with ease, pointing out landmarks that included Bridewell Prison.

"You don't want to end up there. The prisoners walk on treadmills to grind flour for bread. 'Tis said the kitchens are a very inferno," he said darkly.

Will shuddered. He watched the city slip by: warehouses, walled gardens, myriad rooftops, and with them his dreams of being a renowned actor.

The pier at Westminster was so crowded they had to wait in a line to disembark. The buildings with their battlements and high gates projected wealth and importance. The people on the streets moved with greater haste and purpose than their counterparts in London. Who among them, Will wondered, would care about the case of a poor Stratford glover or the fate of his son? What stood between him and prison but his new friend Mack, now whispering Latin phrases and glancing about uneasily?

They located Westminster Hall by the lawyers and clerks entering and exiting, distinguished from one another only by the cut of their black robes and the hats that sat on their heads like overturned porringers.

The hall was more spacious inside than any building Will had ever seen. Trees could have grown there and spread their branches unimpeded. Birds flew around and settled on the high rafters. Their calls and shrieks mingled with the clamor of voices and the clatter of footsteps. Will heard the strains of hautboys and recorders and the beat of a drum.

"What are musicians doing in the hall of justice?" he said.

Mack shook his head slowly, as full of awe as Will himself.

They quickly determined there were three courts in session, and for every fearful defendant and belligerent plaintiff, a dozen or more officials. Will had studied their duties in his handbook but could by no means discern a clerk from a cursitor or a filazer from a prothonotary.

Mack, so confident in the streets, was timid in this new place. "You are better spoken than I am, Will. Why not argue your own case?"

Will held Mack's sleeve. "Be steadfast for me. The judge must respect the defendant who can afford a lawyer."

Will forged a path through the throng of noblemen, merchants, shopkeepers, farmers, and foreigners. He could identify the French by their nasal tones and fashionable dress, the Dutch by their thick speech and dirty boots.

"The whole world is at Westminster!" he mused aloud.

Finally he located the Queen's Bench, where his case was to be heard. His fingers fumbled through the handbook. "Remember, Mack, *quid pro quo.* This for that," he murmured. "The settlement I offered Burbage. A fair judge will accept it."

"He must," said Mack. "How do you say in Latin, 'One cannot squeeze blood from a stone'?"

"I don't know, but say it in English and he will see the point."

The court's business moved quickly. Some cases took only minutes. The judge's eyebrows formed a long black caterpillar as he interrupted the lawyers and questioned the witnesses himself. The jurymen shrugged as they pronounced their verdicts; some even slept. Will trembled to think of his fate resting in their careless hands.

"This judge behaves like a king," said Mack. "He tells the jury how to rule and they obey him."

"Everyone has been found guilty. I shall find no mercy here," Will said, dismayed.

"*Burbage versus Shakespeare!*" cried out a clerk with a red badge on his robe.

"Remember to speak in a low and manly voice," Will reminded Mack. "Otherwise you betray your youth."

Will stepped up to the bench with Mack at his elbow. He saw Burbage across from them with his arms folded, sneering. The judge snatched a document from the clerk.

"Are you the defendant, John Shakespeare?"

"No, I appear in my father's stead," Will replied. "I am—"

"Another damnable debtor!" said the judge. "Have you the money upon you?"

Will motioned to Mack. "Speak!" he hissed.

"No, Your Majesty—I mean, Your Honor," began Mack. "My client proposes a *quod pro qua*—I mean, a *prid quid quo*—something for something!"

Will grimaced. He saw the sweat beading Mack's brow.

"What my lawyer means—" he began.

"Does not matter!" roared the judge. "*Lex remedium dabit.* The law gives a remedy. Shakespeare, I sentence you to Bridewell. Learn to work like an honest man."

Bridewell? Will saw himself tied to a harness like an ox and straining against a heavy millstone.

"Your Honor! Hear me," cried Mack.

Will's heart sank. He had made a terrible mistake in trying to teach Mack too quickly! He should have devoted all his time to this Burbage matter, not to writing verses.

"You may not punish my client, William Shakespeare, in lieu of his father, John Shakespeare, for *debita sequuntur perso-*

nam debitoria; debts follow the debtor," said Mack with perfect clarity. "Not the debtor's kin."

"Well spoken, Mack!" Will cried, hope rising in him.

The judge, however, was deaf to all pleas. He thrust a document at his clerk, who passed it to a marshal, who seized Will roughly. Too stunned to protest, Will let himself be led away.

"Here is no justice!" Mack was shouting now. "This is cruel rigor. *Per vinculum ad venitum et rigor mortis.*"

Will knew the phrase was nonsense invented on the spot by Mack. His friend's voice rose in pitch. He pounded the bar. Will feared he would soon commit mayhem. God forbid they should both be arrested! Who would help them then?

"I came to the Queen's Bench for mercy. For equity!" Will cried over his shoulder. "Will no one hear me? I am not John Shakespeare!" He struggled against the marshal, who only tightened his grip and pushed him onward. Through the sea of startled faces eager for new sensation and relishing this tragedy.

To Bridewell.

Will ducked his head. A tide of shame surged in him and he saw his every hope and ambition washed away.

~⊙ Chapter 31 ⊙~

Meg heard her own voice rise, catch, and betray her. Will must not go to prison! He could die there like her father. She turned back to the bench but the judge was already hearing a new case. That quickly, Will was forgotten as if he had never been there.

Meg saw the smug and smiling William Burbage leaving the court. Had he bribed the judge? If he could afford that, he did not need Shakespeare's money! She fell into step behind him. In her lawyer's robe she resembled a thousand other men who scurried like ants in their service of their hidden queen, Justice. It would be an easy matter to rob a fat-gut like William Burbage. Then as Meg she would go to him and pay Will's debt—with Burbage's own money! The justice of it pleased her.

The debt paid, Will must be released from prison.

As she tried to discern where Burbage wore his purse, she saw his brother approaching. She slipped behind a pillar and strained to hear their conversation.

"Is the case concluded already?" James Burbage asked.

"Aye," said William. "The law does not wait on you or any man."

"Where is the young man? Did the judge agreed to our terms?"

Our terms? Meg frowned. Was James also a party to this injustice?

"I did it on my terms, not yours," said William harshly. "Shakespeare is off to Bridewell."

"Damn your greed!" said James. "You know he does not deserve prison."

"Brother, you would forgive the devil himself for cheating you." William's laugh was scornful. "Come now; we have a meeting with Lord Leicester."

Meg knew who was the head of the brothers' enterprise and who was its heart. Quickly she contrived a new plan to aid Will. Coming forth, she greeted James Burbage.

"I am Matthew Mandamus and I would speak with you, sir." Her manner was polite but determined.

"Mandamus? We command?" said James, amused. Evidently he knew Latin.

"He is Shakespeare's attorney," William muttered. "I've finished with him."

"The judge is deaf in both ears; I pray you are not," said Meg.

"Go on," said James, peering at her.

"My client esteems you greatly. He did earnestly desire to be employed by you."

"I would not hire a son of John Shakespeare to clean my boots," said William.

"One day you will gladly pay for the privilege of licking *his* boots," Meg shot back in a very unlawyerlike way.

James stepped in front of his brother and drew Meg apart. "Speak your purpose and be quick. I have other business."

"Sir, your business ought to be with this actor destined to blaze across London like a comet through the sky. O the stage of an inn is too narrow for his greatness! Do you know he is a poet too? His pen is sharper than a sword and his words sink deep into every listener's heart."

Meg hardly knew where her words came from, but the feeling behind them was true. She went on. "Would you let this most excellent poet languish in prison when he could grace your stage? If you give Will Shakespeare a place in your company, you shall earn a hundred times the paltry sum his father owes." She was trembling at having said so much.

James Burbage stroked his beard and regarded Meg. "I swear, but for your garb you resemble the young woman who came with Will Shakespeare to my theater."

Meg reached up and touched her cap nervously.

"Pay him no heed," said William in a surly tone. "Lawyers, like actors, are skilled liars."

James shook his head slowly. "I doubt this is a lawyer, William."

Meg gulped. Despite the two layers of disguise she felt suddenly naked.

"What do you mean?" said William. "He is Mandamus, a green lawyer barely out of his boyhood."

"Nay, I have transformed many a fellow into the fashion of a woman. I know all the tricks. This is the most excellent disguise I have yet beheld," said James in a low voice. He smiled at Meg like a conspirator.

Meg's heart was pounding. "I do not understand you,"

she said, though she understood perfectly well that Burbage recognized her.

"Mandamus," said James, "I insist you join my players." He leaned closer and whispered in Meg's ear, "No one but you and I will know your secret, I promise."

This was not the outcome Meg was aiming for. She was pleading on *Will's* behalf. It took her a moment to fashion a reply.

"I will. If you free Will Shakespeare and hire him today."

In the silence that followed, Meg feared she had over-played her part.

"Come, Lord Leicester awaits us," said William impatiently.

"Then go to him; say I will come anon." James waved his brother away.

"Stay, William!" ordered Meg. "Write here that the debt is paid and sign your name." She offered the reverse side of the summons.

"I will not!" he said.

"Do it!" said James. "Leicester will not be pleased to lose two promising players over a small legal matter."

A scowling William signed the paper and threw it at Meg.

"Come, Mistress Mandamus," said James, taking Meg's arm. "Let us redeem the prisoner and restore his freedom."

Only with difficulty could Meg restrain herself from leaping for joy.

After obtaining the services of a moneylender and emptying his own purse, James Burbage had in hand the funds neces-sary for Will's release.

"This would make a most excellent device," said Burbage as they hastened to Bridewell prison. "The hero, a rural fellow, is wrongly arrested and imprisoned, whereupon his beloved, disguised as a lawyer, argues his innocence and frees him. In the end they are married." He rubbed his hands together in delight. "Your Will shall pen this and you and he play the principal parts."

Meg blushed. "You misunderstand our friendship."

Burbage gave her a sharp, knowing look. "I do not."

Is this man a soothsayer? Meg wondered how he could know what she had not admitted even to herself.

They reached the prison to find Will not yet chained to the terrible millstone. He was relieved to see Meg, surprised to see Burbage, and stunned by the news that he and Mack were now members of Burbage's company. James took his leave of them to attend on Leicester while Will and Meg—still wearing her lawyer's robe—repaired to a nearby alehouse to celebrate.

"You must call yourself Matthew Mandamus," Will said, raising his cup. "'Tis a fine name for a player. You will command the stage."

Meg smiled, trying to hide her misgivings. How could she keep her disguise from Will and the other players when Burbage knew she was a woman? And why, O why keep up the pretense of being Mack now that Will's debt was settled? How sorely she wanted to tear off her cap, shake out her hair, and speak in her own voice!

"Why did Burbage hire me? What if I disappoint him?" she mused.

"Pishery-pashery!" Will dismissed her concerns with a

wave of his hand. "Today you proved your skill in feigning. Not a soul suspected you were no lawyer."

But Burbage had known, so why not Will?

"Just think, Mack. You and I shall work together every day!"

"Too much closeness may rub and fray our friendship," said Meg. It was a mild way to sum up her fears.

Will shook his head. "Rather, by such closeness we shall grow one conjoined heart, like twins." He tilted his head and winked at her.

What does he mean by that? "You are in love with your own cleverness, Will. And I am in love with my mattress, for it has been a long and wearisome day."

She rose to leave and Will followed her into the street. The brisk air sent Meg's thoughts skittering like leaves. If she worked for Burbage, would she have to leave the Boar's Head, leave Gwin and Violetta? And for what? A double life even more confusing than her present one. With Will, she would be Mack feigning to be Matthew Mandamus. With Burbage, she would be Meg feigning to be Matthew feigning to be whatever character he made her play.

"I'm going off to piss," said Will, a little drunk.

Meg continued on her way, ruminating. If Will decided to visit Meg at the Boar's Head, she would have to run ahead of him and become Long Meg again. Had she purchased Will's freedom at the price of her own sanity?

"Stop there, scoundrel," someone said. She paid no heed, for she was just a confused young woman on her way home.

But when she heard "I know you, Mack," she paused. Her heart pounded with alarm. Slowly she turned to find herself facing a man with a scarred hollow at his temple, a very ugsome fellow.

"I don't know you," she said. "Leave me alone."

The street was crowded with people. Will was somewhere nearby. No one would assault her in the presence of so many witnesses. Still her hand touched her leg where the dagger was hidden.

The man opened his greasy jerkin to reveal a pistol in his belt. He waved a document at Meg and said in a tone of smug triumph, "Under this warrant and in the name of the Queen's Majesty, I arrest you, Mack, alias Long Meg de Galle, for the assault upon one Roger Ruffneck."

~⌐ Chapter 32 ⌐~

Thomas Valentine had traversed the length and breadth of London searching for the lady he longed to marry. His hopes never faltered, for he was of a sanguine nature. Sir Percival, to the contrary, had an excess of black bile that made him choleric. Every day Thomas was forced to listen to the same complaint: "O a serpent's tooth is not so sharp as a daughter's ingratitude!"

At first Thomas believed Olivia had run away to escape her father, who kept her like a bird in a cage. But if Olivia wanted to fly away, why did she not fly to him, her betrothed? Every day after finishing his studies, he would bring her a posy of sweet flowers and describe to her the wonders of the heart, the liver, and the blood. She would close her eyes and bury her nose in the bouquet.

One day he considered that perhaps Olivia had fled from *him*. The thought caused a pang like a surgeon's knife nicking his heart. He understood the body's humors and the causes of fever better than he understood how Olivia could disdain his love. He held her always in his mind's eye. She was his star by night—but which one among the distant, shimmering multitude? By day she was the invisible moon. Where among the earthly multitude of this mazelike city had she concealed herself?

Thomas wandered that mid-October day as dusk drew on. The ailing Sir Percival lay in his bed at the Red Lion Inn with a mustard poultice on his chest. The doctor stroked his beard, a new feature of his appearance. He reasoned that since Olivia was fleeing him, he might have better luck catching her if she did not recognize him. Finding himself near Aldgate, he remembered the day he had arrived in London and bandaged the head of a young man. Will was his name and he had been writing a play. Was not the fellow lodging at a nearby inn? He had not yet inquired there for Olivia, an oversight he decided to remedy.

Just at the city gate he was knocked to his knees by someone in a great hurry.

"Pardon me," the fellow said and paused to help him up. "Are you the doctor? By your beard I hardly know you. Have you found your love yet?"

"How can this be? I was just thinking of you," Thomas said. "If I could conjure my beloved with my thoughts, there would be a thousand Olivias before me, but there is not one."

Will Shakespeare—for that was his name, as Thomas recalled—said, "What does she look like? Maybe I have seen her."

Thomas frowned to aid his thinking. "Her eyes are evenly spaced, her flesh as white as bone, and her hair falls about her shoulders. In brief, she is the most proper size and proportion for a woman such as herself."

"She beggars all description," said Will with great

seriousness. "If I see her I will say that you seek her." He touched his cap in farewell.

Thomas did not want to be alone. Nor did he want to return to the sickroom of Sir Percival. "Shall we sup together at your lodging?"

Will groaned and pressed his hand to his forehead. "I cannot eat or sleep tonight—"

"Your head! Does it still hurt you?"

"No, but I must be up all night with my law book, good doctor. For the ruffian who beat me up now sues my dearest friend for beating *him* up. I have just got out of prison, but my friend is locked up and I must contrive a way to free him by morning."

Thomas drew back, wary of being mixed up with people who were always being assaulted, sued, and jailed. Perhaps Sir Percival was right that Will was bad company.

"I shall take no more of your time tonight, Will Shakespeare. Good luck against your foe. He did seem a ruthless one."

"Wait!" Will laid a hand on his arm. "You saw my assailant that night, did you not?"

Thomas could not deny it, for he was an honest man. And before he knew it he had been persuaded to appear as a witness against Roger Ruffneck, who, by the deeds Will described, was undoubtedly a villain. He had no choice now but to trust Will, for without bleeding him and analyzing his humors he had no way to judge his nature.

"When this mistaken affair is ended, Thomas, I shall be forever your debtor."

"I want no money, only my Olivia," said Thomas with a sigh. "I will meet you tomorrow at the guildhall."

Thomas went back to the inn and tended Sir Percival's rheumy chest. He did not tell him about his appointment the next day, knowing the old man would try to dissuade him from it. As the night wore on, doubt and hope battled within him. He was a man of reason who did not easily comprehend strong feeling, much less succumb to it. But he almost believed his meeting with Will Shakespeare was preordained and that an event of great moment would soon occur to change his destiny.

He heard Sir Percival grinding his teeth and murmuring in his sleep, "Olivia, Olivia, ungrateful daughter!"

Thomas could not rest. He rose from his bed and leaned on the windowsill, gazing up at the winking stars.

Chapter 33

"Will! Help me," Meg cried as the bailiff swiftly bound her wrists with a leather thong. She berated herself for being so heedless. Had she seen him in time, she could easily have outrun him.

Summoned by Meg's shouts, Will followed her and the bailiff all the way to the Wood Street prison.

"Listen to me, you wretched catchpole," Will said to the bailiff. "This man is no criminal. It's Roger Ruffneck you should be arresting."

"Stop barking at my heels, cur," replied the bailiff, jerking Meg forward. She had concluded he was the same rudesby who came looking for her at the Boar's Head, frightening Gwin.

"Keep your hands off my friend, you yellow-bellied sapsucker!" said Will.

Meg strained toward Will. "There's truth in the charge. Ruffneck and Weasle—their testimony will convict me." Her tone was low and urgent. "Find someone to defend me!"

"Mistress Ruffneck will testify against her husband."

"Yes, but she saw me rob him, and I gave her the loot. They will turn her words against me—"

"Oh drat," said Will. "How did we come to be in such a pickle?"

"And Ruffneck will be so angry, he is sure to harm her."

"Away with you!" said the bailiff, menacing Will with his knife.

Will easily skipped out of his reach. "All will be well, Mack! I'll borrow money and get you out just as you did me."

"Don't ask Burbage, or he will take us for base cheaters," Meg called after him.

The Wood Street clink was as horrible as she remembered it, dark and damp and filled with the noise and stench of human misery. The heavy door thudded behind her and the bolt fell into place. As her eyes adjusted to the darkness she could see shapes that stirred, groaned, and subsided again into shadows and stillness. The floor was made of planking and strewn with filthy straw like an untended manger. Bilboes were fixed into the stone walls. At least she was not chained to them. High on one wall was a small grate at the level of the street. It was the only source of light and air. Meg had stood outside that same grate to pass food to her poor father.

She sat down, wrapped her arms around her legs, and rested her chin on her knees. Surely Will would find a way to get her out in the morning. But what if he did not? She would be taken to court, convicted of assault, and returned to prison. Would she die here like her father? The chill of despair crept over her and she began to cry soundlessly.

At the rustling sound all her muscles tensed. From the shadows emerged a boy on his hands and knees. His eyes reflected the scrap of light that came through the grate.

"You don't look like a murderer," he said. "Are you a jarkman?"

"I am not a killer or a forger. Why are you here?" she asked.

"I was nabbed for robbing a peddler. My cuffins left me high and dry. They'll find another foist, one who won't get himself caught." He brushed away a tear. "That Davy Dapper was no true mate! Nor Peter Flick."

Meg leaned forward. "I know those cozeners well. Did they corrupt you?" She felt anger rising in her. The boy was no older than twelve, the age she had been when Davy and Peter deserted her.

He shrugged. "My father tried to teach me but gave up and sent me to their school. Now I wish I had never learned their crafty tricks."

"Have you told the magistrate your story?"

"Yes. He said I was an errant brat and as guilty as Adam." Suddenly wary, he frowned. "How do you know my cuffins?"

"It's a long story. What is your name?"

The boy hesitated. "I am called Grabwill Junior."

"Is your father Nick Grabwill?" Meg asked in astonishment.

"Yes. Now who are you?"

"Never mind. Why doesn't he help you?"

"He brings me food sometimes. But he is afraid of being caught himself."

"So Nick Grabwill is still thriving by hook and by crook!"

"How do you know my father?" the boy demanded.

"Have you ever heard of Long Meg?"

Grabwill Junior's eyes, the only part of him Meg could well discern, grew even wider. "Who has not heard of Long Meg? He is hated and feared by Davy and Peter and their band."

"He?" asked Meg.

"Davy and Roger believe Long Meg is a roarer named Mack who disguises himself as a tavern maid to cover his deeds. Others say Long Meg is a woman begotten by the devil."

"And what do you say?" said Meg, hiding her smile.

The boy scratched his head. Fleas were already biting Meg too.

"No woman is strong enough to do what Long Meg does," he said.

"Who says she is a woman?"

"My father. One night a few years ago, a strange cuffin made him steal women's clothing. Soon after, Long Meg began to rough up every rakehell that went to the Boar's Head."

"Indeed!" said Meg. She enjoyed hearing about her own exploits. "But why does your father believe Long Meg—or Mack—to be a woman?"

The boy leaned closer and spoke as if conveying a great secret. "Because he peered at the fellow as he donned the skirt and saw that he lacked a yard. You know, a staff." He pointed to his own lap.

In the darkness Meg blushed. "By my beard I don't believe it!"

Young Grabwill shrugged. "My father has the eyes of an owl. He can see in the pitch dark. But he is old and no one heeds him anymore."

"Do you know Roger Ruffneck?" asked Meg, hoping to hear something that might aid her at the next day's trial.

"I hate him with all my guts!" The boy's sudden cry caused the other inmates to clank their chains and curse. "He said my father had not raised me to fear God, but he would remedy that by beating me. He broke my arm. See, it is still crooked."

He held out his misshapen arm. Meg ached at the thought of his suffering.

"I was glad when Long Meg beat up old Ruffy." The boy smiled. "He said a horse trod on him. But he spends all his days grumbling against Mack and devising his death."

"When I see him in court tomorrow, I swear it will be the end of *him*!"

"What? Are *you* Mack?" Grabwill's voice was soft with wonder. "Long Meg!"

"We are one and the same," said Meg.

Now five people knew her secret. Nick Grabwill had been the first. The second was Violetta, who remained her devoted friend. The others—Jane, James Burbage, and now this boy—had responded with admiration, even awe. Why was she afraid of what Will might think?

"Junior! Boy?" The whispered voice came from the overhead grate.

Young Grabwill ran over to the wall and stood on tiptoe. A flattened loaf of bread fell through the grate into his waiting hands. "Father! You will never guess who is here. Mack! I mean Long Meg."

"That she-devil?" came Nick Grabwill's voice. "Let me see her."

Meg approached the grate. She could barely make out the shape of the old curber, black as the night around him.

"So you've been caught at last." He sounded smug. "Not as clever as I am, are you?"

The thief had known her secret for years. Meg was half-afraid of the power it gave him. And then, with a flash of insight, she saw how he might be her best hope.

"Nick Grabwill, I pray you go at once to the Boar's Head Inn and ask for one Will Shakespeare."

"Why should I do your bidding?"

"I've done you no harm, and I can do your son much good."

Grabwill laughed. "It's too late for that. I'm leaving before I get caught."

"Wait! The same villain is the author of your son's misfortune and mine," said Meg in a low and urgent voice. "With your help I can turn the tables on him in court."

"You tricked me once. You won't again."

"Listen, Father! Mack is an upright carl. I trust him."

Nick Grabwill ignored his son and withdrew his face from the grate.

Meg jumped, grabbing the grate with her fingers and bracing her feet against the wall. "Nick!" she shouted into the night. "Go to Will Shakespeare and tell him what you know about me. Tell him *everything*."

~ Chapter 34 ~

Justice Littlewit clapped his moth-eaten periwig over his bald
pate and leaned on the bar in the very guildhall where Lady
Jane Grey had been convicted of treason for conspiring to
become Queen of England. Littlewit longed to try some
renowned defendant, but as a common magistrate he did little more than punish debtors, thieves, and cozeners. With a
groan he eased himself into a worn and ancient armchair.
The jurors rose in an uneven line and sat down again. The
clerk, Nib Squiller, gave him a doubtful look. Littlewit reached
in his pocket to touch the apothecary's flask filled with spirits and determined he would pass a strict and unforgettable
judgment that day.

"Oyez, oyez," intoned the clerk, calling forth the prisoners in the docket. Clerks and attorneys circled around Littlewit like moons, and sergeants stood by with their tipstaves.

"Roger Ruffneck versus Mack, alias Meg de Galle."

Squiller's high voice made Littlewit's head ache. Holding the flask in the crook of his arm, he took a sip.

Led by a bailiff, the defendant approached the bar wearing

a soiled doublet. He was young, of prodigious height, and like any sensible person, scared. A red-eyed wench in a servant's cap began to sob. Women always wept in an effort to move Littlewit to mercy, but today he was implacable. The wench was being consoled by a woman he recognized as Mistress Over–byte of the Boar's Head Inn.

"Where is the plaintiff?" Littlewit said.

A man wearing a ruff so wide and stiff it looked as if his head were surmounted on a platter stood up. Weasle the attorney was beside him, which portended dull and lengthy speeches. Littlewit sighed and took another drink.

Squiller read the charges. "That upon the tenth day of October in the vicinity of St. Paul's, the defendant Mack, alias Meg de Galle, did *malo animo*, with malicious intent, assault the plaintiff, Roger Ruffneck, *vi et armis*, with force and arms, causing bodily harm and stealing from him the sum of forty crowns and jewels worth five pounds."

"How do you answer?" Littlewit asked the defendant.

"I will answer for him. I am his lawyer." A young bearded fellow pushed his way to the surprised defendant's side. They appeared to argue over a point of law.

"Today *I* am the lawyer. Trust me!" He turned to Little-wit, saying, "I, Dick Talio, contest the charge on behalf of my client and plead for a dismissal upon the evidence of this counterclaim." He thrust a writ at the clerk.

Littlewit bristled at the unorthodox procedure. Why did Italians always insist their ways were superior?

"My lord, this claims the plaintiff is a foul abuser of the innocent, a perjurer, and a notorious villain," said Squiller in a bored voice.

Weasle pointed at Talio. *"He* lies. I have two infallible witnesses to this assault besides myself, who was a victim as
well."

"Weasle, you cannot be a lawyer, a witness, and a victim in
the same action," Littlewit said.

"I am the victim here," said Ruffneck, glaring at his
attorney.

Chastened for the moment Weasle said, "I call as witnesses
Davy Dapper and Peter Flick!"

Talio clapped his hands. "Bring them on!"

The two witnesses came forward, glancing uncertainly at
Talio. Yes, they said in reply to Littlewit's questions, they
had seen the defendant strike Roger Ruffneck with a sword
and deprive him of his purse and jewels.

"Let me question them," said Talio, proceeding without
waiting for Littlewit's permission. "Why did you not help
your friend?"

"We did not want to suffer his fate," said Davy.

"Mack was beating Roger bloody and saying he would
murder him!" said Peter.

"Stow it," said Davy out of the side of his mouth.

"Peter Flick, you perjure yourself!" cried the defendant.

Talio continued, ignoring the interruptions. "Ha! Neither of
you denies Roger was your friend. Was he not in fact paying
you for your lying testimony that helped him divorce his wife?
And did you not run away *before* the alleged assault occurred?"

Littlewit pretended to cough in order to gulp some spirits.
This confused case was demanding all his attention. "How
do you know they ran away?" he asked Talio.

"Because I was present and gave chase."

"If I cannot be both a witness and an advocate, neither can you, Dick Talio," complained Weasle.

Now the defendant spoke up. "Then *I* attest that Davy and Peter are arrant liars, and Roger also, for I was at the bawdy court with Dick Talio when he unlawfully divorced his wife."

"You are the defendant; you cannot be a witness either," said Weasle.

Littlewit rose from his chair and shook his fist at Weasle. "I am the magistrate. Let me ask the questions!"

Weasle ignored him and shouted at the defendant. "You waylaid my client in the churchyard *animo furandi*, with the intention of robbing him, and your lawyer chased his companions away so that you could assault him without witnesses!"

"Aha! You are admitting that Davy and Peter did not, could not, see what befell Roger!" cried Talio in triumph. "*Quod est demonstratum.* There were no witnesses; therefore there was no assault. The charges must be dismissed."

"Not so fast," said Littlewit. Talio was a clever youth, but Littlewit had been a judge for a long time and that counted for something. "Weasle, describe what happened."

Weasle related the incident at length, including the defendant's threats to carve out his heart and drive a sword through Roger's guts. Littlewit glanced at Mack-alias-Meg, who looked sheepish. *Guilty*, he decided.

"Why did you chase them away when they might have prevented the assault?" Littlewit asked Talio.

"The *alleged* assault," said Mack-alias-Meg.

"The reason touches an unrelated action," said Talio with a slight smile. "But since you ask . . ." He paused.

Littlewit leaned forward.

"On the seventh day of September," Talio continued loudly, "at the Boar's Head Inn, Davy Dapper and Peter Flick stole from me twenty-five crowns. Here is the warrant sworn out this very morning for their arrest."

Quick as rabbits, the two witnesses bolted from the bar. They shoved the bailiff, skirted the sergeant with his tipstaff, and made for the door. They would have escaped had Mistress Over-byte not stepped into the aisle and blocked their path with her outstretched arms. Davy put his head down like a bull and rammed into her. She caught him in a fleshy embrace and staggered backward. A second bystander—was it the host of the Boar's Head?—tackled Peter from behind.

"Take that, you cowardly cozeners. Hurrah for Mistress Gwin and Overby!" Dick Talio shouted, drawing cheers and the deafening sound of feet stomping on timber floors.

Littlewit rose to his feet slowly. He flushed as warmth spread through his chest. What should he do? He could not release Davy and Peter without starting a riot. "Arrest them!" he ordered.

"We never should have robbed a lawyer," said Peter to Davy.

"Shut your stupid trap," said Davy. He shook his fist at Talio. "You stole my best satin boots!" This brought a peal of laughter from the defendant. "And my purse too."

"So I did," admitted Talio, "and with its contents paid the man whose cart you wrecked. That day I spared your lives so that you could be here this day." He smiled with sly delight.

Was this a new wrinkle in the case? Littlewit took a sip to help him think more clearly and said, "Oyez! Attention.

Remove those two to prison. All return to the present action lest you confuse the jury. Are there further witnesses to the assault upon Roger Ruffneck?"

At once the plaintiff shot to his feet and pointed to a woman in the crowd. "My wife! Jane Ruffneck. She was there."

The woman came forward, shaking her fist. "If he was assaulted, I swear he deserved every blow he got."

"Quiet, woman, until you are questioned," said Littlewit. "Did you see Mack-alias-Meg attack your husband?"

"No, for that man is not my husband." She pointed to the plaintiff.

"Don't let her speak. Her truth will dig my grave," the defendant begged Talio.

"Admit he *was* your husband, Jane," said Talio gently. "Until he defamed your good name in order to divorce you."

This was a provocative case after all, Littlewit decided. A harsh judgment against one of the parties would be necessary to teach these wrangling foes a lesson. But first he had to settle a simple question.

"Mistress Ruffneck, did you see this person"—he pointed to the defendant—"assault that person?" He pointed to Ruffneck. "As Cuthbert Weasle described it?"

The still-defiant witness said, "I did."

"There you have it," said Weasle in triumph.

"Finally a plain answer from a witness! How does the defendant reply?" Littlewit asked.

"It is true; Mack de Galle assaulted Roger Ruffneck," said the defendant.

A gasp rose from the onlookers. The weeping began again. Littlewit scratched his head.

"But there are compelling reasons—" said Mack-alias-Meg.

"Mitigating circumstances," Talio whispered.

"Mitigating circumstances," the defendant repeated, "that a magistrate and jury ought to take into account, namely that the plaintiff abused his wife, destroyed her good name, and cheated his family of a livelihood—injustices that the law did not remedy but rather permitted!"

"Yea, when Justice sleeps, the wakeful citizen must see that the law is obeyed," Talio said with the air of a sage.

Littlewit's patience and his drink were almost gone. "What, are you *both* lawyers, with your mitigating this and that?"

"Your Honor," whispered Nib, "I would conclude this action before it is entirely out of your control."

Littlewit shifted, let out a fart, and spoke loudly to cover the sound. "I see no reason why the plaintiff should not prevail in this matter. No disinterested person has come forth to credibly discredit him."

"Wait," said Mack-alias-Meg. "Send a bailiff to the Wood Street prison to fetch a boy named Grabwill Junior. He will testify to Roger Ruffneck's criminal abuses."

"What is being abused here, Justice Littlewit, is the civil procedure itself," said Weasle. "This case concerns not whether my client has assaulted anyone, but by whom *he* was assaulted. Mack de Galle has admitted guilt. Dispense with the trial and proceed to judgment!"

"Fie upon the procedures!" Littlewit said. "I am the judge here."

"And I am still a witness!" It was the woman again. "I will have my say."

"Speak, woman!" shouted Littlewit, hoping to frighten her into silence.

"Being no longer the wife of Roger Ruffneck, I have no

duty to obey him. My obligation is to the truth, a duty that compels me to reveal a heinous and long-hidden crime."

Littlewit rose from his seat, blinking away the dulling effects of the wine. What terrible crime could this insignificant woman have committed? Would he get to hang someone yet today?

"My husband was ever a jealous and violent man," she began. "Three years ago, when we lived in the parish of St. Alphage, he accused me without any cause of lying with the priest, who was no godly man. He went out one night and came back with blood on his hands, and he threatened to kill me if I ever revealed to anyone that he had murdered the priest in his bed."

There was not a sound in the hall until the defendant let out a high, womanish cry and fell senseless to the ground.

∽ Chapter 35 ∾

For several minutes Littlewit beheld the mayhem.

"I'll have your life!" shouted Roger Ruffneck, leaping toward his former wife.

"Seize that murderer!" someone cried. Two sergeants and a bailiff tackled Ruffneck.

Talio, Mistress Overbyte, and the wench crowded around the defendant. At least Mack could go nowhere.

"Is there a doctor here?" Talio's voice rose over the hubbub.

Ruffneck cursed his wife as the sergeant led him from the hall. Some bystanders drew back as if from the devil himself. Others jeered and shook their fists. A rotten apple soared through the air and struck Ruffneck in the back of the head.

"Oyez, oyez!" cried Nib, but no one heeded him.

A man with a bag shoved his way through the throng and knelt beside the defendant, who revived and sat up.

"My mother is innocent!" he said, tears coursing down his cheeks. "And by that knowledge I am made new. I am reborn!"

Littlewit wondered if the defendant had sustained an injury to his brain. If so, could he still be found guilty?

Talio clapped the doctor on the back. "You are late, Thomas Valentine, but all is well."

"Thomas—my love?" The wench collapsed against Mistress Over-byte. Had she not been pining for Mack-alias-Meg only moments before?

The doctor whirled around. He snatched the cap from the girl and her dark hair sprang out. "Olivia!" he cried. The girl moved her lips soundlessly as the doctor took her into his arms.

"Olivia? You are not Violetta?" the defendant was saying, still deranged from his fall. Then he smiled. "Ah! Now I understand the reason for your strange melancholy."

"You are obstructing my courtroom. Away with you both," Littlewit said, flapping his arms at the two lovers.

The mad hubbub had subsided into cheers of delight as the doctor led Olivia from the bench, not taking his eyes from her. But she looked back at the defendant, saying, "Wait, for I must be sure that Mack goes free."

This domestic drama was interfering with Littlewit's judgment. "Now to conclude this case." He stood up and glanced around. The plaintiff and his witnesses were gone—three new malefactors in custody, one of them for murder! The present case appeared to be moot. But Littlewit was not ready to give up. He raised his voice for the benefit of the jury, though he knew none of them would understand his words. "*Habemus optimum testem confitentem reum.*"

"What does that mean?" whispered Mack-alias-Meg.

Talio shook his head and shrugged.

Pleased that his Latin had confounded even the Italian, Littlewit translated. "'We have the best witness, a confessing defendant.' Though the plaintiff now stands accused of murder, that does not mitigate your crime, de Galle." He had no idea if this were a valid point of the law, but who could gainsay him?

Talio placed his hands on the bar and leaned forward, his face inches from Littlewit's. "Your Honor, my client has not made a full confession."

"Will!" said the defendant, sounding distressed. Littlewit decided he was still touched in the head, for wasn't the lawyer's name Dick?

Talio tipped his head toward his client and gave him a long and searching look.

"The truth will come out, howsoever it seeks to hide itself," said the defendant to Talio in a voice free of fear or distress. "I am not who you think I am. I am not Mack de Galle, as I have claimed to be."

Littlewit decided that Bedlam Hospital would be a better place than Fleet Prison for the lunatic Mack.

"I ask your pardon for the deceit, which was undertaken with the best of motives. Let Violetta be my witness." The defendant gestured toward the servant girl, who left the doctor's side and approached the bar.

"I thought you were called Olivia," said Littlewit sharply.

"I am. I was pretending to be Violetta. As was she." She pointed to the defendant. "I mean, she was pretending not to be Violetta but Mack de Galle, who is no such person." Her hand and her voice both trembled.

"Are you all mad?" cried Littlewit. He struck himself on the head and his periwig flew off and landed on the floor.

Talio picked up the periwig and considered it as if it held some grave meaning. "If there is no such person as Mack de Galle, then it is impossible he should have committed any crime." He peered at Littlewit. "Because there was no crime, then today's action must *ipso facto* be dismissed."

"Give me that." Littlewit half stood, seized his wig from Talio, and sat down again. If there was no such person as Mack de Galle, then who was this person at the bar?

"Since coming into this hall, has my client admitted to being Mack de Galle?" asked Talio.

Nib Squiller shuffled through his papers. He gave Littlewit an apologetic look. "Your Honor, he was identified as Mack, alias Meg de Galle, and he stated that Mack de Galle struck the victim, but he did not say *he* was Mack de Galle."

Littlewit bolted out of his seat, waving his periwig at Talio. "No more of your subtle quibbles!" He turned to the prisoner and shouted, "If you're not de Galle, then who are you?"

For a long moment the silence held. Finally the defendant replied, "I am Meg Macdougall, called Long Meg by my friends at the Boar's Head Inn." As he spoke his whole demeanor changed. His voice grew reedy, like a young boy's.

"Yea, I'll vouch for you, my dear!" cried Mistress Over-byte.

Was this Mack-alias-Meg a devil? And all these people his minions, come to provoke him to madness and turn Justice on its head? Littlewit fumbled for his flask and put it to his mouth before remembering it was empty.

The defendant gazed at Talio with eyebrows raised beseechingly. "I have no brother; there is only me. That, Will, is the simple truth," he said, reaching up to pull off his cap. Out tumbled long, golden locks.

The onlookers gasped as one. Only Talio smiled.

"'Tis a man-woman!" said Nib Squiller.

"Nay, 'tis our Long Meg," someone shouted. "Huzzah for Talio; Meg is free!"

"I have not dismissed the charges yet," protested Littlewit. He placed his periwig back on his head. "Draw up the dismissal," he said to his clerk.

One of the jurors broke out in song.

> *Here's to our hero, Long Meg.*
> *She of the mile-long leg.*
> *Sing high, sing low, heigh-ho!*
> *To the Boar's Head we go.*

The doctor and Talio hoisted the defendant to their shoulders. Mistress Over-byte and her husband, the doctor and his wench, and the witness Jane Ruffneck danced like lunatics under a full moon.

"Arrest the defendant for . . . for impersonating a criminal!" Littlewit cried. "Arrest everyone for rioting in the courtroom! Unlawful assembly. Nib, draw up new charges post haste."

But Nib was in the midst of the revelers. Even the sergeants were celebrating by pounding their staves in time with the singing.

"Oyez!" shouted Littlewit, banging his chair against the bar in frustration. He knew with a magistrate's infallible reckoning that young Talio would one day be a renowned and admired judge, while he himself would die an obscure magistrate. As the joyous party trailed from the hall, he tore at his periwig with both hands and threw clumps of the false hair to the floor.

Chapter 36

Will had every reason to be jubilant. Dick Talio was his best performance ever. *Talio* was Latin for "retaliation," but not even the judge had suspected his alias. He had kept his dearest friend from prison and seen three of his tormentors apprehended for their crimes. He relished the paradox that Justice was done even as its procedures were so riotously overturned. Will smiled at the memory of Littlewit tearing his wig while the officers of the court danced with the victors.

Despite what the old thief had told him, Will was startled to hear Long Meg's voice coming from his friend Mack. More so to see his familiar face change into Meg's and her golden hair tumble forth. Then admiration stirred him. This goddess of the Boar's Head had proved as adept at transformations as one of Ovid's shape-shifting gods! He was elated, for her timely disclosure had sealed their triumph.

Bearing her from the courtroom, Will was aware of Meg's rump on his shoulder, her thigh alongside his cheek, her ankle in his grasp. Her presence made his blood quicken. They had cavorted all the way to the Boar's Head, where she disappeared, returning in a bodice and skirt. Will sneaked fur-tive glances at her full, round breasts and wondered how they could have been so well hidden under Mack's doublet. How many times had he unknowingly brushed against them? Now their curves were visible, but alas her strong, shapely legs were hidden beneath a skirt. His new interest in Meg confused him, and he was uncertain how to speak to her now. She gave him no help, rather avoided meeting his eyes.

Why, he wanted to ask, *did you do this? Was it only for fun?*

Master Overby opened the taps, pouring free ale for all. The drink filled Will with warmth. He reveled in his sudden and satisfying revenge against Peter Flick and Davy Dapper.

"Let's drink to Justice, which prevails despite the law!" he said, raising his cup.

"To villains and thieves hoist with their own petard!" crowed Meg.

"Brought down by this arm they were!" said Overby, shak-ing a fist, proud to have proved useful at last.

"Nay, more by my great girth," boasted Gwin. "My gut still hurts from the force of his head."

Will could tell that this story would grow with each telling until it was a legend at the Boar's Head. Like Long Meg her-self, already larger than life and glowing with pleasure. He could not look at her for long.

"To Jane," said Will, "for delivering the blow that felled the fatal Ruffneck!"

Meg raised her cup to Jane and said, "The truth that con-demns the guilty, sets the innocent free."

Will wondered why Jane's testimony had caused Mack to collapse, then rise up again suffused with joy. It had something to do with his—rather, *her*—mother. The only time Meg had spoken of her past was while they were watching the play. He knew so little about her, really.

A tipsy Jane Ruffneck promised to redeem Grabwill Junior from prison and take care of him. She told how Meg once came into the Boar's Head unaware of the man's cap still on her head. Ned mimicked Violetta—rather, *Olivia*—gesturing wildly for her to remove it. Olivia giggled and turned her face toward Thomas Valentine.

"O how my throat ached after so many hours of speaking in a low voice," said Meg. "It is a relief to be myself again."

Will understood that Meg had to disclose her sex in order to defeat the charges against Mack. He realized now that in court, Mack had been mutely beseeching Will to reveal him as Meg. While he admired the strategy he had to ask himself, *How did she expect me to know?* And that led to the inevitable question, *Why did she disguise herself in the first place?* He sensed it was a mystery tied up with everything that was dark and inscrutable in the species womankind.

It was Thomas Valentine, still holding Olivia's hand, who asked the question uppermost in Will's mind. "Meg, why *did* you invent this Mack and pretend to be him?"

All were waiting for her answer. She hesitated and lifted her shoulders. "Is your Thomas a jealous man?" she asked Violetta.

Before she could speak Thomas said, "There is not a jealous bone in my body."

"Now that you know Mack is no rival suitor," said Gwin with a wry laugh.

"It was a silly plot we dreamed up!" said Olivia in her

high, quick voice. "Meg invented a brother and disguised herself in order—"

Meg interrupted. "To tempt Will to woo you."

Will's hands gripped the edge of the table. He had not expected Meg to say that.

"To *trick* Will Shakespeare rather. For I did not love him," Olivia said hastily, giving Thomas the full force of her beauteous smile.

"Not love him? Who here does not love Will Shakespeare?" Meg spoke lightly, but Will noted her blushing.

Her comment renewed the merry laughter. Will felt his own face redden. How had he become the butt of the joke? He smiled to hide his hurt. No man likes to be rejected, even by a woman he does not love. Or teased, especially by a woman he admires.

"I thought we would be friends, Will," said Thomas Valentine in a tone of rebuke. "You with your broken head and I with my broken heart. But while I was looking for my Olivia, you were concealing her and wooing her for yourself. O broken faith!"

"You wrong me, Valentine," said Will.

"My love, I did not know you were in London until I saw you in the courtroom," insisted Olivia. She turned on Will. "Why did you not tell me when you first met my Thomas?"

Will's triumphant mood was quickly fading. "Am I on trial now? I must protest my innocence. How was I to know that *our* Violetta was *your* Olivia?" He pointed his forefingers in opposite directions. "Had you accepted my invitation to dine, you would have discovered her yourself. Or had you described her better, I might have guessed who she was."

Olivia stood up and withdrew her hand from her lover's. "Thomas! Could you not even describe me?" she said, anguished. "I suppose you told him I had a set of bones, a stomach, and a liver within me, expecting him to say, 'O that must be Olivia!'" She closed her eyes and lowered her face to his. "Of what color are my eyes?"

This should not be a test of love, Will thought. He had stared into the lady's eyes often enough while playing Pyramus but could not say what color they were. He tried in vain to remember the color of Anne Hathaway's eyes. And Meg's? He glanced at her. Blue, just as he thought.

Softly Thomas said, "Why, they are brown. Like . . ." He faltered. "Like nothing in the body I can think of, except themselves."

"Ahh," sighed Gwin.

Olivia opened her eyes and blinked back tears. She favored Thomas with a look more ardent than any she had bestowed on Pyramus. "I have been so cruel!" she said. "There is so much for you to forgive, I fear you will decide not to love me after all."

"Sit down. You must tell me all, like a patient his every hurt," said Thomas with gentle authority.

Will hoped she would not tell Thomas how often she had kissed Will onstage. That might move even the mildest of men to jealousy. And from there to a challenge and a duel.

"But first know this," Thomas was saying, having seized Olivia's hand again. "Nothing you say will diminish one jot my love for you. Therefore I state before these good witnesses that I wish to marry you, Olivia, if you will consent."

The lady's free hand fluttered to her neck. "I shall upon

certain conditions. One, that you will refrain from writing poetry or destroying flowers for my benefit."

Thomas nodded. His eyes were bright with hope, for he was a man about to realize his dearest ambition. Will almost envied him. His own desires were at that moment hopelessly muddled.

"And two, that you not hold my hand at all times."

Thomas frowned, considering the request. He opened his hand and released Olivia's.

"In truth a hot and moist palm is a detriment to good health. Your hand shall henceforth be free."

"Thus mine to freely give again." Olivia extended her hand, palm upward. Thomas lightly took it up and kissed it.

"And now, let's away to your father and share this news," he said.

"Love's favor falls on those who freely choose." The words sprang from Will's lips. He smiled an apology. "Thomas may not rhyme their love, but the lady put no such constraint upon me."

The glad company broke up, and Meg embraced Olivia at their parting. Watching Meg, Will decided he did not believe she pretended to be Mack only as a jest. As Long Meg she had been kind to him. As Mack she seemed to relish their adventures as much as he did. Mack had been a boon companion; they had helped and trusted one another like the truest of friends. No, there was more to her disguise than mere trickery. He approached Meg, saw her wary look, and turned away. Did he want to know the truth?

"Will?" she said, surprising him. "Do you have a question for me?"

More than one. Too many for this moment. He shook his head. "No, I am going to my room to write my father. He will want to know his affair is settled."

"I am glad of the outcome," she said.

Which outcome? He kept his expression blank.

"We should talk, Will. I want to explain."

Will shook his head. He was no longer able to speak freely to her. *What did I tell Mack about myself that Meg now knows?*

Meg persisted. "You must have known. When did you figure it out?"

Was it only yesterday that he and Mack were at Westminster and in and out of jail? Today he no longer had a friend named Mack. And the Long Meg standing before him was a cipher. A mystery.

"Truly I don't know," he murmured, turning away.

Writing the letter did nothing to ease his confusion. Every incident related to his father's debt was tied to Mack. To *Meg.* Rather than explain he chose to relay the barest facts, omitting the theft of the twenty-five crowns because it reflected poorly on himself. There was left only the outcome, for which a few sentences would suffice.

The Boar's Head Inn, Whitechapel
16 October 1582
To John Shakespeare, Henley Street, Stratford-upon-Avon

Honored father, I hereby inform you that the debt to
William Burbage is settled and the matter concluded
with an offer of employment by his brother, one James
Burbage, the proprietor of the Theatre in Shoreditch.

Where if I am successful, our family's financial woes
will in a short time be relieved and my own ambitions
realized.

Thus while sad necessity drove me hither, glad
Fortune greeted me and now contrives to keep me in
this paradise of possibility,
Where you may find your dutiful son,
William.

Will knew his father would never come to London to see him disgrace the name of Shakespeare on a stage. He in turn had even less reason to return to Stratford. Glovemaking was his past. His future lay with James Burbage's company. The lucky break he owed to Meg. To *Mack.* It was Mack whom Burbage wanted to hire; Will's job was merely part of the bargain. He began to worry: When Burbage learned that Mack was really a woman, would he refuse to hire either of them? Could Will persuade him he was not a party to Mack's trickery?

Uncertainty clawed at his earlier confidence. He had gone from having two friends to having none. Mack was a brave and goodly fellow. But by revealing himself to be Meg, he had deprived Will of all the delights of their friendship and possibly jeopardized his new job. *Fie upon him! And fie upon Meg.* He had enjoyed her witty companionship at the Boar's Head and at the Theatre. What fortitude she displayed in her trials! She was a brave sight in doublet and hose with her golden hair about her shoulders. Now a misunderstanding as thick as the morning fog in the forest of Arden hung between them.

A small voice spoke to Will, the same one that warned him when he was in the woods with Anne, the insistent voice he often chose to ignore. It said: *What right do you have to be angry at her?* He could not shake it out of his head. It chastened him, forcing him to admit that he had suspected the truth—then about Anne and now about Meg. To be still more honest, he had *known* the truth and pretended not to. Had played the very game he accused Meg of playing.

You must have known, she said. *When did you know?*

When, indeed? It was a fair question. He would have to think about it and undeceive himself before he could undeceive Meg de Galle.

Chapter 37

The padded doublet and soiled hose lay on Meg's bed like the lifeless body of Mack. He was a roaring boy no more, Will's friend no more, and a defendant no more, though he *had* robbed Roger Ruffneck, who deserved far worse. The loss of her other self saddened Meg. During the trial she realized it was necessary to shed her disguise or else be convicted. Will's look had reassured her. *Trust me,* he had said when he first saw her in court. When the moment came she did. She admitted that Mack was really Meg. The need for concealment gone, she removed her cap and resumed her natural voice. She expected surprise and revulsion, for mannish women were considered monstrous, yet everyone had cheered. Were they simply happy to see the tables turned and the villain Ruffneck laid low? Or had they all somehow known of her disguise? Even Will did not seem surprised. Was he really such a good actor? Now he would not talk to her. Did he mean to punish her? How unjust! Meg kicked the bed, not caring about the pain that shot up her leg.

Already she missed Violetta, who had gone with Thomas

Valentine to be reunited with her father. Meg found the doctor to be kind and handsome, befitting his euphonious name. Seeing his hand entwined with Violetta's, however, put Meg in mind of a wrist shackle.

"So when did your tears over Will turn into tears for your lost Valentine?" Meg asked as they parted.

"I cannot tell," she said with a shrug. "But I hope Will is not angry with me."

"I think his merry talk hides a broken heart," said Meg with a wink.

Violetta lifted her round, moist eyes. "O Meg, let us always be friends, you and I! Let nothing come between us."

But Thomas Valentine had already come between them. Violetta would marry him and take up her duties as Olivia, the doctor's wife. Her brief role as a tavern maid she would cast off as easily as a soiled apron. But to Meg she would always be Violetta, her first real friend.

At least Jane Ruffneck remained. The news that it was Roger who killed the priest had struck Meg like lightning and shone truth into the dark corners of her soul. Jane recounted the exact and horrifying details, leaving Meg with no doubts. Now she knew that whatever despair had driven her mother to take her life was not compounded by the crime of murder. Her shame melted away. Jane's burden also lifted. Roger Ruffneck would surely hang.

On every side had been such celebration! Meg was full of glee until the evening waned and Will withdrew. Doubts assailed her. Now that she was no longer Mack, did he disdain her very company? Why could they not speak and unfold their hearts and minds to one another? Meg knelt and buried her head in the torn doublet, the symbol of her deceit, and wondered how to ask Will's forgiveness, how to explain the tangled purposes of her disguise.

There was a knock at her door. Meg's heart leaped up. It had to be Will! He had finished his letter and was thinking of her too. She jumped up, smoothed her hair and her skirt, and threw open the door. "Forgive me—"

There, huffing from the strain of climbing the stairs, stood her mistress.

"—Gwin?" Fresh remorse flooded Meg, for she had also deceived Gwin.

"Forgive you? Why? For wanting to become a man? What woman does not sometimes wish herself a man?" Gwin said, coming into the room.

"But I don't! I want to be a woman. I *am* a woman," cried Meg, closing the door and sinking to her bed. "O I do not understand myself. I only know that Will, who I thought was my friend, acts as if he no longer knows me."

"Can you blame him?" said Gwin. "He realizes all his manly swearing and lewd jesting was done in your company."

Meg squeezed her eyes shut. It had not occurred to her that Will was embarrassed. But what could she do about that now?

"Gwin, do *you* forgive me for deceiving you after all your goodness to me?"

"There's nothing to forgive. No, the master and I thank you." She smiled her gap-toothed smile, which Meg had come to love. "Within days there will be pamphlets and ballads about today's events. You'll soon be a legend. Think of what that will do for our business!"

A fleeting wish that the Boar's Head would burn down crossed Meg's mind. "I am tired of being Long Meg, a freak of nature to be gaped at."

"Not a freak, but rather a *prodigy* of nature," said Gwin. She reached out to touch Meg's arm.

Suddenly Gwin seemed a stranger to her. Meg pulled away. "I won't stay here."

"Nonsense. Where will you go?"

Meg recalled the bargain she had made with James Burbage. What began as a prank now seemed an opportunity.

"To Shoreditch. I'll make my living on the stage."

"God's pittikins, how can you even think such a thing?" said Gwin.

"When every man seeks to profit by me, I must consider how *I* may best thrive. For I have no true friends anymore!"

She hid her face in Mack's clothes and waited for Gwin to contradict her. She wanted Gwin to touch her back and speak some reassurance. All she heard was a sigh, the click of the closing door, and muffled steps vanishing down the stairs.

Chapter 38

In the gray light of dawn before anyone else was stirring, Meg arose and dressed as herself. She stuffed Mack's clothes in a corner. *I am no longer Mack.* Nor was she Long Meg the tavern maid anymore. *I am only Meg.*

Hoarfrost whitened the cobbles of the innyard and she could see her breath as she set out for Shoreditch. She stopped at the Cock and Bull tavern outside the Bishopsgate to warm her hands and break her fast with some cold mutton. She listened as people came in and greeted the host. No one mentioned a prisoner named Mack who turned the tables on his accuser and revealed himself to be Long Meg. But it was early yet. She wondered how long it would take for the news to spread and grow into a tale full of lies. How soon would the curious come flocking to the Boar's Head to the delight of Master Overby? When would Gwin realize Meg was not coming back?

She lingered in the tavern while the thought repeated itself like a stream tumbling over the same rocks: *I am no longer Mack; I am only Meg.* But who exactly was Meg? She pondered that vexed question and came up answerless.

When she left the Cock and Bull the morning sun was melting the hoarfrost. In the fields, flocks of noisy crows fought over the grains left over from the harvest. She rehearsed what she would say to James Burbage. "I confess our bargain was my desperate ploy to aid Will Shakespeare, who was innocent of my deceit," she murmured. "Still, I will honor my word and join your company if you will have me." She hoped this would avert his certain anger. Would he, however, agree to her new stipulation? "I am no longer Mack; I will be only Meg."

She did not realize she had spoken aloud until she heard the familiar voice. "Good. Then I will always recognize you."

Meg whirled around and was surprised to see Will. "Have you been following me?"

"Do you want me to?" He was leaning against a stile, his hand raised to shield his eyes from the morning sun.

Meg's heart fluttered. *Of course I do!*

"I posted my letter to Stratford, then cut across the fields. It seems we now have the same destination." He nodded northward.

Meg had so much she wanted to say to Will. Now his sudden presence had scattered all her words.

"Is silence then your new disguise?" He peered at her. "I preferred Mack for his better conversation."

What could she say? That she preferred the ease of being Mack to this discomfort?

"I hardly slept last night. Tell me, Meg, was your disguise only a trick to tease me?" Will said in a rush.

The accusation jolted Meg. "No, it was not! Violetta said so only to keep Thomas from becoming jealous. It was my idea to disguise myself as Mack. Mocking you was no part of my motive."

"What was your motive?"

"Was it not evident?" cried Meg. "I meant to help you find Davy and Peter. How could Long Meg do that?"

"But why did you feign to be my friend, who is as much a part of a man as his own heart?" Will struck his breast as he spoke.

"I only feigned to be Mack. I did not feign being your friend."

Will crossed his arms over his chest. "That argument does not acquit you."

Meg felt herself growing hot. "If you do not see the distinction, Will Shakespeare, you must believe that no woman can be a man's friend."

"A woman may be a man's wife or his mistress. A man only can be his true friend, his second self," argued Will, dividing the air with his hands.

"In that you are deceived," said Meg. "And may the devil take me, for I believed Mack was mine."

"Your friend was I, Meg de Galle. A woman!"

Will was silent, frowning like a child who thinks himself cheated of a prize.

"We ate and drank together, laughed and roamed the city in search of adventure, and aided each other in danger, did we not?" Meg demanded.

"I thought I did so with Mack, not Meg," Will protested.

"Of course," said Meg, exasperated. "Did you ever look closely at Meg? At *me*?" Meg stopped herself from pleading.

"I did. I noted your strength," said Will. "And I asked for Meg's help that very first night."

"Yes, but you and I know proper women do not run after thieves or thrash villains. We do not swear or even speak in public. Can you comprehend what freedom you men have that we are denied?"

"Being a woman does not constrain you now," Will said.

Meg grew aware of a creaking cart, a dog barking, people passing by. Did they mistake her and Will for quarreling lovers? If only an embrace were sufficient to cut through the misunderstanding between them!

"I have grown accustomed to the freedom of these limbs to move and these lips to speak as I please. But now I am only Meg again, which is almost more difficult than to be both Mack and Meg." She felt herself on the verge of tears.

"You played Mack's part ably," Will said grudgingly.

Meg managed a dejected smile. "No, for Jane and Violetta saw me fail, and James Burbage knew Mack for a woman the first time he saw me."

"Did he really?" said Will.

Meg peered at him closely. "When I declared at the trial that I was not Mack de Galle, you did not seem surprised."

"I played the lawyer's part well, did I not?"

"Aye, but that is not my point. How did you know? And *when*?"

"Old Nick Grabwill came to me the night before your trial and told me a strange story," said Will. "It was then that I knew."

"Did you not suspect earlier? Why did you never ask to see Mack's lodgings or insist on meeting him at the Boar's

Head? Did you ever wonder how Meg could have a twin brother identical in all features? Either you believed we were two, or you knew we were one and the same."

"Ask me no more, for I cannot tell you." Will's tone was plaintive.

"You can but you will not! I think it was you who played *me* for a fool." This possibility sent a wave of shame over Meg. She turned away and started across the road only to find herself surrounded by sheep. She shoved her way through their midst, shouting back at Will, "You wanted to see how far I would go just to be in your company. All the while you were deceiving me into thinking that I was deceiving you!"

"O what a tangled web you are weaving," cried Will. "Like a spider trying to trap me."

Will plowed through the sheep, scattering them. He reached Meg and took her by the shoulders.

"You wrong me with such accusations, Meg. I did wonder why Mack was so like you. I watched you at the inn and admired your strength, your bold manner, and your wit. But I did not know the truth for certain." He paused a moment. "And what if I did? You loved every moment you were in disguise. To be truthful, so did I."

So Will *had* known. It no longer mattered when; Meg was mortified all the same.

"Knowing that I was a woman, you let me debase myself with brawling and drinking?" she said, unable to meet his eyes. "How you must have laughed at my pretense of being a man."

Will put his hand solemnly to his breast. "No, I never

did. You made a better man than most of my sex. But *you* did laugh at *me*, when I came back with Davy's boots."

Meg smiled at the thought of Will with his paltry, ruined trophies. "Didn't you long to tell me of yours and Mack's adventures?"

Will raised his eyebrows. "There was no need, for you took part in them."

Meg buried her face in her hands. "O I am repaid for my deceit and fairly beaten at my own game." She felt Will's hands on hers and let him uncover her face.

"It was a game that required two players," he said and joined his palms to hers. Meg felt her heart pulsing all the way to her fingertips.

"Are we reconciled now? Friends again, despite my being a woman?"

"If you were both Mack and Meg, strength and fairness united in one person," said Will, looking up into her eyes, "then you would be this man's perfect mate."

"Will, I *am* both Mack and Meg. And I don't mean to seem coy, but methinks you are trying to woo me."

"Excellent creature, I am," he said, seizing her eyes with his own and holding her gaze.

Meg's legs turned to jelly. She wobbled, leaning against the fencerow to keep herself standing. Will leaned with her. Was he about to kiss her? Did she not want him to? His hand was touching the front of her neck where her pulse beat. It was almost more than she could bear.

"This is as dangerous as breathing the air during a plague," said Meg, winking to break Will's gaze.

"What do you mean? Is my breath so foul?" said Will.

"I mean you might infect me with longing," she said softly, knowing that she must walk no farther with him lest she be drawn, like a moon, helpless into his orbit. She thought of Violetta's wrist encircled by Valentine's hand. Of the Hathaway sisters Will had left to pursue his ambitions. To be held or to be released; both could cause hurt.

She slipped sideways and turned to face the city.

"Were you not on your way to Shoreditch also?" said Will.

"I was. But I am done with disguising." Meg's voice was barely above a whisper. "Tell Burbage I cannot join his company."

Will looked stricken. "But I have counted on this! If you do not go, then neither will I."

"You must, Will Shakespeare. For what else would you do?"

"I can study law. A lawyer feigns like an actor and lies as well as any poet."

"Foh! I know your ambitions. You would a hundred times rather be a lowly player than a lawyer of the Queen's Bench. Go on without me."

Will stood his ground. Were they about to have another argument? "And I know you would rather command the stage—as you did the streets and the law court—than wait upon drunkards at the Boar's Head Inn. Come, show the strength of your wit as well as your arm. Don't be afraid."

Does Will know me so well? Better than I know myself?

"Your will and your heart are one in this," he said with gentle urgency.

Meg was not used to heeding her heart, which hitherto had demanded so little of her. Was she strong enough to resist its sudden urges?

"You go, Will. Burbage has an idea for a play you must write. I will come and see it performed." How dull and faint that sounded.

"But it is *you* he wants in his company. Without you he won't hire me."

"Is that the reason I must accompany you?" Meg said. "Do you mean to use me for your own benefit?"

Will drew back with a hurt look. "Does a poet exploit his muse? Nay, rather he needs her. Meg, do not divide yourself in two; be one true friend of Will Shakespeare."

Meg felt her heart turning like a flower toward the sun. Her longing to be Will's friend *and* his muse was powerful. But could Will accept her as she was?

"Henceforth the one I must be is Meg the woman," she said firmly.

"And so you shall be. Do I not remain Will though I play Pyramus or Antony? So you can play a man's role and be no less a woman. You can feign Cleopatra or Caesar and still be yourself, Meg de Galle."

"What if Burbage will not let me be Meg? A player who is known to be a woman might bring trouble to his company."

"You said he knew your sex when he offered you employment," Will countered. "He saw what a good player you will make. I'll warrant you'll cause no more trouble than you can easily handle." He winked at her.

The sun had climbed to its apex, dispelling the frost into vapor. Will's words melted Meg's cold fear, making her warm and malleable like soft metal. Who would she become with Will at her side offering true friendship—and perhaps more?

It was time to act while she was filled with praise and confidence. *Now, before I lose my Will!*

She turned around in the road and with a sweeping motion of her arm said, "Let's dally no more in this common way, but hasten to Shoreditch without delay."

Will almost had to run to match his stride to hers.

Chapter 39

Meg's fears were unfounded. Both she and Will were welcomed into Burbage's company. His best player had suffered a concussion in a brawl and could not even remember his own name, so Will was needed to act as well as write plays. Burbage agreed to Meg's stipulation; thus all the players knew her for a woman and were as courteous to her as their rough natures allowed. Meg liked her fellows, especially Bumpass, the clown with the remarkable ability to produce a hundred different sounds by farting, and Wagstaff, a handsome youth who played all the women's roles. The boy was especially glad of Meg's presence, for he was getting a beard and thought himself ready for a man's role. Little Richard Burbage was his father's factotum. He took quickly to Meg, bringing her sweets and offering to do whatever she asked him. Around him Meg felt like a queen. The only fly in the ointment was Rankin Hightower, whose stage name belied his base origins as the son of a butcher. He fancied himself more talented than anyone, especially Will.

James Burbage kept Meg and Will close to him and daily

maligned the proprietors of the Curtain, a rival playhouse. "He is afraid of them luring us away," said Will to Meg. "That's how much he regards us."

"We must prove ourselves worthy of that regard," said Meg. She hesitated to believe their good fortune, which was compounded by the absence of William Burbage from the playhouse. Meg asked Bumpass where he had gone.

"Just before you fell in with our company, it befell that William and the master had a falling out," explained Bumpass, miming the act of stumbling.

Meg took up residence in a tiny cottage in Shoreditch while Will shared a room with one of Burbage's employees, a carpenter named Tom Makeshift. By night Will wrote new scenes and by day the actors rehearsed them, vying for the best lines and the most important parts. Only Meg made no demands, for she saw how tense Will was, how desperate to succeed. She memorized all the players' lines, her brain soaking up Will's words as a sponge soaks up water. She knew by listening when a line did not sound just right, but she never said anything to Will. Invariably he would change it.

Three weeks quickly passed and on the seventh day of November, heralded by trumpet and with flags waving atop the amphitheater, Will's *Tragedy of Cleopatra* saw its first performance. The galleries were filled and the groundlings stood shoulder to shoulder. Peering from behind the curtain Meg saw Burbage's wealthy patron, the Earl of Leicester, seated on a gilded chair on the stage. Beside him on stools sat Master Overby and Gwin, looking as proud as royalty. Will had insisted they be thus honored and admitted free of charge because Overby had been deprived of the income from Will's play.

There were several patrons of the Boar's Head in the audience. Violetta—for Meg still thought of her by that name—and Thomas Valentine waved from the second gallery. Among the groundlings stood Jane Ruffneck. Ned, Dab, and Grabwill Junior rested their chins on the stage. Meg longed to please them all, though her heart was jumping like a frog and she feared she might throw up.

When she stepped onstage as Cleopatra, wearing a wig of black hair, she heard the chanting start up: "Long Meg! Long Meg!" She held her queenly attitude for a long moment before speaking. Will entered, armed as Antony, and the Boar's Head crowd shouted: "Will! Will! Shake your spear!" Meg struggled to keep from smiling. Behind the curtain Burbage would be dancing a jig, for his new players were causing a sensation and the noble Leicester was a witness to it.

It was the final act. Antony fell on his sword. Bumpass and three centurions hoisted Will to their shoulders, carefully avoiding the sheep's blood he squeezed from a bladder onto the stage.

"*I am dying, Egypt, dying,*" Will said, moaning as they laid him on the platform where Cleopatra knelt. "*Give me some wine and let me speak a little.*"

Meg put a cup to Will's lips, and the red liquid spilled out again. She touched her lips to Will's forehead, then to his cheek. She could hear the audience snuffling wetly as if an ague had seized them all.

"*O quicken again with kissing! Had my lips that power, I would wear them out,*" Meg said and kissed Will, closing her eyes and thinking of anything but his lips lest she forget her next lines.

Will was borne away and Rankin strode onstage as the conquering Caesar. Loud booing greeted him. *"Caesar's a merchant that makes a prize of you,"* he said to Cleopatra with contempt. Meg knew he was supposed to say "Caesar's *no* merchant, to make a prize of you." She heard Will behind the curtain, fuming that he was debasing the noble Caesar. But she knew that for all Rankin's strutting, Cleopatra's would be the final victory.

"Give me my robe, put on my crown; I have immortal longings in me," she said.

Wagstaff as Iras minced up the stairs to the platform aloft, carrying a basket. Meg stooped as he put the crown on her head. From the basket she drew out the effigy of a snake. Hidden beneath the stage, Bumpass shook a gourd full of dried peas to moke the hissing sound that filled the amphitheater.

"O thou speak'st and calls great Caesar an ass, outdone in craftiness!" Meg said, imitating the serpent's hiss. She twisted the effigy in her hand to make it writhe. She saw Gwin's mouth open, a wide, dark O, and heard a hundred gasps as she brought the snake to the hollow of her throat.

"Peace, peace," she purred, as if imploring the audience. *"But see the baby at my breast, that sucks the nurse asleep. As sweet as balm its bite, as soft as air—"* With all eyes in the theater raised to her, she sank to the platform with her arms dangling over the stage below.

The rumor that a woman was performing at the Theatre proved a boon to business. The Puritans descended to decry bawdiness, gay apparel, and all forms of deceit, but their preaching and pamphlets only stirred up more interest in the play. The London authorities were powerless to enforce their prohibitions, for the playhouse was beyond the city limits. Nor did the queen show much rigor, for she was said to enjoy plays as much as anyone. Nevertheless a cautious Burbage posted his son at the door to warn him if someone from the Revels Office arrived. He might be a friend wanting to commission a performance or a foe bent on censorship. If the latter, Burbage would replace Meg with one of the other players, and the censor would depart scratching his head.

Between performances and rehearsals, Will and Meg were often in each other's company trying out their new friendship. Gradually their conversation grew easier. Meg told Will about her parents' misfortunes, her exploits with Davy and Peter, and her long-held secret, which had lost its power when she learned the crime was Roger's, not her mother's. Will talked about his family and described Stratford so vividly, Meg felt she knew the town. Once he spoke of the Hathaway sisters and when Meg grew silent, fighting jealousy, he changed the subject.

"Why don't I teach you to write and read?" he offered. "You can be my scribe."

"I would have to write very fast to pin down your quick words," said Meg, smiling. But she was delighted to let Will instruct her and enjoyed the hours they spent in the tiring room after everyone had left the Theatre. They bowed their heads together, sharing the candlelight, their ink-stained fingers sometimes touching as Will guided her hand.

Will was amazed. "How quickly you learn! I was right to prize your wit."

"I can't deceive you, Will! I've been copying letters on my own and teaching myself," she confessed. "I memorize the parts by listening and later match them to your written pages."

He drew back in surprise. "You don't need me then."

"O but I do, because I don't know when I make a mistake."

"And I need you for the same reason," he said, sighing.

Meg would put down her pen and listen while ideas sprouted like grass from Will's fertile brain. She watered the good ideas and plucked the weedy ones. This was what it meant to be a muse.

One day while Meg was doing an inventory of costumes, Will looked up from his writing and said out of the blue, "I miss my old friend Mack." He twirled a man's cap on the tip of his finger. "Do you?"

Meg was a little hurt. Why should Will miss Mack when he had *her*?

"No. It was confusing being Mack. I am more useful to you now, aren't I?" Not liking to beg for praise, she quickly added, "Give me that cap. It needs new feathers."

Will held up two buff jerkins and helmets trimmed with metal.

"Come, let's don this soldier's garb and seek out an adventure to feed my poet's fancy."

Meg saw the light of mischief in his eyes. She countered by tossing a wig and skirt in his direction. "*You* wear the disguise this time. I'll take you where you shall overhear enough privy news to pen a dozen scenes with Mistress Bicker and Goodwife Tattle."

Will threw the costume back at Meg. "I've heard women

gossipping all my life in Stratford. I kept a stall in the marketplace."

"That does not mean you know what it is to be a woman." Meg pressed the skirt against Will's chest. "I am your muse. I know what is good for you." She was good-natured but serious. "We'll stroll through Southwark as two doxies, and you shall witness firsthand how women endure men's fleering and abuse."

"But . . . but . . . ," Will stammered.

"Do you disdain to play the part of a woman?" she asked.

"I do not see the purpose in it," he blurted.

Would he never learn? "You lately told me I was as good as any man you knew," she said. "It was being Mack that made me a stronger Meg."

Will seemed confused. "Therefore I should become a woman to make me a softer Will?"

How could she explain the need? The sexes were not equal. For Meg to behave as a man was brave; Will had admired her for it. But the idea of Will as a woman was simply comical, even to Meg. Still, the reversal was only fair.

"Yes you should," she said firmly. "There's no harm in it."

Will only smiled. "Wherefore do I have you, Meg, if not to teach me what women want from us?" he said with such a gentle manner that Meg could not be angry with him.

At every performance of *The Tragedy of Cleopatra* the Theatre was filled. Barely a week after it opened a stroke of good fortune befell Burbage's company, sending Will and Meg to the Boar's Head to celebrate with their old companions. Any ill feeling over their departure seemed already forgotten. Gwin doted on Ned and Grabwill Junior as she once did Meg and Violetta. Meg cornered young Grabwill and made him understand that if he stole so much as a pie from the oven she would make him regret it. Jane reported that Roger Ruffneck had confessed to killing the priest, and Davy and Peter were still in prison. But Will was past caring about revenge, eager instead to describe the scene of his new triumph.

"Meg was still onstage being applauded, and I was in the tiring room with Burbage when Lord Leicester burst in," said Will.

"He was at three performances this week. Burbage was on tenterhooks the whole time," Meg added.

"Leicester demanded a play for the queen on the twelfth night of Christmas. 'This one is too tragical,' he said, 'dealing as it does with a defeated queen's suicide. But whoever penned it shall write a new one for me.'"

Recounting the story made Will flush with pleasure, which in turn made Meg happy.

"Burbage put his hand on my shoulder and said, 'Here is the author, my newest player, a very skillful man with words.'"

Master Overby thumped the table in approval. Will downed the rest of his ale before continuing his tale.

"Then Burbage promised Leicester a comedy of mistaken love and disguising, accompanied with song to delight Her Majesty."

Meg knew what Burbage was thinking. He had described to her the play he wanted Will to write. The plot would follow their late adventures.

Will winked at Meg and went on. "Burbage told Leicester

he had one who could act the woman's part so well the queen would not know whether to laugh or weep. Leicester nodded and said, 'He who plays Cleopatra, you mean.'"

Gwin squealed and pinched Meg's cheek with her fat fingers.

Meg forced herself to smile. Her heart pounded when she thought of performing before the queen.

"Does Leicester know Meg is a woman?" asked Violetta, a crease marring her happy brow.

Meg had asked Burbage the same question, and now she repeated his reply. "It matters not what Leicester knows. All that matters is the queen's pleasure."

Still, she worried. *And what if the queen is displeased?*

Will lunged at the opportunity for renown. But Meg felt turmoil. How could she perform the very deceits she had forsworn? Could she play herself and Mack, reenact her own life? She might as well go naked on the stage and proclaim her true feelings to all the world! But she must do it. She had a contract with Burbage and an obligation to the company. Will was also counting on her.

"You must give the lovers a happy ending like ours, Will," said Violetta, gazing at Thomas adoringly.

Meg was happy for them yet wistful. *I must think of her as Lady Olivia now.*

"Of course it will end in marriage, being a comedy," Will said.

He smiled at Meg, giving her a look so full of assurance it made her spirits rise and her cheeks turn pink. She was Will's treasured muse! He would not write a part too difficult or painful for her to play. Moreover he promised a happy ending to their tale. Meg would act out deceit and loss but also truth and the discovery of love. Who could fail to be over-joyed by the possibilities of art and life conjoined?

"Will, your play shall please the queen and so shall I," Meg said, reckless with sudden hope. "And if the queen dis-cerns my womanhood, she will be delighted to see one of her own sex on the stage. Is she not also a player? Her stage is the world."

Gwin nodded in amazement. "I remember when she was crowned. You said a woman could not rule England." She frowned at her husband.

"Women are capable of anything, my love," said Overby.

"Huzzah, Long Meg!" shouted Will. "To England's first woman player."

Why not? thought Meg. It followed common sense and per-fect reason that she, as well as Will, could pursue a life on the stage.

⤳ Chapter 40 ⤵

Shoreditch

Will swept clean the desk Tom Makeshift had built for him and moved it closer to the small window to catch the weak November light. He imagined the success that would greet his festive holiday comedy. The queen, Burbage said, loved music, masques, and star-crossed lovers to distract her from the careful business of state. A wise and witty female character was sure to please her as well. Burbage wanted the plot to concern a hero falsely imprisoned and his beloved who disguises herself as a lawyer to obtain his freedom. Will knew he could write such a play, for hadn't he already lived it?

Love's Logical Lawyer, he wrote at the top of the page.

Would anyone in Stratford believe his newfound fortune? A month ago he had been a penniless youth about to go to prison. Now his *Cleopatra* was pulling hundreds to the playhouse and the Earl of Leicester had commissioned a play. He was like the waxing moon, growing toward the day in January when he would shine full upon the queen herself. What if she rewarded him with a pension? Burbage might invite him to be a shareholder in his company. Fame and prosperity would overcome his father's disapproval once and for all.

Love's Logical Lawyer. The title promised dullness. He crossed it out and wrote *Love Disguised.* His pen scratched steadily. Makeshift snored in his bed. A mouse scuttled among the wood shavings, finding stuff for its nest. Will reread his opening scene and with a groan blotted every line. Where should he start then? With a simple ditty. *Lovers know no law/ But the rule of love.* An hour passed and he could think of no rhyme but "flaw" and "glove," which he considered unsuitable.

He wished Meg were beside him. She took seriously her role as a muse—when she was not teasing him. Sometimes he still thought of her as Mack even as he admired her long, golden hair, her ready smile, and the way her lithe figure moved on the stage. From her lips his words fell lightly, like notes from a lute. Hearing them, Will knew what was good and what he needed to revise. Sometimes Meg even suggested a fitter word or rhyme. He had never known such a clever woman. She could now read and write as well as any of Will's peers at Stratford's grammar school.

He had to see her. Quickly he covered the short distance to her cottage. It was almost midnight.

"Meg?" he whispered, tapping at her window. "It's Will."

He felt foolish standing there in the blackness and cold. This was something a lover unable to bear his solitude might do. His inner voice spoke up. *Well, do you love Meg?* Will shifted from one foot to the other, equivocating with himself. Though he was at Meg's cottage at midnight, his intentions were not what they had been in the Forest of Arden at midnight. *Are you certain?* "Yes," Will murmured. This was not a woman to be won in the usual way.

"Meg, are you awake?" He held his breath, listening. He thought he heard a stirring within. The shutter was flung outward and a sleep-touseled head appeared.

"Whatever are you doing here, Will Shakespeare?" Meg rubbed her eyes. She was wearing only a shift and exuding a warmth he could almost smell.

Will felt himself blush, despite the cool night. "I need your help," he said.

At once she was alert. "Is there trouble? Are you in danger?"

Will wished for any reason to embark upon a new adventure. He sighed. "No, my brain is stuck on a rhyme."

Meg rolled her eyes. "Surely it can wait until tomorrow."

"But I'm here now and we're both awake," he said as Meg pulled the shutter closed. "Listen, if only for a moment," he pleaded. Silently he counted to ten. "Please, Meg." How selfish he sounded! At twenty he would leave.

At fifteen Meg opened the window again. She had a blanket around her shoulders. She cocked her head sideways and waited.

Now Will felt foolish. He cleared his throat and began. "*Lovers know no law / But the rule of love.*" He beat the air with his hand. "Flaw? Glove? Above?"

Meg furrowed her brow. Her lips moved as she thought. Finally she said, "How about this? *Lovers know no law / But the rule of love: / Do not withdraw / At a slight rebuff.*"

"That suits the meter," said Will. He leaned on the window ledge. Another rhyme came to him. "*Through lips without flaw / Sings my turtledove,*" he said, wondering what it would be like to kiss Meg. Not on a stage before hundreds of onlookers but now, while they were alone in the darkness.

Will felt Meg's hands on his shoulders. Could she read his thoughts?

"Turtledoves do not have lips," she whispered and pushed him gently backward. Then with a shadowed smile she added, "*Will, despite the riposte / Know all is not lost!*"

Again Will found himself staring at Meg's shuttered window. He wondered if he had been walking in his sleep and dreaming the whole while. He returned home and sat at his desk, where his pen flew across the page as if inspired by the gods who wrought every change on earth and in the heavens.

He filled a sheet, turned it upside down, and wrote between the lines. Some banter between lovers. Two villains cursing. A poetic interlude between acts. He was like the great inventor Nature, ceaselessly contriving new shapes from old and new scenes from old words. When it was almost dawn he fell asleep with his head resting on the desk.

A few hours later he awoke and resumed writing, but his ideas were as sluggish as his sleepless brain. The pounding of Makeshift's hammer distracted him. His characters seemed cut from wood, not made of flesh and blood. How was he to transform his own life into art? Will tossed his papers into a pile of sawdust.

"How do you do that, Makeshift?" he said, gesturing toward a heap of wood. "Assemble a cabinet out of so many pieces without having to tear it apart and rebuild it over and over?"

Makeshift considered his hammer as if it had dropped from the skies into his hand.

"I can't even put a play together with two hands, a brain, and this pen," said Will, disconsolate.

Makeshift nodded. "That stub of a feather is useless as a tool."

"Ha! That's very good," said Will, reaching for his pen as a knocking sounded at the door. It had to be Burbage wanting to see the opening scenes of his play. Will leaped over a stack of wood and crouched behind it. "Tell him I've gone out!" he whispered.

Makeshift opened the door and Will heard a familiar voice.

"Please, don't strike me! I have a message for Will Shakespeare."

Will stood up. It was only Dab Nockney looking terrified at the sight of Makeshift's hammer. "This came to the Boar's Head not two hours ago."

Will recognized his father's handwriting. He unfolded the letter and read:

William, an urgent and personal matter compels me to summon you home. Delay not but come at once upon receiving this. Your father, Jn. Shakespeare.

What did this mean? Was someone in the family gravely ill? He was being *summoned*—was it another legal action? Had his father lost the Henley Street property? Were the Shakespeares about to be evicted?

Will reached into his pocket and drew out three shillings. "Dab, go hire me a good horse, not one with spavins. Makeshift, tell Burbage I will return within a week and show him the first act of my new play."

Will threw his clothes and belongings into a satchel, including the lawyer's handbook, which might prove useful. Next

he ran to Meg's cottage. She was seated before a window reading the poetic miscellany Will had given her. The sun streamed
in the window behind her, illuminating her hair like a crown
of gold.

"Come away with me, Meg," he said, breathless.

She stood up and the book fell from her lap to the floor.
"Now? Where?" Her hand touched her throat, the spot where
her blood pulsed. "What have you done, Will?"

"My father is tangled in some new trouble and needs me
to unravel it again," he explained, holding out the letter. "And
I need your wit to help to solve these woes."

Meg's hand dropped from her throat to her hip. "You
want *Mack* to come with you," she said. "And I have forsworn
being Mack."

She was right. Will's first thought had been that Mack
would accompany him to Stratford and lend him courage and
resourcefulness. But those qualities were . . . Meg's.

"*You* are my friend, Meg. I want you to come with me,"
Will said and found that he meant it.

"And disguise myself as Mack? For how else should I
travel alone in your company and keep my reputation? If you
arrive in Stratford with Meg de Galle, every tongue within
miles will wag right out of its mouth."

Will had not considered this. "How inconvenient that you
are a woman! Will you disguise yourself for my sake?" he
pleaded.

Now her lips tightened. He could see he had angered her.
She blinked rapidly and looked away.

Sudden desolation swept over Will. "Fie, fo, and fum! I do
not blame you for thinking me a knave and a woman-hater.

But I swear, Meg, I revere you as a goddess." His thoughts rushed headlong into words as true as any he had ever written. "I came straight to you, for you are the dearest friend of my heart. I cannot go even a day without the sight of you."

Meg looked at him. Tears marked her cheeks. She lifted her hands and placed her golden hair behind her shoulders like the sun shifting her beams away from him.

"Will, I am your eternal friend. But I will not go with you." She sought for words. "These . . . family matters you must settle alone. Your past is yours, not mine. The present only is ours." She broke off.

"And the future?" said Will.

Meg lifted her shoulders and smiled. "That is up to you."

Now was the time to say it. *I love you.* But the words seemed unsuitable. What he felt for Meg was not the giddy excitement Catherine caused him or the passion he spent on Anne. What should he call the deeper regard that now filled him, body and mind? Maybe this, and not what came before, was love.

There was only one way Will knew to test his feeling. He stepped close and ran his hands from the crown of Meg's head to her shoulders, tangling his hands in her hair. Gently he drew her down to him. He was aiming for her lips, but she tilted her head a wee bit and his mouth grazed her cheek instead. She did not offer her lips but neither did she pull away. She let her cheek, warm and damp, rest against his lips for several long breaths. Finally Will drew away. For the moment he was fully content.

"This is not 'farewell,' for I shall return anon," he said.

Meg reached up her hand and touched his lips. "Promise?"

Will tried to kiss her fingers but she didn't give him the chance.

"Do make haste," she said, tapping his chin. "You have a play to write for the queen and I intend to perform it."

Stern though she sounded, she smiled and blushed crimson like the sky at sunset. Or rather the sky at dawn, for surely this moment was a new beginning for them.

Beshrew the play, Will thought. *It's a sonnet I want to write.*

Chapter 41

Shottery

In November the fields of Hewlands Farms possessed a stark beauty as gray-green thistles and faded, flowerless stalks swayed in the wind. Thousands of finches flitted and chirped while gathering thistledown to line their nests. They were the last birds of the season to breed, for all the sparrows and wrens had fledged and flown away.

Anne Hathaway envied the simple finches their mates, their soft and happy nests, and their wings. She was also breeding. Of this she was now certain. Only she could not sing about it.

For two months she kept her secret even from Catherine. It was not hard, for since Will's betrayal they barely spoke. Though they shared a bed as usual, they slept with their backs to each other. But one morning Catherine came upon Anne retching behind the barn. She knew the truth at once, for there was only one reason for a healthy woman to vomit in the morning.

"You will have to be married now," Catherine said.

"No," Anne moaned.

"Why? Is the father already married?"

Anne shook her head. "Don't be a fool and lie with Gilbert, no matter what he promises."

Catherine ignored this. She stared at Anne's still-flat stomach. "Whose babe is it, then?"

"Whose but Will Shakespeare's?" Anne said, indignant. "I've been with no man before or since."

Catherine stiffened. "You got what you wanted, didn't you?"

"Are you still jealous?" said Anne, her voice rising. "You've forgotten Will."

"Will, I think, has forgotten *you*," Catherine said.

"He does not know about the baby. How could he? Not even his family knows where he is living." Anne sighed. "This is my burden to bear alone."

Soon Anne's stepmother suspected as well. "Are you with child?" she demanded. "Don't lie to me. I have borne six children and know the signs of breeding."

What was the point of lying? Her condition would become evident. Anne admitted she was carrying Will Shakespeare's child.

"That errant son of the ruined glover? Why not some prosperous and upstanding farmer whom it would not be a shame to marry?"

Anne knew her stepmother was thinking of Fulke Sandells, her former suitor. He was twenty years her senior! Who would marry an old man and risk being left a widow with all his children to raise? Such was Joan Hathaway's sorry plight, but it would not be Anne's while she had a voice to say nay.

"I will raise the child myself," said Anne.

"Not in this household! I'll not permit a strumpet and her bastard child to live under my roof." Spittle flew from Joan's lips.

"Our vows were as good as a contract," said Anne defensively. But she trembled.

The very next day her stepmother dragged Sandells into their business. He had been Richard Hathaway's friend and witnessed his will. Thus he bore a sense of duty toward the family.

"Fulke has been to see John Shakespeare and demanded that his son be brought home," said Joan. "The parties agree; Will Shakespeare must be made to marry you."

"Then let those agreeable parties scour all of London looking for him," Anne retorted, glad for once Will's whereabouts were unknown.

Joan smirked. "As it happens, Shakespeare lately received a letter from his son. He replied, ordering him home. Sandells posted the letter himself."

Anne's heart sank even lower. Once she had dreamed of marriage to Will. But he no longer wanted her. Now he was being haled home like an errant schoolboy to answer for their deed. What if he denied it? Could he still be forced to marry her? Under such circumstances how could either of them ever be happy? Will would blame Anne and grow to hate her.

That night she lay in bed with her back to Catherine and her knees drawn up to her chest.

"Do you condemn me too?" she whispered.

Catherine stirred. "I do not condemn you," she said. "It might have been me and not you, had I gone out that night."

"I am sorry for usurping your place in Will's heart," Anne whispered. "But see what sadness I have spared you."

Catherine let out a long, slow breath. "For all the world I would not be in your shoes," she said, touching Anne's hand.

Anne squeezed her sister's fingers. She dared to hope their bond could make her situation bearable. "Catherine?" she ventured. "If Will denies our contract and Joan evicts me, will you come and live with me and the child?"

Catherine sat up in bed, recoiling from Anne. "So shame and her sister must dwell together? What about my good name? I've a small enough dowry as it is; who will marry me then?"

Anne felt the familiar heart-sickness rise up, closing off her throat. She could not speak. Without looking at her sister she got out of the bed, pulled off one of the covers, and wrapped it around herself. Then she went out to sleep on the kitchen hearth, which was also hard and unforgiving yet still held some warmth.

~⌒ Chapter 42 ⌒~

Stratford

Will suspected none of these troubles as he rode toward Stratford on the fine gelding Dab had hired for him. He stopped for the night at an inn near Oxford and wished for some robust company as he ate and drank. Then his thoughts turned to Meg and how she seemed to him more womanly all the time, and he regretted not following up the kiss that had gone awry with a more proper one.

Arriving home in Stratford he stabled his horse in the mews. The familiar smells of urine and tallow greeted him but he didn't even wrinkle his nose, for London smelled far worse. He brushed the dust from his clothes and called, "Heigh! Is anyone about?"

Will's mother emerged from the house and hurried to embrace him. He was relieved to see she was not ill. Behind her stood Will's father, his cheeks surprisingly rosy.

"Good day, Father. The Burbage matter is settled, you know," he said.

His father did not even smile.

How hard it must be, Will thought, for him to acknowledge

that he has become indebted to his son! "I calculated how far my earnings will go toward recovering our lost assets; four pounds when my new play is finished and more if the Master of the Revels licenses it for—"

"Keep all your damned earnings, for you'll need every penny to make the Hathaway wench an honest wife!"

Will was stunned into silence. He had no idea what his father meant. Was his mind afflicted, though he spoke clearly? Then Will heard him say Anne Hathaway was with child. He heard him say she had named Will as the father.

Two months in London, and he had not the least inkling of this trouble!

"I can't, I . . . I *don't* believe it," Will stammered. Could a child result from his single encounter with Anne in the forest? If such was possible then yes, he could be its father. Unless Anne—no. He would not think that of her.

"Marry her," said his father. "That's your debt and your duty."

"I can't marry now," Will said. "How shall I afford a wife and child? I am but newly hired and have yet to prove myself. Everything depends on my next play." His heart sank, knowing this argument would never move his father.

"You *will* marry her," his father insisted. "It's a better match than you deserve."

Everyone knew the Hathaways were wealthy compared to many of their neighbors. Anne and Catherine's father had provided well for them in his will.

"Ah, now I see the matter clearly," said Will. "You expect me to pull you out of debt, not by honest labor but with Anne Hathaway's dowry."

"'Tis the quickest way," he muttered, looking away.

"The quickest way to ruin the Hathaways, that is. No doubt Anne would prefer the shame of being unwed to that of being a penniless Shakespeare laboring in this pisspot glover's shop." Will would have said more to hurt his father, but his mother laid a hand on his arm.

"Will, everything is mortgaged. We must sell this house. It will become an inn, and we will take a few small rooms in the back." Her voice was low, as if she were speaking of someone deceased.

Will pressed his hands to his forehead. He wanted to believe he was in the middle of a feverish dream. But he knew this trouble was real. And it was far worse than being robbed of twenty-five crowns. His family was near ruin. Anne was expecting his child. The neighbors were determined to see them wed. Marriage! Yesterday it was a plot device for a comedy. Today it was a prison in which they would lock him.

"Go see her now," his mother said gently. "Before they find out you are here."

The last thing in the world Will wanted was to face Anne Hathaway. He owed James Burbage and his patron a new play. He had promised Meg he would return. But how could he go back to London now? The news about Anne had turned his world upside down. Instead of gazing at the heavens above the Theatre, his eyes were fixed on the ground at his feet. He was mired in Stratford.

"You thought you got away, didn't you?"

Will looked up to see Gilbert leaning against the door, his arms crossed over his chest.

"I didn't know," Will protested.

"At least it was not the other one or I'd have to marry."

Will stared at his brother. "Have you taken up with Catherine?"

"What you leave behind falls to me," said Gilbert smugly. "All the work, Father's troubles, the shame."

"You dare to complain?" Rage rose in Will. "I've been robbed and beaten and almost jailed trying to settle that damnable debt to William Burbage."

Gilbert smirked. "Then you know a man deserves some pleasure for all his pains."

"A *man* does, but not a coxcomb like you," said Will. In an instant he and Gilbert were wrestling on the ground. Gilbert's fist struck Will's cheek and he tasted blood. But Will was stronger and managed to pin his brother beneath him.

"You can't come home and just take everything back!" said Gilbert, gasping for breath.

"Is *that* why we are fighting?" Will paused to spit out blood and dirt. "I don't want to be a glover. And as for that harpy Catherine, you may keep her. Anne is worth ten of her sister."

Giving his brother a final shove, Will got to his feet and brushed the dirt from his clothes. He turned away from Henley Street and started down the path to Shottery, filled with dread.

~☙ Chapter 43 ☙~

Shottery

Will hardly understood what moved him to defend Anne, but he knew what he had said to Gilbert was true. Anne was worth a dozen of Catherine. But that didn't mean he wanted to marry her. He needed to hear from her lips what was true and what was not. He thought of his ring lying against the soft skin of her neck and he shivered. The biting wind at his back hurried him toward Hewlands Farm. It stirred the withered stalks in the fields, sending up clouds of thistledown that floated through the air like snow unable to settle.

And there she was, meandering through the field. Though she was wrapped in a cloak with her head down, he recognized her gait.

Will had no idea what to say to her. He stepped behind a bush to collect his thoughts. She was approaching; in a moment she would see him and think he was hiding from her.

He came forward. "Anne, 'tis I." He reached up to take off his hat and realized he had lost it in the scuffle with Gilbert.

"I know. I saw you first." She smiled. There were little lines at the corners of her gray-green eyes.

"Why did you pretend not to see me?"

"I wondered if you would turn away from me." She lifted her hand to shade her eyes.

Will stepped to the side so she would not have to look into the sun. He took her hand and brought it down, held it in his own. It was small and cold. He wanted to ask, *Is it true?* But when her eyes met his and he saw such regret and fear there, he knew.

"Believe me, Will, I did not want this to happen. It was not a ruse to trap you into marrying me, no matter what my sister says. I did love you."

"Do you still?" Will blurted out.

"Why should I say yes and add to my own grief?" She paused. "Did you love me?"

"Let's not play games with each other," Will said gently. "What are we going to do?"

"I don't know," she said. "Sit with me and let us talk."

There was a fallen tree nearby and Will led her to it, still holding her hand.

"What happened?" she asked, touching his swelling cheek.

Will groaned. "A fight with my flap-mouthed brother." He didn't tell her what they had argued about. They sat with the sun warming their backs as the wind fell to a mere whisper in the dried grass. Will tried to describe London to Anne, who had never been outside of Warwickshire. He told of his adventures with Mack, though neglected to mention Mack was a woman, an omission that made him feel a little guilty.

"This Mack sounds like a merry friend," said Anne. Her silvery laughter ended in a sigh. Though they sat shoulder to shoulder for warmth, there was something between them holding them apart. Will realized it was the babe growing inside Anne. It was also Meg, whom he had nearly kissed not two days ago.

"I have little news save gossip of poor Anne Hathaway, whose trouble is everybody's business." She said this without self-pity. "So be careful, Will. Once Fulke Sandells knows you are hereabouts, he'll be escorting us to the nearest church."

"I'm not afraid of Sandells. No man will keep me from my ambitions. I've just been hired to act and write plays for a London company." Saying this, Will felt awkward and self-serving, but he had to let Anne know of his situation.

The wind lifted Anne's brown hair and scattered its strands. Her silence rebuked him.

"Neither of us wants to be married, do we?" said Will.

"I do want a husband, but not one who is unwilling."

"And I won't be forced to marry!" said Will in some agitation.

"Nor will I." Anne stood up abruptly. "So marriage is not for us."

"We have taken different paths, Anne."

"*You* took a different path. I am still on this one." She lifted her foot and planted it again. "And I am not free to choose another."

Here was proof of Meg's assertion that women were less free than men. Will could walk away from the child. Anne could not. He stood up but Anne's words stopped him before he could take a single step.

"Why did you come here, Will? Your presence gives me hope, which your words then deny."

"I did not know." He gestured to her lap. "My father summoned me about a legal matter, or so I thought."

Anne looked at him despairingly. "If you had known of the baby—"

The baby. She had spoken of it, finally. Will seemed to see a newborn thing writhing in her arms. *Her baby and his.*

"If you had known, would you have come back?" Her voice became a whisper.

Will could not say yes, nor could he with certainty say no. His eyes began to sting and he realized his cheeks were wet with tears. He sat back down and wiped his eyes with his forearm.

"Did our vows of love mean nothing?" Anne said, staring at her hands in her lap. "I am the same woman who spoke them and you are the same man, yet everything has changed."

"You deserve better than me," said Will. "I fear I would be no good husband, for I have too much mischief and longing still in me." His voice broke with tears. He had not wept like this since he was a boy and cut his arm and saw his own life-blood pouring out.

"Long ago I loved someone," Anne said. She told Will how David Burman had died and that she slept with Will to seize a moment of happiness before it fled. "But I learned I cannot hold someone who is destined to leave me. Therefore go, Will Shakespeare. I will not keep you here."

Sorrow, Will saw, was deep in her bones. It made her strong. Her child would also be strong. He admired Anne yet could summon no words that would not sound like base flattery. She was not the same Anne who had flirted with him, tricked her sister, and lain with him for the purpose of delight. It would take him longer than a November afternoon to know this new Anne.

When Will did not move, Anne said, her voice rising with hope. "If you decide to stay, I'll not cling or be jealous."

Her kindness was too much to bear. He pushed against it. "How can I forgo all my opportunities in London and remain here? You know how miserable I would be."

"Go then, and let me deal with my neighbors," she said. Will heard the disappointment in her voice. "I will say we never vowed our love." She forced a smile. "Perhaps Sandells will marry me. He once wanted to."

Will knew she said this not to make him feel guilty, but to assure him she would be well without him. He stood up again. How should he bid her farewell? No words would suffice. A kiss might mislead her and fail to convey his undefinable passion: his strange sorrow at the loss of her, Anne. Or was it joy he felt to be granted his freedom? A poet he was and yet could not describe his own heart or express its love. For a kind of love it surely was, to long to be as noble and wise as another person.

In the end he said nothing. He kissed his hand to Anne as he withdrew, holding her gaze until she looked away. Then he turned toward the long shadows cast by the setting sun. He began to run as if trying to overtake the dark image of himself.

By the time he reached Henley Street dusk had swallowed every shadow. He saddled up his gelding and took to the road. At Daventry he would find a room for the night and give a false name in case Sandells or his father came searching for him. Perhaps he would ride through the night. Burbage was expecting a play.

Meg, too, would be waiting for him. What should he say when she asked about the crisis in Stratford? Would he lie to her and say nothing about Anne? She was so perceptive he doubted she could be fooled. And think of the consequences of his lie being discovered!

"Fie upon Truth, who in time always shows herself," he said to the night.

Anne's face, bearing a sad smile, floated into his mind. Lying to Meg would doubly disown Anne. Did two lies make one truth? No. Two vows made one marriage though. *The ring*, he thought. *I did not get my ring back from her.* He didn't notice her wearing it. The thought came and left again like a curious creature in the night.

He tried to turn his tired mind to the play and plan it scene by scene, but his troubles distracted him.

He decided to tell Meg the truth: that Anne was carrying his child and had chosen to raise it alone rather than compel Will to marry her. Meg must admire Anne's courage. But what would she say of him? He could guess. *You are no better than Roger Ruffneck, who abandoned his wife and child for his own vile pleasures.* The champion of wronged women and neglected orphans, Meg would have good reason to despise him. She would say the child's misfortune—its bastardy—was his fault, for he had the means to prevent it and did not.

Will remembered as a child seeing a round-bellied woman in a white sheet standing before Holy Trinity Church, her head bowed in shame as the preacher expounded upon her sins. Would Anne suffer the same humiliation and be called a harlot by everyone in the village? It was too harsh a word for one whose only fault was to love Will unwisely. He could keep her from the shame. If he married her.

The gelding had halted in the road while Will's thoughts ran every which way. Will snapped the reins but the stubborn horse did not move. He leaned forward and rested his forehead on its rough mane.

Fulke Sandells must be fifteen years older than Anne. If she married him she would become mistress of his hog farm. Would Sandells be a kind father to her child? To *Will's* son? For surely it would be a boy and might even resemble him. But if he chanced to see Anne and the boy, he could not call him "son." If Anne did not marry, the boy would have no one to call "Father." He would be a bastard. "Whoreson," they would shout at the boy, a word harder than a stone. Was there such a word for him, Will? Varlet. Vile knave. Not for getting Anne Hathaway with child but for leaving her to face the consequences alone.

Will would be nineteen years old when Anne bore their child. *I have too much mischief and longing still in me.* That was his excuse for why he could not be her husband. Was there any time of life or any place of abode free from mischief and longing, trouble and desire? He would be in trouble for certain once Meg discovered why he fled Stratford. As for wooing her, that seemed impossible now, for Anne and the child, though absent, would stand between them like the wall that separated Pyramus and Thisbe. Meg, the best kind of woman, deserved a better man than himself.

Will imagined Anne holding the boy's hand as he learned to walk. The child would totter and he, Will, would take his other hand and steady him. His heart swelled up at the thought. But what if the child was a girl? She would have Anne's strong nature and freckles across her pretty nose. How could he live on and never touch the face of his daughter? Or look at his own face in a glass and not wonder if its features were copied in a son who longed to call him "Father"?

If you stay, I'll not cling to you. What more could Will ask? Anne's generosity shamed him. Would it be so terrible to live near Stratford and raise their child together? One babe would not be much trouble. He might write plays as well in Stratford and send them to Burbage, visiting London from time to time. When the child was old enough and if Anne remained healthy, they would move to the city. It seemed to him possible and even desirable to have a piece of both worlds, Stratford and London. As Antony had Rome and Egypt, knew his duty yet satisfied his desire.

A night owl sounded, interrupting Will's reverie. He tugged the reins. The gelding obeyed his hand and turned around. At Hewlands Farm Anne waited beneath the overhanging thatch of the cottage. She led Will to the barn, where they lay together on fresh, sweet hay. Will found his ring still around her neck and, lifting the ribbon over her head, placed the ring on her finger and said he would marry her.

~ Chapter 44 ~

Shoreditch

"Where the devil is Will Shakespeare? He owes me a play!"

A week had passed since Will's departure and James Burbage was plucking his beard hairs in frustration. Leicester would be coming soon to observe the progress of the new play. But there was no new play.

"He will return anon," said Meg, trying to reassure him. "This play is everything to him. Nothing will keep him from finishing it."

When a second week went by Meg began to worry. Had some terrible accident befallen Will? John Shakespeare's money problems would not keep him away so long. Perhaps someone else was delaying Will. Could it be the rural lass who once deceived him with her charms? Were they even now dallying together, wrapped in a warm cloak against the cold? Meg dismissed the jealous thought. She wanted to believe Will was simply struggling to write. He tended to put off what he was reluctant to do. How maddened she had been by his last-minute preparations for the court case! But writing this play to please Burbage and the queen was all his ambition.

When Will's letter finally arrived, Meg read with dismay and grief that the country lass was expecting Will's child. *It can't be true!* She thought of Will's cheek pressed against her own and his promise to return. He wrote he was contracted to Anne and they would marry at once. *But he doesn't love her! I thought he loved me!* How well they knew each other, she and Will, how close they had become even without sharing a bed. Her longing for him pained her, while his lightness roused her to anger. She gripped the page, almost tearing it. "Who is the fickle deceiver now, Will Shakespeare?" she said, her voice breaking. Hot tears blurred her vision. She dashed them away with her wrist and read: *You must know that I never suspected Anne's condition all the while you and I were friends.*

"Is that supposed to comfort me?" she wailed. Rather it made her feel twice spurned, for Will wrote as if their friendship was over.

Meg tried to read between the lines. Will was marrying Anne without even posting banns. Was such haste necessary to prevent him from running away again? The letter conveyed nothing of the high-spirited, ambitious Will she knew. Its tone was melancholic. In closing he appealed to Meg: *Speak kindly of me to Burbage; say I have been waylaid by the unexpected but will complete the play anon.*

"Anon. How soon is that?" Meg shook the letter. "Because you are too cowardly to write to Burbage yourself, I must tell him?"

With her usual determined stride Meg set out for the Theatre, taking a roundabout way to give herself time to think. She wanted to blame someone. Will, for being weak. Anne, for deceiving and ensnaring him. But she, Meg, had also deceived Will. Was anyone capable of truth? Of constancy? *I am; I will always be your true friend!* Will was inconstant but generous, loving whoever was close at hand and forgetting all else. She could not envy Anne being married to such a man. In truth he was not much more than a boy. Now with a wife and soon with a child to support. Would he have to take up the occupation he hated, that of a glover? When would he find the time to write plays? She must pity him, but could she forgive him?

She found Burbage in a dither and the actors idly playing cards, for they had nothing to rehearse.

"You say he absconded? With a wife?" said Burbage in disbelief.

"He promises to complete the play," said Meg.

"We shall not see it anytime soon, for what man puts his nose to the grindstone when his master is a hundred miles away?" Burbage groaned. "Especially one distracted by a new wife."

"Will is wedded?" said Bumpass. "Then his pen is now put to other purposes!" He thrust his hips forward, causing Wagstaff and the others to laugh.

Meg ignored them. "I thought this was all his desire," she said to Burbage, spreading her arms wide. "This playhouse, these players—"

"And you," said Burbage. "We all thought—"

Meg put up her hand to silence him. "No," she whispered.

What Meg had wanted from Will was more than what anyone might think. She wanted to be his lifelong friend. Now that was impossible. She wondered why the duties of marriage must eclipse the delights of friendship. Would there ever come a time when weddings resulted from friendship, not fleshly weakness?

"He will not disappoint us," said Burbage grimly. "He dares not."

"If he is writing anything, 'tis a sugared sonnet," said Hightower with a disdainful wave of his hand. "All posies and pearls and unmanly sentiment."

Wagstaff said, "He is taking inventory of the lady's charms, but not with ink and paper."

"Silence, you prating fools!" shouted Burbage. "Twelfth Night is the sixth of January. Tomorrow December begins and I. Have. No. Script!"

Everyone fell silent. Meg knew they feared losing the coveted opportunity to perform for the queen.

"Perchance your Will has written some scenes already," said Burbage. "Go to his room and see what you can find."

Meg disliked the idea of going through Will's belongings, but for the sake of Burbage and his company she decided to do it. She followed the carpenter to his lodging. Will's desk was cleared. He had left little of himself behind, not even a book. She lifted the mattress and found some soiled stockings and a pair of long-fingered gloves made of supple white leather and lined in satin. They were nothing like the small braided ones Will had given to Mistress Overby when he first arrived at the Boar's Head. Meg slipped her hand inside. The glove was cool, the fit snug. The stitches in the crooks between the fingers were uneven. Clearly the maker had executed them with difficulty. Had Will sewn these gloves with his own hands? In her mind's eye she saw his short, ink-stained fingers. A pen suited them better than a needle. Meg put on the other glove. She felt in her bones that they had been made for her, that Will had meant for her to keep them.

Meanwhile Makeshift was rummaging on the floor. He stood up and thrust a handful of blotted, crumpled papers at Meg.

"If he had laid plans in his head before scratching away with his pen, he wouldn't have wasted so much paper," said Makeshift. "I wouldn't saw a single plank without knowing what I was building."

Meg took off the gloves and set them aside. She examined the papers, which were covered on both sides with crabbed handwriting. Sawdust spilled from the creases and drifted to the floor.

"If I take these, it's not stealing, is it?" she said more to herself than to Makeshift.

"No, for I heard him curse what he wrote and call it trash," said the carpenter. He scratched his head. "But those nails, though they be on the floor and I curse when I step on them, are not trash but useful to me. Take them and you would be a thief."

Meg assured the carpenter she would not touch his nails. She straightened the pages and went back to the Theatre. Burbage had gone home, where she found him standing before his hearth staring at the pantofles on his feet while his son played with the dog.

"You know as well as I do, he is not coming back," said Burbage, glancing up at Meg as if hoping she would contradict him.

"He will come back, Father," said Richard. "He promised to write a play about a king just for me."

"He's got ten years," said Burbage, "for it will be that long until you are man enough to play a king." He sighed. "No, 'tis tomorrow that concerns me. I have a meeting with Leicester and naught to show him."

"Will did make a start," said Meg, handing Burbage Will's jumbled writings. "He called it *Love Disguised*."

Burbage took the pages from Meg and read quickly through them.

"Not one of the player's parts is complete. Scenes are only half-written," he said in dismay. He regarded Meg with a furrowed brow. "But *you* know the plot."

Meg did. It was her story, after all.

"You and Will worked side by side."

Meg saw where Burbage's thoughts were tending. "I am no poet," she said, shaking her head. "My skill with words is slight compared to his."

"I'll send to Oxford for someone to help you. Poets there are as plentiful as partridges."

"And their wits are smaller than a bird's brain!" Meg protested. "They will turn Will's lively scenes to dumbshows and his comedy to dry philosophy." She was echoing Will, who had once compared scholars in their libraries to dead men in tombs.

Burbage shook the papers in front of her face. "What other choice do I have?"

Meg understood his desperation. Bold measures were called for. She took a deep breath. "Let me go to Stratford and persuade Will to return until this play is performed."

Burbage tugged at his beard. "It does not behoove us to beg," he said. Meg could see that beneath his distress, he was also hurt by Will's departure.

"I need a play now. It must be *this* plot. You understand?" His look was pleading. "Wagstaff will have to do for the hero, though I prefer your Will."

"Master Burbage, do not refer to him as 'my Will,'" Meg blurted out. "For he does not and never did belong to me."

Burbage gave her a wary look. "I think you protest too much. I am not easily fooled. If you discouraged his attentions and drove him off, I am inclined to be angry with you."

"I promise it was no word or deed of mine that made him leave," she said.

Burbage raised his eyebrows. Meg saw he had guessed the truth. "Ah! He had a prior duty, a very pregnant one that prevented your love."

"I tell you I did not love him." Meg felt her voice falter.

"But you do," he said softly. "For friendship, my dear, is the most enduring love, long outlasting the swift-burning passion inflicted by Cupid's darts. Not even absence can destroy it."

"You are almost a poet," said Meg, smiling weakly. "*You* finish Will's play."

"And you are a better match for Will Shakespeare than some country wench. I'll wager you exceed her in beauty, virtue, and especially wit."

"Do not forget length," said Meg, feeling secretly pleased. No one had ever remarked upon her beauty before her height. But this was no time for flattery and preening. "Give me Will's play and let me read it through," she said, snatching the pages.

At her cottage Meg pored over the work by the light of a small lamp. With painstaking care she deciphered Will's careless hand and every troublesome word. Reading the scenes and fragments, she could almost hear Will's voice. She recognized Davy Dapper, Violetta, and Justice Littlewit. Meg herself was on the page, tearing off her disguise and saying to the hero, *I am no longer Mack; I am only Meg.* Will had not even changed her name. But elsewhere the hero said to his beloved words Meg did not remember hearing: *I have got my wish and you, your Will. So let us kiss and love each other still.* Had Will said this to Anne?

Her lamp flickered and consumed its last drop of oil. Meg sat in the dark, her bosom aching. Will was gone from her life. He had briefly trod the stage with her, then exited, leaving Meg standing alone. But there was no applause, for the play was not over. Indeed it was barely begun. Why should she not go on with it? So many parts she had played in her sixteen years. She started out as little Meg Macdougall, who became an orphan and a thievish boy. Then she was a tavern maid, her own twin brother, an avenger of injustice, and a lawyer. She became the friend of Will Shakespeare. Now she was becoming an actor. She had even played a queen, Cleopatra.

Meg smiled, remembering Will's confusion when she had said, *I am not Mack; I am only Meg.* Now it struck her—there was no such person as "only Meg." She was everyone she had ever been or pretended to be. All her roles were as much a part of her as her long arms and legs and her mind with its myriad thoughts and desires. Within herself she now identified a longing that must be unique, for no one else stood where she did at this moment, brought hither by circumstances that were hers alone. No one had seen with her eyes, spoken with her tongue, or imagined her thoughts. No one had known Will Shakespeare the way she knew him.

She realized she could see not only what Will had written, but also what was missing. She knew what was necessary to make the play complete. The awareness was like a bud that heralded a flower, fruit, seeds, and a whole tree. Meg leaped to her feet. Despite the late hour she ran back to Burbage's house and pounded on the door. He opened it wearing a night-cap, beneath which his eyebrows lifted in hope.

"*Love Disguised,*" she said, panting. "The name is apt. The pieces are there."

"I already know that." He sagged with disappointment. "I cannot sleep. What shall I tell Leicester?"

"Tell him the promised play shall be finished in time. We are in the game together, you and I, Wagstaff, Bumpass, and all the company." Meg waved her arms in a circle. "Even Rankin Hightower will not disdain to be part of this endeavor."

Richard appeared behind his father, rubbing his eyes. "Is there a part for me, Meg?"

"Yes. There is a stable boy. You might also play a young thief," said Meg. Richard was a well-featured child, she realized. In ten years he would indeed make a fine actor.

Faced with Meg's sudden exuberance, Burbage stepped back. "But who will finish it?" he said.

"Fear not. By hook or by crook, by Will or by me, come hell or high water it will be done. Give me a pen, ink, and new paper. Some wit besides my own. A horse perchance; I'll ride to Stratford in my thoughts." Meg's mind overflowed. She hardly knew what she was saying.

"Can you really finish Will's scenes?" Burbage's tired eyes grew bright again.

"Conceived and partly written is more than halfway to birth. I am no Shakespeare, but my will is strong and my words as true as angels," she said.

"I knew there was profit to be had." Burbage rubbed his fingers together in anticipation of the gold coins. "And much delight too, when you play the woman's part."

The woman's part. Meg knew that did not include speaking on a stage. Or seeking adventure, pursuing villains in the street, and pleading before a judge. In ordinary life, a woman's proper part—unwritten but set in stone—was marriage, subordination, and silence. This was Anne Hathaway's destiny. Maybe it pleased Anne, but it would not satisfy Meg.

"I'll play a woman, a man, or any part you provide me, and do my utmost to please. The queen herself shall reward us all beyond what we imagine or deserve." She winked at Burbage. "As long as I am Meg, so shall this be."

Burbage rubbed his hands, smiled, and held up a finger. He left her standing there. In a moment she heard the lid of a box slam. Burbage returned carrying a portable writing desk with papers sticking out.

"Here is everything you will need."

"I'm out of lamp oil," she said.

"Take mine. Richard, light her way home." Burbage shoved the half-asleep boy out the door.

Meg hurried after Richard, clutching the desk to her chest. It was so cold she could see her breath in the air, but she burned inside like a furnace. In the dark sky a million stars twinkled while the rest of creation slept below: birds, fish, lovers, dreamers, and even the night thieves. The moon was a narrow crescent, a smile on the face of heaven. At Meg's cottage Richard placed the lamp on the table. Its flame cast shadows that leaped and flickered like ideas eager to take form, like players in the wings waiting to come onstage.

Meg sent the tired boy home. She opened Burbage's writing desk, took out the pen and the jar of ink. She laid out Will's pages before her, smoothed them flat. She was ready to begin. But for one thing.

The gloves were on her bed, two white shapes in the dim light. Laying down the pen, she reached for them, pulled their softness over her fingers. Took a deep breath and caught her lower lip in her teeth. She picked up the pen again and with Will's hands holding her own, Meg began to write.

Postscript

March 1583

Sonnet to *M. M.* by *W. S.*

I can't deny Anne hath a way with me,
And I had mine with her, though by her leave,
The consequence whereof, 'tis plain to see;
I relinquish thee, and to her cleave,

Yet not forswear ambition or thee deceive,
My friend—both man and maid, soul's twin!—
But from thee both a while myself bereave,
T' bestow heart's wealth on wife and kin.

In time my useless wit shall rise again,
With mem'ries of thee made strong, and conceive
Brave heroines, offspring of this pen,
Disguised for love in plots that interweave.

Thus our lively deeds and loves I'll use.
Tho' Anne be my wife, thou Meg art my Muse.

~Author's Note~

Love Disguised is a work of fiction, built on a few solid facts and fleshed out with airy imagination. While my earlier novels *Ophelia* and *Lady Macbeth's Daughter* reimagine *Hamlet* and *Macbeth*, this is an original story featuring Will Shakespeare himself before he became a renowned playwright. Every author's youth provides experiences that are later shaped—not always consciously—into art. This novel plays with that premise, inventing a youth for Shakespeare by looking backward from his best-loved comedies. Those who know his comedies might recognize elements of them here. Readers who are new to Shakespeare can enjoy this story on its own terms. If this novel were a play, it would be called a "city comedy," for it deals with everyday life in London and often satirizes its citizens.

What are the facts behind my fiction? We know a fair amount about Shakespeare's early life. He was born in 1564 and went to Stratford grammar school, which is still standing. There he would have studied the poetry of Ovid, which he loved. His father was a glovemaker and former alderman of Stratford who ran into financial troubles in the 1570s. John Shakespeare owed a debt to William Burbage, one of his tenants. No one knows if this Burbage was related to James Burbage, owner of the Theatre in Shoreditch where Shakespeare got his start in the 1590s. But for the sake of the story I assume they were brothers, and that Will traveled to London to settle the debt, where he met the theatrical Burbage and felt the first stirrings of his ambition. (Later, in 1598, Burbage lost his lease on the Theatre, and his men—Will included—dismantled the building, ferried the wood across the Thames, and used it it to build the Globe Theatre associated with Shakespeare's greatest plays.) Before such playhouses were built, plays were performed in innyards. There were several inns named the Boar's Head, one located right where I have placed it just east of Aldgate. It was first used as a playhouse in 1557.

We don't know what occupied William Shakespeare between the time he left school in 1578 and turned up on the London theater scene around 1592. Scholars call these the Lost Years, because documentation is extremely scarce. At the time I have set this story, young Will was most likely an apprentice to his father. He was a long way from writing his first plays, but he surely knew Ovid's tale of Pyramus and Thisbe (translated by Arthur Golding) and the history of ancient Rome from his schooling. Some of the verses my Will writes are my own invention; others are adapted from *Midsummer Night's Dream* and *Antony and Cleopatra* to suggest very early drafts by a talented but inexperienced writer.

This is a documented fact: in November of 1582, eighteen-year-old Will married Anne Hathaway of Shottery, who was twenty-six and pregnant with his child. A bond, or assurance of the marriage, was posted by Fulke Sandells, a neighbor of the Hathaways.

It surprised me to learn (from Germaine Greer's book) that Anne Hathaway had a younger sister, Catherine, who was Will's age. I wondered if both sisters had set their sights on Will. This gave me the idea for the rivalry between them that culminates in the "bed trick" (see chapter 6), a dramatic convention of the time. Incidentally, vows spoken between a man and a woman, followed by consummation, constituted a legal marriage, though a somewhat irregular one. (Deception might complicate the matter.)

I employed several conventions of Elizabethan comedy. Perhaps the most obvious one is disguise: Meg pretends to be her brother, Mack, in order to befriend Will more freely. (No virtuous woman would freely roam about the city, except in the company of a male relative.) We may wonder how characters in disguise managed to pass undetected, but the illusion must have been convincing because audiences loved it. Disguise was common onstage anyway, for young men acted the female roles because women were prohibited from the stage. Or so everyone assumes, though I haven't found any mention of an actual law to that effect. I think it possible—and some Shakespeare scholars agree with me—that women did act onstage (probably pretending to be boys pretending to be women). Imagine the gender confusion! (Thank you, Ellen Mackay, for our stimulating conversation on the subject.)

There is evidence that women in men's clothing and men in women's clothing did roam the streets of London, causing controversy. Satirists like George Gascoigne, writing in 1576, and Philip Stubbes, writing in 1583, denounced the wearing of doublets and jerkins by women as an extravagant fashion or worse, a sign of degeneracy. In 1620 two pamphlets were published, *The Man-Woman* and a reply, *The Womanish Man*, criticizing those who dressed and behaved like members of the opposite sex. In making Meg a cross-dressing heroine, I justified her behavior on the basis of her difficult past and her desire for freedom as well as secrecy.

I drew inspiration for Long Meg from two sources. One is *The Life of Long Meg of Westminster* (1635). Long Meg was a legendary figure born during the reign of Henry VIII, the subject of ballads and a play performed in 1590 but now lost. The second source is a 1662 account of *The Life and Death of Mrs. Mary Frith.* Born around 1580, Frith was "a very Tomrig or Rumpscuttle [who] delighted and sported only in boys' play and pastime." Known as Moll Cutpurse, she went to plays dressed in men's clothing and was reputed to be, as her nickname implied, a thief. In 1608 Thomas Middleton and Thomas Dekker wrote a play called *The Roaring Girl*, with Moll Cutpurse as the main character, a prankster and defender of women against the slander of men. Most comedies end in marriage, but Moll vows she won't be married until honesty and truth reign—which is to say, doomsday.

Like Portia in Shakespeare's *Merchant of Venice*, Long Meg takes the role of a lawyer. Although much has been written about Shakespeare and the law, finding out how an actual case was prosecuted in his day is no easy task. The handbook Will uses is an invention based on other sources. Shakespeare himself, judging from the courtroom scenes in his plays, was more interested in mocking the law than in representing it realistically. I'm grateful to Luke Wilson for his "legal advice" and terminology. Ultimately the legal scenes reflect what I was able to tease out of my reading on English common law, which was slow to change. Early modern England was a very litigious society and the education of lawyers not so formal as it is today, so it's likely that a modestly educated man like Will would be capable of defending himself or an acquaintance in a legal matter.

It is possible to get a sense of what London was like at the end of the sixteenth century by reading John Stow's *Survey of London* (1598) together with the fascinating Agas map, made between 1561 and 1570 (reprinted in *The A to Z of Elizabethan London*). It shows every church and street and gate, details such as cows, archers, and clothes drying in the fields, the steps leading down into the Thames River, armaments outside the Tower of London, and the great high houses along the London Bridge.

But don't go to London looking for the city of Shakespeare's day. It is completely overbuilt by modern London, though artifacts and displays in the Museum of London and in the Globe Theatre Museum are like tickets to travel back in time—so are the many sites associated with Shakespeare in and around Stratford-upon-Avon. If you have the good fortune to visit when these sites are not crowded, you can question the historical interpreters to your heart's content, wander among the foxgloves in Anne Hathaway's cottage garden, and even hear the cuckoo sing, announcing the coming of summer.

In such a setting it's not hard to imagine that Will Shakespeare really did go to London in 1582 to settle his father's debt, met the cross-dressing Long Meg of the Boar's Head

Inn, and embarked on adventures that drew them closer than the best of friends. Why not?

I am grateful to so many people who have helped make this a better book than it would have otherwise been. Thanks to Melanie Cecka, for her expert editorial guidance; to Michelle Nagler and Brett Wright, for bringing this project to completion; to Ken Wright and Michele Rubin for being in my corner and Susan Cohen, my safety net at Writer's House. To Regina Flath, Jill Amack, Beth Eller, Katy Hershberger, Erica Barmash, and Patricia McHugh, who make and market such beautiful books at Bloomsbury. And to Rob, David, and Adam, for indulging my whims and making me laugh.

~⊙ For Further Reading ⊙~

Greer, Germaine. *Shakespeare's Wife.* New York: Harper
  Collins, 2009.
Picard, Liza. *Elizabeth's London: Everyday Life in Elizabethan
  London.* New York: St. Martin's, 2004.
Powell, Thomas. *The Attorney's Academy.* London 1623.
Prockter, Adrian, and Robert Taylor. *The A to Z of Elizabethan
  London.* London Topographical Society, 1979.
Salgado, Gamini. *The Elizabethan Underworld.* London: J. M.
  Dent & Sons, 1977.
Schoenbaum, S. *Shakespeare: A Compact Documentary Life.*
  Oxford: Oxford University Press, 1977.
Shakespeare, William. *Collected Works.* (Any edition with
  good notes.)
Wood, Michael. *Shakespeare.* New York: Basic Books, 2003.